THE MOONSHINER
AND THE
PREACHER

SAM PEMBERTON

Editor – Nancy B. Dailey
Publishing Coordinator – Sharon Kizziah-Holmes
Cover Design – Sharon Kizziah-Holmes

Paperback-Press
an imprint of A & S Publishing
A & S Holmes, Inc.

ISBN -13: 978-1-956806-54-0

DEDICATION

To the memory of Arvel Pemberton{January 1, 1911 – January 14, 1967}, and all circuit ministers that pastored the little churches at Big Flat, Hickory Hollow, Cozy Home and throughout the area around Big Flat.

ACKNOWLEDGEMENTS

Nancy B. Dailey, thank you for all the effort and time you put in to finding my original writings typing it and editing it. You did a great job, and your endeavors are greatly appreciated.

Sharon Kizziah-Holmes, if you hadn't guided me to Nancy, this book may never have happened. With your expertise and direction as my publishing coordinator, it is now done.

To both of you ladies, without you this project the manuscript would still be in a closet somewhere. You two deserve all the praise for your special talents and understanding of the intent and purpose of this novel.

To my wife Pat, thank you for standing beside me all these years. Your love and support mean the world to me. I don't know what I'd do without you.

INTRODUCTION

While the book is a work of fiction, writings are my best attempt to portray the struggle of a minister dedicated to his profession and dealing with a moonshiner.

The preacher was modeled after great uncle Paster Jess Rose and my father who was also a preacher.

The moonshiner was modeled after my moonshiner, grandfather William Henry Sutterfield.

Uncle Jess Rose and Grandpa Sutterfield represent characters that made their living farming and moonshining.

All the characters are based on people I grew up hearing stories about. I committed them to memory for the time I used them for this novel. None of the characters are referred to by their true name. While there isn't anything written in the book based on real events it is his best attempt to portray the struggle between a minister and the moonshine liquor. They believed strongly in their religion, while at the same time, enjoyed the liquor.

I sincerely hope you enjoy the read and take away a bit of how our present-day faith is influenced by these men's dedication.

CHAPTER 1

The ringing of the bell above the door slowly faded away after the last customer left the store.

Edward Tice was busy counting the money from the day's receipts at the hardware store on the corner of Main and Commerce, two blocks from the train depot in Batesville, Arkansas.

The clouds had gotten heavier all afternoon and it looked like it could start raining any minute.

Ed finished posting the sales totals in the ledger and went to lock the front door. He moved the box of ax handles inside before locking up. He silently wished the rain would begin and be a downpour. Maybe then he wouldn't have to go to church with his boss tonight.

At nineteen years old Ed was learning a lot about managing the hardware store from his boss, Joseph Carr. He knew Mr. Carr trusted him a lot before he had finished his first week. In the last two months Ed had been by himself most of the time at the store, with only the two colored laborers that helped him.

Mr. Carr was more interested in the college and the church than he was in making money with the store. He would come to the store early in the morning and help catch up the orders, but as soon as possible he was gone to work for some project at the college or the church.

Ed knew the old man had not worked this hard for the church very long because he could see by the books that he had really gotten involved since his oldest son drowned in a boating accident last summer.

As the sales decreased, the donations to the church increased. Until Ed went to work it appeared Mr. Carr might go broke trying to support the efforts of the Presbyterian church and college.

Now the business was doing better, but his zeal for the church was growing also. Ed Tice had become a new target for that zeal. For the last month Ed had listened to Mr. Carr talk about church every morning. He had never asked Ed about his convictions, he just assumed Ed was a wayward soul that arrived the same day as a shipment of wire and nails came up the river on a barge.

Ed had been sitting on one of the nail kegs when the barge docked. Mr. Carr, a little gray- haired man who met the boat, hired him to help unload the supplies for his hardware store. After the supplies were unloaded, Ed had gone home with Mr. Carr and hired out to work in the store. Ed never told him anything about where he came from or why he had come to Batesville.

During the last two months Ed had questioned himself time and again why he had been hired by a man who was so zealous about religion.

Mr. Carr wasn't forceful in his efforts to get Ed into the church, but for over a month he had told every story of conversion he knew at least twice. Ed almost told him about his own experience, but didn't because he was trying to forget about his conversion in the Baptist church and the problems since.

But tonight, he'd promised to go to church, and that brought back those memories from almost three years ago.

Ed remembered the night when he had gone to church with his mom. The revival had been going on since the last week in June and his mom had begged him to go every night for almost a week until he finally agreed.

He had sat on the back seat with a girl he knew from school a couple years earlier. Since completing the eighth grade Ed had not seen her, and while sitting by her he decided going to church wasn't nearly as bad as he'd imagined it to be.

The second night he began to listen as the old evangelist warned everyone about how bad hell was going to be.

Ed wasn't sure how he got to the front of the church that night. He remembered seeing his mom start toward him, then he remembered everybody hanging onto him and telling him how much he needed the Lord, and before the night was over he'd nodded his head yes when they asked if he was saved, and the church had counted him as a new convert.

The new Bible his mom bought for him was easy to read and understand, and Ed enjoyed explaining what he'd read to his mom and her friends.

In a couple of months, he was teaching Bible study on weekends. The preacher only came to the old school house once a month, and Ed taught Bible study when he wasn't there.

It was only natural that he began to "preach." Ed was into the preaching business before he realized it, just like he'd gotten religion.

As he sat remembering those days, Ed knew he'd enjoyed them, but he didn't know why he was dreading going to church with Mr. Carr, unless it was the other things.

Ed continued to recall the days after he started

preaching.

The old circuit riding preacher who had preached for years in Wayne County, Tennessee, became sick not long after Ed began to preach.

For over three months Ed had filled in for him and held revivals when there wasn't too much work on the farm. The ministry was going great and Ed enjoyed the attention from all the people.

The only real disagreement among people in the hills of Tennessee was whether religious people could use the whiskey they made for medicinal purposes. Ed enjoyed the hot toddies his mom made with hot water, sugar and a "shot" of the liquor. He finally gave it up except for times when his throat would get really raspy and hoarse after preaching. But he kept it a secret from the people in his churches. He didn't see anything wrong with it, but if it was going to hinder the people, he wouldn't do it. At least not where they could catch him.

Mr. Carr came in the back door. "Ed, you ready to go to church?"

"Yes."

"Well, let's go. We're having a fellowship dinner before prayer meeting tonight. Just wait 'til you see the food."

Ed looked around to see if he'd put the cash in the safe. He wasn't sure what he'd gotten done before he started daydreaming.

CHAPTER 2

Ed followed the Carrs to the third pew from the front and sat down beside them. The pews were more comfortable than the old homemade benches that were in the churches back home.

The dinner had been good but Ed thought everyone was too polite. They didn't relax like the folks at home.

This whole evening reminded him of the life he was trying to forget.

He watched as the minister approached the pulpit. As the preacher laid his Bible on the pulpit, Ed remembered the thrill of being on the podium. His thoughts went back to when he was preaching all over Wayne County, Tennessee. The four little churches had been so impressed by. a seventeen-year-old boy who could preach.

After the regular preacher was able to take his appointments again, the people had offered to send Ed to a seminary in Memphis.

As the preacher began to admonish the small group of

people in attendance at the church in Batesville, Ed continued to think about his own experience.

He'd ridden the train to Memphis. In his pocket was four hundred dollars, a hundred from each of the churches that were paying his way through Bible school. The money had been more than enough because he'd been invited to stay with one of the instructors at the school.

The first week at the school was exciting. Ed took his turn giving the devotion, and the feeling of power that he'd enjoyed back home was even greater at the school.

Always proud of his ability to express himself while he was in grammar school, Ed never gave a thought to becoming a preacher until his mom gave him the Bible. Now he was learning to preach, not just loud talk, but smooth oration.

He'd enjoyed Bible school until....

The problem was two-fold; on one hand there was the school's position on liquor, on the other there was the beautiful daughter of the instructor Ed was boarding with.

Ed had a girlfriend back home and he tried not to notice the sixteen-year-old daughter of his favorite instructor. But then, it wasn't really his fault that he started seeing her as a girlfriend. Ed slumped in the pew as he thought about the girl, Elizabeth. He still got excited when he thought of her.

They began going for walks down Poplar Avenue after supper each night. The walks became dates, and it wasn't long until they were more than friends.

After yielding to the temptation of seeing Elizabeth, Ed began to wish for one of his mom's hot toddies. The use of liquor in Wayne County was accepted by several of his friend in the church, but the continual talk against it in Memphis made Ed ashamed of wanting a drink.

Prohibition league members were everywhere, and the more they fought liquor, the more Ed wanted a drink. He finally bought a pint of bonded liquor and hid it in the suitcase under his bed.

Elizabeth came into his room without knocking and caught him making a "cold" toddy. She thought it was exciting and joined him. But that night was the beginning of the end for Ed at Bible School.

The problem came to a head when Elizabeth asked Ed to go for a walk two weeks later. He said no because he needed to study for an exam on the four gospels the next morning. He was going over the notes when he heard Elizabeth and her dad climbing the stairs.

The knock on the door was a banging thud. When Ed answered the door, the preacher and his daughter burst into the room.

"Elizabeth says you're keeping liquor in the house!" Her dad's red face said more than the words.

"I am." Ed refused to lie.

"You mean you admit it?"

"Yes."

"Well! Get out of this house this minute!" Elizabeth's Dad pointed to the door.

The church service was over and Ed could not recall any part of it, he'd been so lost in his thoughts. The ride home in the car was the biggest reason Ed had gone to church.

The year was 1913, but Ed's first ride in an automobile was after he went to Memphis. The car ride home from church made five times he'd ridden in a car. Two of those were tonight.

When Mr. Carr asked how he liked the church, Ed's answer didn't seem convincing.

"Just fine,...oh just fine." He excused himself and went to his room.

The memories of that night four months ago were stronger tonight than any time since he left Memphis.

He thought of when he left the seminary. Leaving had

been a nightmare. He couldn't forget the surprised look on Elizabeth's face when her dad ordered him to leave. She stood watching him pack the suitcase, knowing the liquor had been in his room for a month, and he had over half of it left. He remembered looking at the bottle as he piled his clothes in the suitcase. The amber colored liquid was costing him a lot, his hope of becoming a real "preacher-man."

Ed went to the train station planning to catch the train home. While he was waiting to buy his ticket, he thought how much he dreaded facing the people back home.

On the board listing the arrival and departure times of the trains was: Next departure Newport, Arkansas 9:52. Ed asked for a ticket on the 9:52 without knowing why he did it.

He arrived in Newport before day break. He had over three hundred dollars left from the money from the churches, but no plans at all. He just wanted to disappear for a while. He certainly wasn't interested in going to church after this mess.

For three weeks Ed worked on a farm north of Newport on the Cache river. He couldn't believe the conditions the farm hands worked and lived in. The shacks had dirt floors and were the same quarters slaves had lived in before the war between the states.

Ed listened to the colored folks complain during the day as they worked on the farm. They said they were being treated worse than when they were slaves.

"Why, Mr. Ed, my master always took care of me, but now I don't even get paid 'cept when they feel like it," was the way one of the men described it.

After the third week Ed couldn't stand the mosquitoes, the filth, and the arrogance of the field boss anymore, so he left and caught the barge to Batesville.

CHAPTER 3

Ed had gone to sleep thinking about when he had left Memphis. When he dreamed, his dreams were nightmares. In them he was always trying to explain that he'd done nothing wrong, and that he'd hurt only himself if he did commit a sin. When he woke up after the dreams, he lay awake thinking about his mom and the shame she must be going through. Her son had run away after taking the people's money to go to Bible School. No wonder it was so hard to convert people.

Ed heard Mrs. Carr starting to cook breakfast. At last he could get up.

A guilty conscience had to be the worst company anyone ever had to keep. While he was in bed his memories and dreams were torment, during the day he could forget by staying busy, but there was no running away from himself. He was mad, ashamed and embarrassed by the mess he was in, and going to church last night only made it worse. Maybe he wouldn't go anymore.

"Son, you liked church, didn't you?" Mr. Carr didn't wait for an answer. "I know you were scared at being in church 'cause you sat so quiet, but you'll get over it." Ed looked at the old man and nodded, afraid of what he would think if he knew the truth.

"Me and the wife will just be patient; don't let anyone push you into church." He passed Ed the plate of eggs as he talked. "Religion ain't worth a dime unless it's coming from the heart. You just make a confession when you feel like it."

Ed lowered his head and ate in silence. *Oh, Lord, why did I have to go to work for a man so obsessed by church?* he prayed softly. The pain of his memories would be eased by not having to listen to this old man talk about church all the time.

Ed guessed the religion was Mr. Carr's way of trying to make up for the years he'd neglected his family. A customer at the store said the old man didn't really get into religion until after his boy drowned. Ed listened and nodded every time Mr. Carr asked a question. He didn't really pay attention to anything Mr. Carr said, but the remark he made as they finished breakfast made Ed wish he'd listened.

"I'm proud you're going with us this Sunday, too." Mr. Carr went to the bathroom to shave.

Ed didn't know when he'd agreed to go to church on Sunday. It must've been one of the times he said "uh huh" and nodded during breakfast. How was he going to get out of this? Time would provide the answer.

The store was busy for a Thursday. Usually there wasn't much traffic until Friday, but today four wagons had been loaded with wire and nails.

Ed was proud he was working hard; at least he was not worrying about religion.

Right after the wagons were loaded, Mr, Carr left without even mentioning the church again. Most of the time he spent at least ten minutes telling Ed about his plans for the afternoon.

The bookwork from the morning sales kept Ed busy for an hour after lunch. As he posted the ledger he noticed the names Massey, Rose, Sutterfield. All of these names were common in Wayne and Hardin County, Tennessee. Maybe they were kin folks.

Ed's mom was a Massey, and she had talked about her relatives in Arkansas. He didn't know where they lived, but all the invoices were for supplies shipped by train to the Sylamore depot over thirty miles up the river. He'd gone with one boxcar load of supplies, and was amazed at all the hill farmers that came to pick the stuff up from the train depot. Some came over fifty miles to the depot. If they were kin he had no idea where they lived in the hills.

After finishing the bookwork, Ed began straightening up the store. The wagons had been unloaded in such a rush the store's stock was left in an untidy mess. He hated trying to find what he needed after a customer got there. Besides, Mr. Carr had raised his pay to $15 a week because he kept the store in order.

He was sorting the horseshoes according to their size when the minister came in. He looked different without the collar he'd worn last night, but Ed recognized him.

"You all right today?"

"Sure."

"Glad you came to church last night."

Ed nodded.

"What did you think of our Bible study?"

Ed felt his heart pound. He was afraid to admit he didn't listen to any of it. "It was interesting," he finally answered. The lie amused Eddie. How could he tell this old preacher his Bible study was interesting when he'd not listened even two minutes?

"Brother Carr said you were coming again Sunday, that right?"

"I promised him I would this morning." Ed wished again he'd listened better this morning. Maybe he could have thought of a way to say no about Sunday.

"OK, son." The preacher started to leave. "We'll see you Sunday."

After the preacher left, Ed tried to imagine that little meek fellow preaching. He would go Sunday and listen to him. "I'll bet he can't preach a lick," he said to himself.

CHAPTER 4

Ed sat by the youth leader waiting for Sunday School to start. The crowd was going to be a large one this pretty morning.

Since Thursday Ed had been confused about church. He was anxious to go but he was afraid his past experience might keep him from enjoying church again.

The piano player began playing a hymn; the crowd became very quiet as a hush came over everyone. A big muscular fellow went to the podium.

Ed was amazed at how different this church was from the churches at home. The women all sat beside their husbands. They were dressed very proper in their best dresses and hats. They sat very stiff, not looking to either side, and certainly not whispering like Ed remembered his mother and her friends doing before and sometimes during church.

The church was brought to order by the big red headed man standing like a giant above the pulpit.

Ed always liked to guess at people's occupations while they were in church, dressed in their best clothes.

The big muscular red headed man trying to serve as Sunday School Superintendent was definitely not accustomed to wearing a suit and tie. He was uncomfortable, and looked out of place on the podium where he dwarfed the pastor sitting meekly waiting for the preliminaries to be over.

After eliminating banker, lawyer, doctor and any other profession, Ed decided he must be a butcher at the slaughterhouse. He was too pale to be a farmer or anyone who worked outside, but from looking at his muscles, he definitely was doing some kind of strenuous job. Hanging quarters of beef would build muscle.

Ed followed a group of young people out for Bible study.

Why would a church put a big bruiser like that in charge on Sunday morning? One thing Ed had learned at the seminary was for a pastor to make sure the church leaders were attractive but ordinary, so people wouldn't be distracted by their appearance.

Ed almost laughed aloud when he remembered the old instructor telling about a church in Alabama that had a midget for a pastor. The church grew really fast as people came to see the tiny pastor, but when they got over the shock, the crowd dropped off in a hurry. The church split up over the little runt, with some people so hurt by the fuss they quit church for good.

Ed listened as the teacher stammered beginning the Bible study for this morning. The lesson was in First Corinthians, one of Ed's favorite books, and he almost spoke up several times. The teacher got better after the first few minutes. He wasn't so nervous, and some of the college students in attendance helped with the discussion.

Ed's opinion of the church improved. The Bible teacher became relaxed, leading the discussion by asking questions and then respecting everyone's ideas. Ed was still nervous but he felt an urge to study his Bible for the first time since leaving the seminary.

After the class was over, Ed went back in the sanctuary for the morning sermon.

The big fellow finished with receiving the morning offering, and the pale little preacher walked slowly to the podium.

If this church was trying to create interest by using leaders of diverse characteristics, they were successful.

The little preacher read more scripture than Ed had ever heard read for one sermon. *If he preaches all of that, half of this crowd will starve to death and the other half will go to sleep,* Ed thought as the preacher finished reading.

The preacher pulled his glasses off, hooked the lenses over the Bible and laid the wire ear pieces on top. He slowly wiped his brow with the pale-yellow handkerchief from his pocket.

What's he doing with a yellow one when his suit is blue? Eddie was still inspecting the church and its pastor.

After almost two minutes the preacher began to exhort his congregation to live by the principles of the three chapters from second Peter. The little preacher was good in spite of his poor delivery. As Ed watched the little preacher make mistakes in his posture, use of hands, turning the wrong way when he crossed the podium, raising his arms at the wrong time, the urge to preach again became so strong he was barely able to sit and listen.

Ed would have loved to have preached the verses giving the promises to the elect of Christ. He would have raised his voice to a crescendo as he emphasized the promise of "ye shall never fall" in verse ten of the first chapter.

He couldn't believe it when the little fellow slowly put his glasses back on and read the verse quietly.

Ed was already planning how he was going to preach that in his "next sermon."

The thought embarrassed him. He looked around the church, afraid someone was able to sense what he'd been thinking. He sat listening closely for the rest of the sermon, trying not to compare the preacher to anyone. He was going to go to church and try not to think of his own ministry. After all, he had failed miserably.

The church service ended abruptly. Ed was used to the long appeal for converts to come forward. Today they stood, the preacher prayed a benediction and the people left, treating each other politely but not anything close to the warm, exuberant fellowship Ed remembered from Wayne County's churches.

He was quiet as he rode home with the Carrs. Ed had no way of knowing Mr. Carr was interpreting his quiet mood as a spirit of conviction. The old man was plotting the next approach at closing in on Ed for the conversion. Ed was in a pensive mood, realizing his religion was still alive. Today the urge to preach had been reborn.

Chapter 5

Ed Tice, a preacher. The thought haunted him all afternoon.

When it came time for the night service, he made an excuse not to go. While the Carrs were preparing to leave, he heard the old man whisper "He's just running from the Lord." Ed knew he would have to tell Mr. Carr about his problem or he would be pestering him to get "saved."

"Saved." Ed thought of the traditional term used by most southern evangelicals. He had never been able to explain his feelings about conversion. He knew the goal of everyone in Wayne County, Tennessee, had been to either miss Hell or make Heaven.

He'd come up with a description for each type of Christian although he didn't have the nerve to share his opinion with anyone, especially people in the church.

The ones who continually talked about being "saved" were scared of Hell and wanted to be "saved" from it. The ones who were carried away with the prospects of going to

Heaven were converts to the idea of working their way to some glorious reward. Most of the last ones seemed to think they needed a special work of their own to justify their admittance to Heaven.

Ed wasn't sure which description fit Mr. Carr. The old fellow didn't seem scared of Hell, nor did he spout off about how righteous he was or how he was going to Heaven. This Christian might be different. Ed was trying to decide what kind of church worker his boss was when he began to think about himself.

Before he even thought about getting back into the church, he needed to straighten out the mess he'd left behind. The only thing he knew for sure he could do was send back the money the churches had given him. When he had come to Batesville he still had over two hundred and fifty dollars.

Tomorrow I'll go to the bank and see how I can get that much of it sent back, Eddie thought as he dug the tabacco sack with the money in it from his suit pocket. He looked at the bull on the sack. This was a vice he'd never tried, nor had he wanted to, but the other one.... Ed stopped himself in mid-thought, refusing to even recall the problem again.

The money with what he'd saved since going to work totaled $318. He could send $70 to each of the churches. *Never heard of making payments on a sin before.* Eddie was amused, then flushed with anger at himself. He might be wasting his time even thinking about preaching again. Then he envisioned Elijah taunting the profits of Baal. *God permitted him a sense of humor.* Ed thought there might be hope for him, even though he did seem to have a knack for foolish thoughts when reverence was more appropriate.

Mr. Carr was in a good mood for a Monday morning. The rain last week had allowed all the people a chance to come to town, and business this week was going to be slow for a change.

"Mr. Carr, can I take off for a few minutes? I need to go to the bank." Ed had finished listing the items they needed to order on Wednesday.

"I'm going to the bank, I'll make your deposit." Mr. Carr looked at Ed. "When did you open an account?"

"I didn't."

"You'll need to go, then."

Ed left the store feeling guilty again for allowing Mr. Carr to believe he was going to open a bank account.

Ed went through the door of the fanciest building he'd ever seen. Memphis had some nice banks, but the marble works at Batesville had been a good source for materials, and this building was beautiful.

"I'd like to know how I can send money to four churches in Wayne County, Tennessee, and it be safe 'til it gets there." Ed's voice was quivering as he asked.

"Why son, just open an account and send them checks." The banker stared at Ed over the top of his glasses.

As Ed looked at the wire rimmed glasses, he thought how well the optician had done in the month since he came to town. The preacher, every banker, Mr. Carr, and he didn't know how many other businessmen were wearing the same style glasses. The thought about the glasses allowed him to regain his composure enough to overcome the questioning stare.

"Yes, open me an account."

A few minutes later Eddie was in the post office addressing envelopes to each of the churches. He enclosed a check for $68 in each one, and a note: "I'm sorry the way things turned out, and I'll send the rest as soon as I can." Eddie signed his name, paid for the postage, and mailed the letters. He felt better as he went back to the store.

The day passed without Mr. Carr leaving the store; he even worked while Ed went home for lunch.

"Has Joseph bothered you today, son?" Mrs. Carr asked as she fixed sandwiches for Ed to take to the store.

The question was unexpected, and Ed was stumped for a minute.

"Well, no...why?"

"You know he wants you to join the church. He never mentioned the church to our Billy before he drowned, and now he's trying to ask everyone." Mrs. Carr turned to face Ed. "Son, he means well, but I don't want him bothering you. I want you here...if you go to church or not."

Ed took the sandwiches and left for the store. He considered what Mrs. Carr had said. She knew her husband's zeal for religion was a guilt complex. *How can I tell when I'm doing that?* Ed asked himself, knowing the question, afraid of the answer. He understood now why the Carrs wanted him with them, but could he live with someone very long who was trying to compensate to the world for a son they'd lost?

Mr. Carr was sitting on the bench in front of the store. He'd placed a keg in front of the bench for them to spread lunch on. Ed sat the basket down and they began eating without saying a word.

"Ed, you get your account opened?"

"Yes."

"The postmaster came by to get some hinges for a door." The tone of Mr. Carr's voice was full of meaning.

Ed gazed at the buildings across the street. He knew sooner or later, if he stayed here long enough, he would have to tell someone about where he came from and why he was here.

The Carrs were good people; he knew Mr. Carr would understand, and he knew the postmaster had told him about the four letters. Small towns were not good places for keeping secrets.

"I went to the post office after I opened my bank account." Ed couldn't find a way to start telling the story.

"I sent money to some people I owed."

"To churches?" Mr. Carr's answer was more curious than questioning.

Over an hour later Ed had finished the story not leaving out even one detail.

"Son, you're going to write your folks." The stern sound to the little gray-haired man's voice, after Ed finished telling about why he was in Batesville, was the first time Ed ever heard him sound forceful.

They finished the day without mentioning the church or Ed's problem, but they both spent the rest of the day thinking about what should be done.

CHAPTER 6

On Thursday night Ed sat down to try to write his mother. The effort to say something that would explain how he ran away without bothering to tell anyone was going to be hard...too hard.

He was trying to block out the bad memories, but why had he ignored his mother? Ed had tried to forget everybody from home because of his embarrassment, and his mother was just one of the people he was ashamed to face. He dreaded facing her more than anyone. She had fought so hard with his dad to let him preach. His dad actually blackened her eye once during one of their arguments before Ed left for the seminary.

How could I hurt her after all she did? Ed asked himself, and threw the pencil down. *I can't just write home and say Hi Mom, I'm living in Arkansas,* and he didn't want to go over the whole ordeal again, not in a letter.

While he thought about all that happened before going to church with Mr. Carr, Ed saw another side to religion...confession. Also, thinking during the time since Sunday gave Ed another look at church goers, members, and Christians.

He knew now what kind of Christian he wanted to be: a believer, someone who knew God as love. He'd read the writings of Paul to the Ephesians every day since Sunday. The sixth verse of the first chapter said what Ed felt: "To the praise of the glory of his grace, wherein he hath made us accepted in the beloved." A confessing Christian, a preacher that knew it was God whose love had provided a way for everyone to confess and be forgiven.

Now if he could write his mother and ask her forgiveness, if he could forgive the girl in Memphis....

The girl, Elizabeth. Ed knew he must be feeling better toward her. At least he could say her name, and a couple of times this week he'd even been able to imagine her face, pretty and radiant, as they had walked along Poplar Avenue, not the raging spoiled brat who caused all of his trouble just because he refused to go for a walk.

Tomorrow night...I'll write Mom a letter. Ed read most of First John, and went to sleep.

Mr. Carr let Ed open the store on Friday mornings; he met with the other businessmen for breakfast, and usually got to the store around the middle of the morning, after stops at the bank and post office.

When Mr Carr got to the store, Ed was checking the harnesses for moths and any other parasite that might feed on the leather.

"Morning." Ed spoke without turning to look. He knew the sound of his boss walking across the boards of the floor in front of the seed counter.

"Morning. You got a letter."

Ed almost dropped the brush he'd been using to dust the harness. How could he get a letter?

Mr. Carr handed him the envelope. It was from his mother.

The letter began with his mother trying to explain how the secretaries of each of the churches had received the checks.

"Son, it hurt me real bad that you didn't bother to write me first. I've worried so much, afraid you were dead and I would never know what happened to you. I'm writing this letter just hoping you'll get it. Brother Payne, our new pastor, said I might be able to get a letter to you by just sending it to the post office in Batesville, Arkansas. Please, son, write me…." The letter went on for four pages.

Ed had gone to the storage shed behind the store to read the letter. He was not crying, he just felt rotten after reading it.

He re-read the part about Elizabeth writing him a letter. "Eddie, the way I found out you were gone was when the minister's daughter wrote you those letters. I wrote her asking why she'd written you at home when you were still in Memphis."

Ed read the next few sentences real slow.

"That poor girl is almost crazy, she even made her daddy bring her up here. Son, she's sorry about what happened, but I don't blame her, I blame myself for using liquor all of those years. Son, it's wrong. A Christian just can't use liquor, not even a little for a cold. It's a sin. I want you to forgive me for not teaching you better. Son, promise me you'll never touch it again. Are you going to church?" The letter was not very well written because the pages were crumpled, and the handwriting at times was just scrawls, barely legible.

Ed went back to the store.

"Son, go home." Mr. Carr was not ordering him to go, just a suggestion. "Answer your letter."

"It's from Mom." Ed squeezed the letter against him as he answered Mr. Carr. "I'll go write her."

Ed spent the rest of the day writing and re-writing the letter to his mom. He didn't know how to answer her question about him going to church. Church to her meant a Baptist fundamentalist church, not a Presbyterian church. He finally wrote, "I am going to church with the people I work for," without bothering to tell her the denomination.

He spent most of his time writing another letter...to Elizabeth. He asked her to send the Bible he'd left in Memphis, the Bible his mother bought for him when he first started to church.

The letter to Elizabeth was harder to write than the one to his mother because as he faced up to the past, he was forgiving everyone, including himself, and most of all, Elizabeth. Once he forgave her, he realized he missed her and loved her, but it would be rather forward to write all that in this first letter.

The letter to Elizabeth had four sentences when he finally mailed it. One asking about the Bible, one telling where he was, one apologizing to her family for what he did, and the last one asking how she was.

As Ed read it over before sealing it, he knew it had to be the worst letter ever written.

CHAPTER 7

The relief of finally knowing the people at home missed him made Eddie feel better than he had since leaving Memphis.

While he worked on Saturday morning, his mind was on going to church this Sunday. He was going because he wanted to!

The big red-headed fellow didn't look or sound as awkward when Ed watched him come to the pulpit and begin the morning service.

The Bible class was even more interesting than the week before, and it was obvious everyone in the class knew enough of his story to know he was a preacher...or rather, he used to be. He made several comments about the lesson, and was very pleased that his knack for explaining his point of view hadn't suffered from his bad experience.

Ed listened to the little preacher. He didn't sound any better. His voice was too shrill for a minister, his manners were awful, but he was well prepared and his content was excellent.

Maybe going to the Seminary was bad for me. I learned some about the Bible, but now I can't enjoy listening to a preacher because I'm always criticizing him. Eddie stopped the thought as the minister asked the people to stand for the benediction.

Mr. Carr introduced him to the same people he'd met last week, but this time they seemed to look him over from head to toe. Ed felt like a prized horse being appraised before a race. One old lady said, "And you have preached, boy; can you still do it?"

The question seemed so cold.

That's it, Ed thought. Ever since the beginning of his religion he'd felt uncomfortable around some people in the church. Now he knew what it was. He was going to read some scripture he thought applied to his feeling as soon as he got home.

Meanwhile he considered the feeling he had when the little old lady made the comment and asked the question. First, there wasn't really anything wrong in her asking, but he knew it was the attitude a lot of people seemed to have toward church. *Too casual, not sincere, too familiar, lack of reverence, too much thinking and talking, not enough spiritual....* Ed paused. He didn't know what he was searching for. When he thought of his spiritual experience he was at a loss to explain it, even to himself.

That's it! That's it! He almost spoke aloud as the car stopped in front of the house. *If you could explain the relationship of the soul to God, it wouldn't mean much.*

Ed went to the house, asking Mr. Carr for his Bible as they went through the living room. He went upstairs to his room and immediately began to search the Bible for what he knew had to be the thing he'd just discovered.

Faith was the basis of salvation through the love of God. Now could he find a scripture to explain or confirm it? After reading all the scriptures he'd preached from, he began to read Romans, the eighth chapter. *I never preached from this because it always seemed hard to explain it.* Eddie read the 14th verse: "For as many as are led by the spirit of God, they are the sons of God."

He went to the window, watching the wind blow the leaves on a maple tree. He knew what he needed to say. He remembered the third chapter of John. He believed it was the eighth verse that told how being born of the spirit was like trying to answer where the wind came from and where it went.

"Lord, I know now." Ed began praying for the first time in a long time.

The sun was going down when he realized he'd been praying and reading the Bible for most of the afternoon.

"Ed, you want to eat?" Mrs. Carr seemed far away to Ed. He wondered why.

"Yes, I'll be right down."

Ed realized he'd been in his room all afternoon. He wondered what the Carrs thought when he'd missed lunch. Did they come to get him?

He ate in silence. The peace he felt didn't need a description. He'd read Christ's answer to Nicodemus several times, over and over again, this afternoon. His mind was at peace for the first time, maybe ever.

The meal was finished, and Ed got dressed to go to the night service without being asked.

As he sat by himself waiting for the choir to begin the service, he missed Elizabeth. After they'd started dating, he'd enjoyed their walk to the church on Sunday night more than anytime they'd spent together. They'd always left early and got to the church in time to watch all the people come in.

He watched Mr. Carr as he talked to the pastor. He heard part of the conversation.

"Pastor, I mean he prayed all afternoon."

Eddie's face flushed in embarrassment at first, then he

smiled, content to let them discuss him.

After the pastor finished visiting the Carrs he made his way over to the side of the church where more of the young people always sat. He spoke to each one of them hurriedly until he got to Ed.

"Son...." He leaned over toward Ed as if he was trying to think of what to say. He clutched Ed's hand between both of his while he tried to phrase the question. After a long pause he said, "Can...I come by the store tomorrow?"

The pastor had asked the question rather loudly, and most of the congregation turned to look at them. Ed nodded, pulling his hand away from the pastor's. He was sure the pastor had meant to say more.

The service was a blessing and Ed felt a zeal to preach as he watched the pastor try to tell the story of Abraham and Isaac. He was sure when he preached the "spirit" would lead him. He'd found out this afternoon what his ministry had been lacking. He couldn't wait for his second chance.

He didn't have to wait long before he got his chance. On Monday the first person in the store was the preacher.

"Son, just give us a few minutes testimony before the Bible Study on Wednesday. It don't have to last a minute, or take thirty if you want to." That had been the way the pastor left it, for Ed to decide if he would like to speak at the church on Wednesday.

Ed smiled as he went through Mr. Carr's Bible trying to decide if he was going to read scripture or just testify and sit down.

He wished he had his own Bible. He knew they were both King Janes versions, and every word was the same, but he could almost feel the pages of his Bible and find any book or chapter immediately. With Mr. Carr's Bible, it seemed like some books tried to hide from him as he turned to them.

He finally decided to take the Bible to the pulpit. When

he got up there he'd do whatever he felt like, but he was studying for more than a testimony.

CHAPTER 8

"Will they ever quit singing?" Eddie thought as he rubbed his sweaty palms together. They felt sticky.

He remembered his first week at the Seminary in the pulpit class. The instructor had told them if they were so nervous that their hands were sticking together to always preach a simple sermon, something that couldn't be messed up. He'd promptly gone to a church in Fraizer and felt just that way. Beads of sweat had been on his forehead an hour before church started.

He'd decided to switch to Noah and the flood rather than trying to preach the story of Paul's conversion. He knew it was probably the only time Noah had ever sailed the ark with Adam and Eve as members of his crew. But tonight, he wasn't afraid of the pulpit, just eager to get started.

Since the church had been built there probably had never been a crowd to compare to this Wednesday night, not even Sunday mornings. Ed watched as the people continued to come in during the song service.

Mr. Carr hadn't been in the store an hour altogether since the pastor asked Ed to testify, and the crowd was here to hear "the runaway preacher." Mr. Carr had done a good job of getting the people out.

The choir finally finished singing. As most churches back home did, this one sang until everybody got there.

Ed knew a good pastor never started the rest of the service until the people had stopped coming in The rule of thumb in preaching was to keep singing until there was a complete hymn sung without any additional people coming into the church during the song.

The church was full. When the pastor got to the pulpit, he didn't say anything. Looking from side to side he finally found Ed and looked straight at him.

"Ed," he said, motioning for Ed to join him on the podium.

"Tonight we're privileged to have Edward Tice from Wayne County, Tennessee. Most of you know him from Brother Carr's hardware store." The preacher took his Bible, turned from the pulpit and went to sit by his wife in the front pew.

During the walk up the aisle, Ed's knees felt weak, and he wasn't sure he could say a word, his mouth was so dry.

"Lord," he muttered as he stepped onto the podium. The choir was sitting behind him. They usually went back to their pews, but tonight they had to stay on the stage because the pews were full. *Why did all these people come? I'll bet there wasn't thirty people here last Wednesday night*, Ed thought as he laid his Bible on the pulpit.

"Let us stand and pray!" Eddie's voice boomed as he prayed for God to bless those in attendance.

As soon as the crowd was seated, Ed began his testimony. The feel of the power on him was awesome. The crowd's eyes were glued to him.

"I am nothing tonight except for the mercy and grace of the God I serve." Eddie began to tell about his relationship with God.

He exhorted the crowd to avoid thinking of God as being limited to a building. He reminded them that God's work was a reality, done with real things like buildings, books, and people. But his services required obedience to Christ through the spirit being able also to lead his people.

The longer he talked, the more comfortable he became. "The spirit is here, but not because of Ed Tice." Ed was coming to his conclusion. "God intends we testify of his son, that we believe him for our salvation, that we get serious and realize he loves all people and is not willing that any should perish, but that all should come to repentance."

Ed waved his arms, asking the crowd to stand. He very quietly asked each person to search their heart.

"I don't want anyone asking anyone to come to the front. If the spirit is drawing you, if you feel a need for Christ, come...right now because God loves you." Ed bowed his head. Closing his eyes, he began praying quietly.

He could hear the crowd moving. Were they leaving? Ed opened his eyes, and there, standing in front of the pulpit was over fifty people.

What do I do now? he thought. Ed was perplexed. He'd never seen more than two or three people come forward at one time.

The pastor and several other men joined the people standing at the altar. The crowd was so quiet, the people were all praying. They needed some kind of leadership.

Ed began to pray: "Lord, I don't know how to ask for what these people need. You know their hearts, you love them, they've been drawn by the power of your Holy spirit. As each one of them confesses to you, Lord, forgive them. Lord, as I preached your word I felt the power of Your spirit. Please forgive them, everyone."

Ed cried as he finished the prayer; everyone in the church cried with him.

He went back to the pew where Mrs. Carr was sitting. As he sat down by her, she reached over and squeezed his hand. She didn't say a word, but her smile told Ed how proud she was of him. He bowed his head, waiting for the pastor to end the service.

Ed felt relieved as the choir sang the closing hymn. He'd always questioned if he was really called to preach. Tonight, he'd gotten his answer. He was called to serve God, not to preach but to serve as a preacher. It was going to be hard to make it, at best, but maybe.... His thoughts went back to Memphis and Elizabeth.

CHAPTER 9

Thursday morning at the store was hectic; it seemed everyone that was in the church had the same idea about coming by the store to see "preacher Ed."

Ed savored this attention, but was afraid to say very much about what he'd accomplished in just one sermon. He could remember stammering through sermons the next service after he'd done really well and people had bragged on him.

One old man had really impressed Ed when he told him he reminded him of preachers back home years ago.

"Where is home?" Ed asked.

"Tennessee."

"Where in Tennessee?"

"Wayne County, around Waynesboro." The old gentleman hadn't noticed the surprised look on Ed's face when he'd said Wayne County.

"You know anybody named Tice when you lived in Tennessee?" Ed asked, expecting the fellow to know some of his family if he was from back home.

"Tice? You mean your name is Tice?" The shock of Ed being a Tice had just soaked in on the old man.

"Sure am. From Waynesboro, too." Ed was enjoying watching the old man's expression as he began to study him closer trying to see if he could place him as somebody he knew from Wayne County.

"I don't remember you. 'Course I've been gone 'nigh on to twenty years. You wouldn't even have been born when I left, would you?"

"Afraid not. I'll just be twenty next month."

"You been in Arkansas very long?"

"Just this summer."

"Ever been up the river?"

"As far as Sylamore."

"I live in Big Flat. You know where that is?"

"No. Where is it from Sylamore?"

"Just up on the top of the mountain…ah, that's not really the right way to describe it." The old man stopped for a minute. "It's about twenty-five miles through the roughest country in northern Arkansas."

"What's your name?"

"Why, son, I'm sorry, excuse me. I'm Jim Rhodes. I run the cotton gin at Big Flat. I just came to town to pick up some things for the gin and got to hear you preach while I was here. You ought to come up to Big Flat and preach for us some time."

"I just might do that. You think the pastor would invite me to preach if I come some weekend?"

Ed was anxious to go see if the folks around Big Flat were from back in Tennessee.

"I'll tell the preacher about you and get him to write you a letter when to come. OK?" Mr. Rhodes reached for the pencil to write down Eddie's address.

After Mr. Rhodes left, Ed began to think what a small world this was. When he left Memphis, he was sure he could hide forever in Arkansas. Now he knew there was no way to hide from people, or the Lord. It was good, though, to meet someone who knew his folks. Ed felt almost like he'd been visiting with a member of the family while he talked to the old man from Big Flat.

Maybe they'd let him come to Big Flat to preach. Ed was wishing they would write him before the old fellow got out of sight.

The visitors were fewer in the afternoon. It was a good thing, or they might've had to close the store.

Ed began to think about Elizabeth. He wished he knew how long it should take for her to write him back. She might not even care anymore That thought made him feel empty and cold. She would write.

It amazed Ed how fast Elizabeth had taken over his mind after he'd gotten over the guilty feelings he'd carried since leaving Memphis. Now he couldn't wait to see her, where before he'd shuddered in shame at the thought of having to face her or her father.

If I hear from her I'll catch the train and go to Memphis. He was already planning a trip, and he wasn't even sure she would read his letter if she got it.

For the rest of the day Ed made plans for the trip to Memphis. His imagination was very vivid, the trip was a success. And before the afternoon was over he could see Elizabeth as Mrs. Tice, and them pastoring a church...after they were married, of course.

When Mr. Carr came back to the store just before closing time, his face showed excitement as he hurriedly filled an order.

"Son, you want to preach us a revival?"

"I don't know...." Ed was almost overcome by how fast things were happening.

"Now, you don't have to answer right now." Mr. Carr began helping carry the boxes of supplies they always displayed on the sidewalk inside the store. "It may be too soon to expect you to just take off preaching again." The old store keeper couldn't hide his pride at having gotten Ed back in church.

"There's never been a time since I've been going to church when people really got excited like they did last night." Mr. Carr couldn't stop talking about the sermon Ed preached. He'd talked for two hours after they got home last night and all day today.

Ed was beginning to think he'd made a mistake by preaching. If he listened to his boss, he'd get the big head for sure, and he knew one sure way to not ever do any good as a preacher was to start thinking he knew all about it. He could almost see the instructor the day he had told the class how hard it would be to handle the praise of the people.

"You'll handle your failures, don't ever worry if you mess up a sermon. The ones to get concerned about is when you do real good and the people begin to tell you how great you are. Then be careful. If you believe them, you'll be in trouble. Remember, pride goeth before destruction, and a haughty spirit before a fall."

Today was a day Ed'd tried hard not to take what the folks said too serious. The pastor was a good man, but these people didn't have a preacher. The reason Ed had seemed so good was the little meek fellow was so far from being what a preacher should be. But how could he tell them that? Maybe if he said, *Now, look, I can't preach. It's just that the pastor you've got is way too meek. He needs to get prayed up and preach with a little bit more fire.*

The thought was the first time Ed ever came close to being critical all day. He felt bad, but he knew he was partially right. The man wasn't a preacher.

Ed thought about himself. He'd gone in to the ministry too quick. After he got to Bible school, he'd read the qualifications of a bishop for the first time. He'd been amazed that the churches let him preach the first year he started attending church.

He knew very few people at home realized the apostle Paul didn't just take off on his journey right after his conversion He'd discovered the years between Paul's conversion and when Barnabas went to Tarsus to get him was almost eight full years. It scared Ed; was he ready to preach, even now?

The church was never ready for a beginner. They were always too easily attracted to a young minister, but he knew he'd do himself and the church more harm than good if he tried to preach again and wasn't ready. Then he remembered how he felt when the old man from Big Flat suggested he might be able to come to their church and preach.

I'll go if I get an invitation. Now if I only knew how to handle this revival thing. They'd finished closing the store while he was lost in his thoughts. He knew now how he would do it. *I'll agree to preach on Wednesdays as long as they want me to.*

"Mr. Carr, I'll preach every Wednesday, but let's wait about any revival, OK."

"Sure, son, I'll tell the pastor. He'll be glad to have you do anything; he needs help."

It was the first time Ed ever heard the old man even come close to criticizing anyone in the church. He also knew now there was more to Mr. Carr calling him "son" all the time than just a figure of speech. The old man was transferring his love for the son he lost in the boating accident to him. Life sure had an unusual way for things to turn out. He'd left Memphis sure that he'd never have another friend, and now he had a fine old gentleman trying to help him, and a church ready for him to start preaching again.

Now if tomorrow.... He started to wish for "his letter" from Elizabeth.

They ate supper in silence. It was the first time since Sunday that Ed got a chance to let his mind rest. He went upstairs and went to bed not long after finishing eating. The night's sleep was the first one for Ed Tice in a long time when he didn't dream about some horrible thing he'd done. There was just a girl he dreamed of all night. He prayed he'd get a letter.

The mail always came in on the ten o'clock train, and Ed watched for the postman to go to the depot. Was he ever going to go?

The sun was shining bright on the red brick of the street this morning. The postman was certainly taking his time walking to the depot. Ed had swept the walk twice while he waited for him to start to the depot, and he was ashamed to sweep it anymore, but he wanted to know as soon as the mail got back.

"Ed, why don't you just go wait at the post office for the mail?" Mr. Carr was sincere, he never teased Ed, and that was the one thing Ed like the most about the Carrs. They either lost their sense of humor after their son died, or they never had one. But Ed didn't need to be around anyone who was always joking, not while he had his problems.

He laid the broom on the sidewalk and crossed the street to the post office. He watched as the postman pushed the cart loaded with mail up the hill from the train station.

There has got to be some mail for me in all of that, Eddie thought as he looked at the pile of mail sacks on the cart as it got closer.

He didn't realize how anxious he'd become to hear from home until this morning. Now his heart was pounding. Would that postman ever quit visiting and get on back with the mail? Ed was fidgeting as he stood in the doorway watching the mail being carried inside through the side door.

He went back to the store. The wait was killing him, and it might be all morning before the mail was sorted.

"You get anything?"

Ed looked back toward the post office before he

answered Mr. Carr. "Don't know yet."

"I thought you went to wait on the mail."

"I did, but I got tired of waiting. I'll go back after while." He started to tell Mr. Carr how nervous he was waiting at the post office, but didn't.

Ed waited on a customer, but his mind was on the mail being sorted across the street.

The customer was another member of the Wednesday night crowd, who talked continuously about the "sermon" while Ed counted each kind of bolt her husband had written on the order. She had no idea what a carriage bolt was, and Ed couldn't read the writing, but Mr. Carr knew her husband's writing, and when Ed asked for his help, they got the order filled.

If one more person comes in and starts telling me how good I preached, I'm gonna start screaming, Ed thought as he finished the order. *Why can't people realize that when church goes good it's the spirit?*

Ed was questioning himself, but at least he'd forgotten the mail…for just a minute.

"Edward Tice." The postman's voice was the loudest, coarsest voice Ed could ever remember hearing. "You got some mail. Two letters and a package." The postman laid them on the counter next to the box of bolts.

The lady was still talking, and it looked like she planned to stay. She bent over and read the writing on both of Eddie letters and his package.

"Now, son, don't you go running back to Tennessee. I'll bet that letter there is from your Mama,…and this one…." She picked up Elizabeth's letter and smelled of it. "Yep, it's from your girl."

She turned to Mr. Carr. "Joseph, you just tell him now that we get him back in church. Those people can't have him back, no way."

She left the store mumbling to herself, and the box of bolts she'd come to get was sitting by Ed's package.

Ed's face was crimson. He'd never seen anyone so nosy, but she was so…well…he was at a loss to describe her.

"Ed, that woman is the finest person you'll ever meet…if you can stand her." The postman winked at Ed and left.

Ed had been staring at the package and the two letters, and hadn't seen the dozen or so people that followed the postmaster to deliver his mail.

He picked up his mail and left the store.

"Now you folks get out a here." Ed heard Mr. Carr telling people they were going to have to "quit pestering the boy, or he'll leave."

The voices faded in the background as Ed walked toward the river. He didn't know if he would have any privacy there or not, but he knew he couldn't read his letter or open the package at the store.

CHAPTER 10

The letter from Elizabeth lay on Ed's bed. He'd finished reading it for the fourth time. He couldn't believe she was so upset over his leaving Memphis.

"And Eddie I cried all night after you left. I was afraid to tell Daddy the truth, but after I realized you were gone, I told him. I wrote you a letter telling you if you'd come back we could straighten everything out, but your mother didn't even know you were gone.

"Eddie I was never so happy as when I got your letter today. I came home and Mama had laid it beside my plate, and I found it when we started to eat supper. When I recognized your writing I got so excited I spilled a pitcher of tea all over the table.

"Daddy laughed, he thought it was funny, but Mama is still mad."

The letter was written just the way he remembered Elizabeth talking. She gave every detail and didn't make any attempt to pretend she wasn't in love with him, nor did she seem worried that he might not feel the same.

"Daddy said for you to come on back and finish your schooling at the Seminary. Your mother wrote him a letter that got here the same day mine did telling about you sending the money back to the churches. He says you won't need money if you stay with us, but Mama said you couldn't stay here because I was too sweet on you."

Ed had stopped reading after that line for a minute.

He wasn't going back to the Seminary, but he'd go to Memphis and get Liz. He smiled when he thought of her as Liz; she hated that name.

I'll have to do something about her temper tantrums.

He folded the letter and placed it in the bottom of his trunk.

His mother's letter was a newsy letter from home. It gave a list of all the births and marriages, followed by the deaths in the communities for a ten-mile radius. She'd written a full page of questions at the end.

He'd been busy writing her for the last hour. Some of the questions couldn't be answered.

He didn't know if he would go back to Memphis. He wasn't going to the seminary because he didn't think he could with his reputation; they'd always remember he'd drunk the liquor.

He didn't really have a desire to go back to Wayne County. He knew the scripture said a prophet had honor except in his own country, and he didn't believe a preacher should preach to his own kin. But still, he'd like to be around people like his family. He felt an urge to go to Big Flat. He was sure it was the place he'd heard everybody talk about, where their relatives lived.

If Ed remembered the stories right, the Rhodes family helped survey the northern part of Arkansas just after the Louisiana Purchase. They came back to Tennessee telling stories about all the game, the good timber and good farm land.

His dad always said it was just stories, that Arkansas was half swamp and the other half was a rockpile covered by a briar patch. He had to admit he was beginning to believe the part about the swamp during the time he'd spent in the bottoms above Newport.

But the rockpiles didn't completely cover the hills. There were rich fertile valleys and some of the upland was flat plateaus. He believed Big Flat was one of those level plateaus that was so beautiful. At least he was going to see, if he got invited.

He tried to answer his mother's questions. He was going to have a long letter written just answering them, and he needed enough time to answer Elizabeth's letter tonight.

It was going to take some thought before he wrote Elizabeth. Was she mature enough to get married? He didn't have a home, and on his salary at the store they couldn't possibly live and buy a house.

He sat trying to decide what to write. Finally, he began the letter. He always believed the best way to do anything was to come right to the point and say or do exactly what he felt.

After he finished the letter, he began to worry about being so forward. He'd told Liz he didn't blame her for his problem in the first paragraph, and then for two pages he told her his plans to find a church to pastor somewhere and get married as soon as possible.

He almost tore the letter up a couple of times when he woke up during the night and thought of all he'd written.

His heart was beating fast and his palms were sticky when he mailed the letter the next morning. Like they were before he preached on Wednesday. It was done. Now he'd wait for his reply.

CHAPTER 11

A limb hung against the tin roof. The wind had been blowing hard since sundown. March 1923 was coming in like a lion. Ed had meant to trim the tree last year but just didn't get around to it.

Tonight, the beating of the big limb followed by the scraping of the smaller limbs as they slid back and forth squeaking against the tin were not the kind of noises Ed Tice really liked to hear while he tried to prepare a sermon for Sunday morning.

Liz lay sleeping peacefully, the smile she'd given him when she said good night was an expression of happiness. The flickering lamp gave the room a peaceful feeling even though the wind was roaring outside. Ed was happy, but the sermon might never get finished if he didn't stop daydreaming.

Sometimes he would just sit and watch Liz sleep on Saturday nights. She knew he seldom slept more than a couple of hours because of his "Sunday nerves."

Tonight, he'd been remembering how they got here.

The week after he answered her letter over ten years ago was probably the longest week he'd ever spent.

He would never forget the day he got her reply. She'd invited him to Memphis for the next weekend. He was excited and was planning to go when he opened the second letter. It was from Jim Rhodes inviting him to preach at Big Flat, the same weekend he was supposed to go to Memphis.

The letter from Jim ended with "We'll expect you on Saturday. I've made arrangements for you to get from Sylamore. Just ask the man at the depot when you get off the train. He'll have a good horse for you to ride, and directions how to get to my place."

Ed remembered the frustration he'd felt when he realized he would have to write Liz and tell her he would come to Memphis another weekend. Preaching came first.

Ed looked out the window of the little parsonage. The moon was bright on the other tin roofs; the dark shingles of some houses gave the town a checkerboard appearance on this clear night.

This place had been good to them. That first trip went better than he'd ever imagined, and when the pastor decided to move to California three weeks later, Ed bought most of the furniture in the parsonage for twenty-five dollars.

They'd been married in Memphis on Tuesday, and he'd preached in Big Flat the next Sunday.

Town bookkeeper, preacher, and barber. Ed smiled as he thought of how he'd expanded his services in the last ten years just to keep food on their table. He started as pastor, bookkeeper for the general store and part time clerk. Barbering came along after the town barber got too old and quit.

During the years he'd learned to live on whatever they made each week. Some people thought the preacher didn't need any money, while others felt they could pay the preacher and maybe the Lord would ignore one of their sins. Ed would prefer his congregation just heed his sermons on stewardship, then he wouldn't notice the ones who gave and those who didn't.

Preaching? Ed was proud to do it most of the time. After ten years the zeal he experienced while praying the Sunday afternoon at the Carrs was still with him.

But he wished for children so Liz wouldn't be alone while he was off preaching. He'd taken the pastorate without knowing he would have to go to Hickory one Sunday morning a month and to Cozahome another one. All the people in Big Flat were kin to those at Hickory and "Cozy;" they didn't want but one preacher for all three places.

The real serious church goers went to wherever the preacher was on Sunday, while the old folks had Bible study for the kids at Hickory, Cozy, or Big Flat, regardless of where the preacher was. Ed knew a lot of people liked the system. There were always Wednesday and Sunday night services in Big Flat, plus the first and third Sunday mornings. The second Sunday of each month at Hickory and fourth Sunday at Cozy gave everybody a break except him.

Neither Ed nor Liz realized what life was going to be like as "ministers" when they got married.

He turned back from the window. He remembered her temper tantrums the first year. She'd thrown his best suit in the yard during one of their fights. But then he came home one day and found her crying. She'd stopped crying when he came in. She went to the door and closed it.

"Ed, sit down, I've got something to say. I knew you were a preacher when I married you. I was raised by a preacher and I knew what I was getting into. I won't fuss anymore when you have to leave me to go see people. I won't complain when people don't allow us any privacy. Just forgive me for the way I've been acting, I knew better."

The day she'd said that, Ed remembered thinking, *She'll forget she said it by tomorrow.* But for ten years she'd lived up to her promise.

Ed went back to his Bible and began thumbing through the books of the old testament, hoping some scripture would jump out at him for tomorrow's sermon.

The desk and chair crowded the bedroom, but he hadn't said a word when he came home a few days after Liz made her promise, and found it sitting by her side of their bed.

She knew he spent a lot of nights studying and praying, but she wanted him in here by her, whether she could sleep or not.

Ed just wished the churches' problems would smooth out as well as his marriage.

He began to read in Psalms, and as he read he thought about his last sermon. He'd preached a sermon the prohibitionists would have been proud of.

When he met Jim Rhodes he was so glad to find someone from Wayne County. When he came to Big Flat the first time, he was equally impressed with the people. It was just like back home. Now as he sat thinking about preaching so hard against liquor last week at Cozy, he realized the problem was these people were too much like the people at home. They farmed little patches of land. They ran their stock loose in the woods. They hunted and trapped during the winter, and they made moonshine liquor...and drank it.

Ed never thought he'd see the day he'd hate liquor as much as the prohibition people he'd met in Memphis, but now he wondered about the law. Since the law went into effect over two years ago, every still in the hills for twenty miles in any direction had been running full time. The liquor was ruining the people and their way of life.

For the first time last Sunday he'd really preached hard against "shine." He wondered if it did any good at all.

Tomorrow morning he'd know when he saw the crowd. If any of the folks from Cozy came to hear him this Sunday, he'd know he didn't make any of them mad.

Of course, the problem wasn't with people who came to church, it was the people who didn't, or rather, the men who didn't.

Ed began thinking of the Sitton clan here. Like the ones in Wayne County, they made most of the illegal liquor. He liked Willie Sitton the few times he'd been around him. And Ellen, Willie's wife, brought their children to Hickory for church every time he preached. He thought about how pretty the three little girls were, dressed up and sitting by their mother. It was hard to believe their dad was selling more "shine" than anyone in the country.

If I could convert Willie,... The thought had never occurred to Ed before. *That's it! That's it. I can't preach enough sermons to change it, but if Willie started coming to....*

He thought of the times he'd gone to members of his congregation's homes to try to help settle a problem. All the stories usually started the same. "Brother Tice, he doesn't usually do this, but he stopped at Willie Sitton's barn above the bridge...." And then the wife would tell how bad the problem had been since her husband got home drunk.

I'll get Willie in the church. Ed made himself that vow, and went to bed. As he lay down beside Liz, he didn't have any idea what he'd preach tomorrow, but if he could come up with a plan to convert Willie Sitton, the drinking problems would be solved.

CHAPTER 12

Ever since Saturday night Ed had been planning his visit with Willie Sitton.

Monday would have been a good day for him to go since the drunks were usually hung over from the weekend, and not too many around the barn, but he had to go down on the lower end of Big Creek to see a woman who was dying from cancer.

Tomorrow morning I'll go see him, Ed thought as he unsaddled his horse. He turned the gelding loose with the mule in the field behind the parsonage.

He had three means of transportation and the horse was his favorite of the three. The car was so undependable, seldom started, and besides half the people lived in places impossible to drive to. That was the reason for the mule; he was better at going along the edges of the bluffs and the deep hollows than the horse. He rode the mule to see most of the people around Hickory.

Since supper Ed had sat with his Bible open in front of

him, but he'd read very little. He'd spent most of his time trying to decide how to approach Willie. He turned the lamp out and went to bed. *I'll just listen this trip,* he thought.

Ed took a lot of pride in being a preacher that listened to his people. Each time he went to visit the Carrs since moving to Big Flat, he'd appreciated Mr. Carr more than when he stayed with them because he'd learned to listen to the people when he went to invite them to church.

"Why son, all I did for a month was go by the new barber's place and listen to him. 'Course each time I'd invite him to church before I left. He's the best church worker we've got now."

Mr. Carr had stopped saying, "Son, you listen to your people, can't learn a thing about 'em talking to 'em. You can learn everything there is to know about 'em by listening. It'll pay dividends if you'll listen."

Ed decided not to take the car to Willie's. He needed to see several people along the creek, and he'd make it better by riding the mule.

As he put the old army saddle on the mule he knew he must look unusual with the big black leather saddle on the little red mule, but he wasn't about to put his good saddle on and get it scratched up by all the limbs along the creek.

The mule gave a couple of jumps as he got in the saddle; he was full of vigor this morning. They'd be at the bridge in a half hour. Now, if Willie would only be at the big barn so they could visit.

"Have a seat if you can get off that varmint you're ridin'." Willie Sitton was mending a set of harnesses.

Ed got off the mule and tied him to the gate post.

"Preacher, where you going this mornin'?" Willie's face showed the surprise at having him stop at the bridge.

"I've come to see you."

"Me?"

"Yes, if you'll let me, I'd like to visit a while."

Willie hung the harness he'd been mending on the wall of the tack room. He studied the harness for a minute, holding in his hand one of the pieces of frayed leather that still needed mending.

"Go ahead, Willie, and fix that. I don't want to hinder you."

"Preacher, it can wait. Ain't very often this place gets a real preacher for a visitor." Willie's gesture when he said "real preacher" was toward the barn as a whole, and the side room in particular. He started toward the side room and then stopped.

"Preacher, you want to go in there? Willie was confused about how to handle Ed's visit.

"It doesn't matter." Ed knew Willie was ashamed for him to go in the room where all of his liquor sales were made.

Willie turned the key in the padlock and slid the latch pin back. The chain was left dangling from the door, and the lock fell to the ground as the door swung open. Willie hurried into the dark side room.

Ed picked up the lock and hooked it through one of the links of the chain.

"Preacher, we can go up to the house." Willie was nervous with the preacher being there in his side room.

"No, this is fine," Ed answered as he sat down on one of the blocks of wood. His eyes had grown accustomed to the darkness.

The room was about 10 feet wide and 20 feet long. The side next to the barn was logs, but the exterior walls were heavy oak boards nailed to the hewn log frame. The ceiling was the bottom of the shingles and lath. The room's dirt floor was as smooth as glass.

Ed knew the men standing and spitting tobacco juice on the dirt had caused the floor to be so smooth. He remembered rooms like this in Wayne County.

The big block of wood in the center was taller than the

smaller ones. It was the table. Cards had probably decided the owner of money placed on that block of wood. Money for liquor was probably exchanged on it. The shorter blocks like he was sitting on were for visiting.

Willie was still nervous as he walked circles around the room, stopping each time he passed the door to look out.

"Preacher, you really think we ought to visit here?"

"Why not?"

Willie stood, studying the preacher. They were about the same age. Willie was thirty-one last October, and he was guessing the Preacher to be about the same. But after their age there wasn't much they had in common. The preacher was over six feet tall, while Willie had to stretch with his shoes on to be able to claim the five foot and six inches he told everyone he was.

Willie guessed they both weighed close to two hundred pounds; at least he knew he did, but he couldn't really say their weight was close to the same when he compared his short stubby arms with the long arms of the preacher. When he came through the door, Willie knew why he'd always looked like he covered the front of the church at Hickory. *That preacher is long,* thought Willie. *I mean tall.* He was too nervous to even think straight.

Ed watched Willie as he nervously paced the room until he stopped to study him. Willie stared at him for a full minute.

"Say something, Preacher." Willie's voice showed his irritation. "I don't know how to talk to no preacher."

"Willie, just sit down. We'll talk about me if you want to." Ed felt better as Willie finally sat down.

"How come you're a preacher?"

"I don't know, Willie. Most of the time I'm trying to answer that question myself." Ed wished he hadn't answered the question when he saw the delight in Willie's eyes at his answer.

"You mean you're not sure?"

"I'm sure why I preach. I just don't know why the Lord picked me."

Willie's eyes had not left Ed since he stopped pacing the floor.

"Preaching is not easy, Willie."

"Why?"

Ed wondered about his plan to listen; this was turning into a cross examination of himself.

"Is your job easy?" Ed hoped to turn this conversation around.

"Yeah, most of the time."

They both became silent. Willie took out his pocket knife and began whittling on the block of wood he was sitting on. Ed watched him closely, realizing how awkward this was, a preacher visiting the bootlegger.

"You're from Wayne County?"

"Yes." Ed was shocked that Willie knew that.

"My folks and your used to make…" Willie stopped.

"Shine together," Ed finished the sentence, and they laughed for the first time together.

Ed decided to try a direct approach. "Wille, I came to ask you to come to church."

"I come to church."

"I've not seen you there over a half dozen times since I've been here."

"That's all I've been."

Ed wasn't sure he was ever going to be able to talk to Willie, or if Willie was going to say enough for them to get acquainted.

"Preacher, I've got to have a drink, you want one?" Willie went through the back door of the side room and came back with a quart of his 'shine.

Ed was never more disturbed. Why had he come up with this stupid idea of visiting Willie in the first place?

"Willie, I've got to go." Ed got up to leave.

"I'm sorry, Preacher. I didn't mean it when I asked you

to drink with me." Willie got ahold of his arm. "I just didn't know what to say. Your coming here where I ...." Willie's eyes left the preacher and stared at the dirt floor. "... sell my whiskey," he said, finishing the sentence.

"Willie, I'm sorry, too. I just thought we could visit and then maybe you'd come to church."

"I will, Preacher, I will." Willie's nerves were getting some better, but he still hadn't recovered from the shock of Ed's visit.

Outside in the sunlight Willie seemed to relax as he walked over to Ed's mule.

"You buy that mule from old man Reece?"

"Yeah, sure did."

"I raised that mule, broke him to ride going up and down this creek. He's almost seven years old." Willie slapped the mule on the shoulder as he talked. "Thought he would get bigger than this, though. Sold him 'cause he wasn't big enough for me to ride."

"I wish he weighed a couple hundred pounds more, maybe, but I don't ride him much." Ed agreed with Willie.

"Preacher, you're one of the few men that ever come out of that room dry."

Ed ignored the remark and got on his mule.

Willie stepped back as the mule turned. "Preacher, come back," he said.

"I'm planning on it." Ed answered as he rode off.

CHAPTER 13

It's been almost a year, Ed thought as he recalled his visit with Willie. He'd tried to forget about the visit, but having Willie for church Sunday reminded him of that morning at the barn.

Now as he drove along the rocky trail of a road that wound its way to the bridge, he thought about his visit with Willie.

He might go visit him again. He'd enjoyed the piercing stare Willie gave him during his sermon yesterday.

I could handle it better, Ed thought as he pulled onto the swinging bridge. He liked driving across the new bridge; it swayed and flexed under the weight of the car. He slowed to look at the water.

"Come on, Preacher, you're blocking the road!" Willie's voice could be heard above the noise of the car motor.

Ed pulled on over to the end of the bridge where Willie was standing, smiling, and wiping his brow.

"How you doing, Willie?"

"Better."

"Glad to see you in church."

"I promised you I'd come."

"I know, Willie, but it sure took a while."

"Park your car, I'd like to talk to you."

Ed pulled the car over to the side of the road and followed Willie to his tool shed.

"I was just taking a break from sharpening a plow." Willie pointed to the smoldering coals in the forge next to the anvil. "I used to let Jim Davis do all my smithin' 'til his wife got tired of me paying him in 'shine."

Ed leaned against the corner of the shop and watched Willie turn the blower until the coals in the forge turned a bright red.

"I hate doing this in hot weather. The fire gets me too hot and then I take a cold." Willie talked as he turned the plow over in the forge.

"Hand me that pot." Willie pointed to a tin pot setting by the post Ed was leaning against. Willie set the pot by the forge and poured some water in it. Ed watched without saying a word while Willie hammered a new edge on the plow.

After he finished the hammering he stuck the plow in the water, letting it sizzle until the steam stopped rising from the water.

"Boy, I'm proud that's finished." Willie took a tin cup from a nail and poured some of the hot water into it from the pot by the forge. He paused for a second, glancing toward Ed as he poured some liquor from a jar he took from behind the anvil.

"Want a toddy?" Willie sipped the hot mixture of 'shine and water.

Ed turned his back, staring back toward his car. *Lord, why do I have to face this?* Since he'd been preaching at Big Flat Ed had never thought of his old problem, but today as he watched Willie, the memories and temptations all came back.

"Preacher, most people 'round here use a toddy for a cold." Willie's face was red from the heat and the embarrassment of having asked the preacher to drink again.

"Let's go down to the end of the bridge. There's always a breeze under the shade of that big sycamore."

Ed followed Willie to the end of the bridge and leaned against the rail, without saying anything, while Willie finished the toddy.

"Preacher, I'm worried."

"About what?"

"People are buying too much 'shine."

Ed stood up. He couldn't understand a man in the business of making whiskey complaining about having too much business.

"Willie, I wish they wouldn't buy any."

"I know, preacher." Willie leaned against the rail on the other side of the bridge, "I asked a preacher years ago why God let things like whiskey be made. He said he thought alcohol was necessary, 'cept people abused it. I know it helps my cold."

"Willie, let's not talk about liquor."

"I know, Preacher. I liked your sermon yesterday." Willie looked away from Ed.

"You liked it?"

"Uh-huh." Willie walked over to Ed's side of the bridge. "Ma always read about David killin' the giant. I used to practice with a sling after I heard the story. Couldn't never hit a thing."

Ed was surprised to learn Willie knew anything about the Bible.

"Your mother read the Bible to you?"

"All of it, one winter when I's twelve."

"How much of it do you remember?"

"All of it. When I hear it."

Ed needed to go. He had to be in Marshall by ten to

meet the train.

"Willie, you need anything from town?"

"No, don't reckon."

Ed went to his car while Willie continued to watch him. As he started the car, Willie waved and turned away.

The drive to Marshall gave Ed a chance to think about this morning. Was it another coincidence that Willie offered the toddy? Did he know about the problem years before? How could he have found out?

"I sometimes believe he can read my mind." Ed was talking aloud to himself as he remembered the way Willie seemed to stare into his mind.

Ed still believed if he could convert Willie, the liquor problems around Big Flat and Hickory would lessen.

But today liquor wasn't his biggest concern. His mother was coming on the train to stay until Liz had their baby. The excitement of the baby, his mom's first trip to Arkansas, and the addition to the parsonage would keep him busy.

CHAPTER 14

Noah Franklin Tice; a big name for a little fellow that might weigh seven pounds after his second week as a resident of the parsonage at Big Flat.

Ed leaned back from his desk. It was hard to concentrate with a baby crying.

He sure has a good set of lungs, Ed thought as he listened to the baby screaming even louder.

Liz was trying to change a diaper. Her mother had stayed until yesterday, but now they were on their own.

The past two months had been exciting. Ed's mother stayed until the baby was born, then Liz's mother had stayed for two weeks. The people in the churches had helped, too. Ed wondered if any baby ever got this much attention around Big Flat before.

Of course, everyone knew they'd wished for children ever since they got married.

If a new baby was brought to church, Liz would get it and bring it to him and go on forever about how sweet it was. She'd stopped doing that so much last year, like she'd given up on them ever having one of their own. And then she got pregnant.

The women from Big Flat gave the baby more clothes than either of the other churches, and there was no way he cold wear all of the things that had been knitted for him. When Ellen Sitton brought her gifts she left an envelope for the preacher. Ed opened it and found a ten-dollar bill with a note saying, "Sorry you didn't make it to preach last Sunday, proud you got a boy. Willie."

Ed looked at the ten-dollar bill. He had his answer to a mystery. While he preached his first sermon at Hickory, Willie and some of the other men had sat across the yard from the old school building under an oak tree. The offering had been $2.03, about normal for a church with a couple of men and the rest women and kids. But after that there was always a ten-dollar bill plus the rest of the money. Sometimes the total would be seventeen or eighteen dollars. Ed suspicioned Willie gave the money, but he'd never known for sure. Why would a bootlegger support the church?

Ed began to think of when he'd stopped with Willie the last time. He'd been so excited to see his mother, and the time since, that he'd forgotten the visit, nor had he thought of it much since. He took the ten dollars from his pocket. It had always been there every Sunday since he got here. *Why didn't I think of Willie giving it before?* Ed wasn't sure he'd ever understand people.

I should of listened to Willie that day I went to pick up Mama. Ed's thoughts went back to the tool shed. *Even if he did want to talk about his liquor.* He had wondered all day what the point was Willie would have made about people buying too much 'shine.

When I go back.... Ed stopped at that thought. Fear seemed to grip him at the thought of going back to see Willie.

The liquor problems were growing worse. Prohibition wasn't working out for anybody. It seemed to Ed people who never drank a drop were trying to drink all they could since it became illegal.

It reminded him of when he was a boy going to school at the Oak Grove School above Waynesboro. He never thought of climbing on the hedge until the teacher made a rule against it. Before the term was over, he'd been whipped twice with the paddle after being caught trying to walk the hedge by stepping on the stubs of the cut limbs. In addition to the whipping he still had a scar on his leg from falling through the stubble.

I don't guess this is much different. Ed needed to study instead of day dreaming.

The church. When he thought of the church, he usually thought of everybody in all three communities. Jim Rhodes was still the leader at Big Flat. John Rhodes , his brother, was the leader at Hickory. Cozy's influence was split between Coy Bryant and Wayne Blair, the Rhodes' brother-in-law. Ed found out his first month that the kin folks stuck together even closer than back in Wayne County.

Ellen Sitton was John Rhode's daughter, which made it even more complicated to try to preach against Willie selling liquor.

After that one hard sermon last year, he was glad he'd decided to convert Willie instead of trying to stop it from the pulpit. He knew these people were worse than the ones in Wayne County for using their liquor.

Mrs. Rhodes brought catnip tea to make sure little Noah's hives "broke out real good." She brought a camphor made from a combination of grease, sugar, 'shine, and Lord knows what else. In addition, she brought a tonic guaranteed to cure the colic.

Ed tapped his pencil on the desk, remembering the taste of the tonic. It was obviously made from some of Willie's best liquor.

Lord, how do I handle this? Ed knew the answer before he said it. He could do nothing except point out the problem.

The problem…if only he could define the problem. Jim Rhodes was the best Sunday School leader and teacher he'd ever seen or heard. He could read as well from the Bible or anyone who ever played in one of Shakespeare's plays. Ed wasn't surprised to learn he'd studied at Vanderbilt. And then there was how he would very subtly tell the congregation their drinking habits were a matter of conscience.

I could preach forever, but until these people are convicted in their hearts, it won't do any good. Ed closed his Bible and got his coat to go for a walk in the cold night air.

For eleven years he'd walked the length of the town on clear, mild nights. The dogs didn't bother to bark any more when he passed the houses. This was his town.

Ed often wondered if any preacher ever won a town completely. He knew the church was stronger in numbers than when he came. But he didn't know about the spiritual side. How could he ever know?

He was yet to meet a man around here who didn't plan on making things right with God. He'd heard about atheists, but they were not a problem in these hills. *Since I've been here every man or woman that died has somebody willing to vouch for their convictions.*

Ed stopped by the Rhodes General Store. He kept Jim's books. He knew he gave a lot of groceries to people. Oh, they were posted on accounts, but there were accounts that there hadn't been a cent paid on in years.

Ed remembered pointing out an account that was over four years in arrears. Jim had totaled it up; the total was only $260. "That's Mrs. Still," was all he'd said, and walked away. "Preacher, she'll pay sometime if she can.

Until then we'll let her have what she needs."

Ed had gone to visit her after that and learned her husband fell off the bluff while he was coon hunting. Then he learned her husband had been to Willie's before he left to go on the hunt.

As he walked back to the house he felt of the ten-dollar bill in his pocket. He knew he couldn't win by fighting their way of life, but if the Lord could win Willie.... He began to think of going on one more visit.

CHAPTER 15

"Willie, are you here?" Ed yelled as he rode the horse through the barn gate.

The side room was locked, the gate to the barn lot was closed. Willie was not around the barn. Ed had always wondered how much time Willie spent at the barn. This was the first time he'd ever been here and not found Willie around, but it was still early.

Ed turned his horse back out the gate and started toward the Sitton house on top of the ledge above the barn.

Willie's mules were hooked to a wagon loaded with hay and tied to the hitch rail in front of the house. Willie came out of the house just as the preacher rode up.

"Come on, Preach, get down off that horse." Willie stuck out his hand before Ed turned loose of the saddle horn. "Too cold to bring that boy?" Willie shook his hand as he teased about Noah.

"I just stopped by to thank you."

"Forget it, forget it." Willie walked toward the wagon.

"Hop on, Preacher. You can go with me to feed the steers up the creek."

Ed hesitated. He wasn't sure he wanted to go with Willie to feed the steers. How much should he have to do with the old bootlegger? Then he thought of Christ's answer when he was questioned for mingling with the wrong crowd. If he remembered right, the twelfth verse, chapter nine, in Luke said the "whole need not a physician but they that are sick."

Ed climbed on the wagon.

"Preacher, why were you arguing with yourself about getting on the wagon?"

Ed stared at the bright brass knobs on the mules' harness. He wasn't sure he was capable of visiting Willie because Willie seemed to know his every thought.

"Willie, I just wondered if I should ride around with you while you feed the steers." Ed paused, and took the reins from Willie. "Let me drive the mules. I got my answer from the scripture while I balked." Ed thought his answer would give Willie something to consider.

"Preacher, how'd you get here this early? That's twice you've come before the sun got up over the hill."

Ed had left Big Flat by the light of the moon and the breaking of dawn, but the deep hollow of Big Creek wouldn't be under the bright December sun for another half hour.

"I get up early," Ed answered.

"Preacher, you wuz smart, taking the reins," Willie said as the mules stopped at the wire gate at the top of the bluff. Willie jumped off and opened the gate. Ed drove the mules and wagon through and waited for Willie to close the gate.

Willie came back to the wagon. Ed drove the mules on toward the creek.

"Preacher, stop right down here. See the fog?" Willie pointed at the haze rising from the water. It would only make it three to four feet above the water before the air turned it to vapor and it disappeared.

"I like to watch it do that. As the sun gets higher, the fog doesn't last as long. Just before it quits, it'll look like smoke right on top of the water."

They sat quiet, watching the fog rise from the water that was clear. The only sign of moving was the ripples made at the rapids below the still pool. The sounds coming from the shoal defied description; sometimes they sounded like a gurgle, then the tones would become sharper, almost a chime as the water made its own music.

"Let's go." Willie pointed up the creek. They rode in silence across the creek and along the gravel bar, until they came to another gate. Willie opened the gate and left it open, jumping on the wagon as the preacher drove through.

"I used to ride a mule by myself up through here when I was just a tot. It was four miles from the house to John Rhodes' mill.

"That's where I met Ellen." Willie pointed to a bare spot in the bottom field they'd just pulled into. "We'll throw the hay off there. I'll call the steers while you untie the wire."

Ed began pulling the wire from the bales and throwing the blocks of hay on the bare ground Willie had pointed to. He couldn't believe how loud Willie could yell as he called the steers. Of course, standing on top of the wagon seat made him seem taller and probably louder. Ed was beginning to like Willie. Willie respected him as a preacher, but he still treated him like a man.

A lot of people were so uncomfortable that they never let the preacher get acquainted, but while they watched the fog rise from the creek, he'd seen a side to Willie that was deeper than most folks, and he'd enjoyed Willie's way of putting him to work, even if he was a little bossy.

After the steers heard Willie, the bawling and running of the herd toward the wagon had become louder than Willie.

Ed finished untying the last bale before the first steer arrived. There must have been fifty of the critters trying to get to the hay strewn over an area too small for twenty of them to stand.

"Preacher, I should a told you to spread the hay out more." Willie gave the reins to Ed, and they sat down on the wagon seat to watch the steers fight for position to get their share of the hay.

"Let's go, Preacher, I've got another load to take to the cows down the creek."

Willie began telling the history of his family settling the farm. The Sitton family came to Arkansas in 1831, according to the family Bible. They'd been one of five families that left Waynesboro in the spring of 1830, but returned after finding the Mississippi River flooded for miles in every direction from Memphis. In 1831 they'd tried again, only this time they went to Paducah, Kentucky, and crossed the Ohio into Illinois and then crossed the Mississippi above the bottoms coming across the hills of Missouri. According to Willie the trip took two tries and four months to finally make it just about 300 miles from Wayne County.

"But the Lord only knew how far they actually came, because the five families' descendants all told about the trip differently." Willie ended the story by saying, "Preacher, all I know is they made it. I'm proof of that."

They'd made it back to the barn. Willie went to the side room and unlocked and then opened the door at the back.

"Come on in here."

Ed was uncomfortable in the side room. He remembered Willie pacing the floor around the room until he finally went to get the quart of moonshine liquor. As he stepped up on the boards of the floor of what was obviously a grain bin, Ed felt even more uncomfortable.

Willie began putting corn cobs in the little pot-bellied stove in the center of the bin.

"I build a fire in here almost every morning, keeps the moisture out of the grain." Willie pointed to the sacks of wheat.

Ed became aware that he'd spoken only once since they got on the wagon. He remembered planning to listen to Willie during their first visit. He was listening today.

CHAPTER 16

"Ed, a lot of people think I'll burn my barn with this stove, but I never put wood in it except for a little bit of red cedar. Mostly I just burn corn cobs. They don't last but barely long enough to make my toddy." Willie put a pot on to heat some water.

Ed watched as he put two spoons full of sugar into the water. He noticed Willie had called him Ed for the first time. He'd always said Preacher or Preach before.

The sound of the spoon stirring the sugar water reminded him of his mother making a toddy years before at home.

"Preacher, you want one this morning?"

Ed dropped his head and stared at the boards of the floor. *Why does he do that?* Ed thought as he slowly raised his head.

"No, Willie." His answer was resolute, leaving no doubt.

"Preacher, I need to know something."

"What?'

"Well, you come over here a year ago last July. You come again this last June. Now you're back and this is December." Willie stopped to get a pint of 'shine from under the sack Ed was sitting on.

Ed watched him pour the clear liquid into the steaming cup of sugar water. He sat down across from Ed. Staring over the cup, he switched it from hand to hand until it got cool enough for him to hold.

"I've asked you all three times to take a drink. The first time I watched you swallow as I unscrewed the lid on that quart of 'shine." Willie sipped his toddy. "That day I's sharpening the plow your eyes lit up like other fellers do when they want a drink. Today you dropped your head. Preacher, has liquor ever been your problem?"

Ed stood up. He went to the little stove. It was like the coal burner stove at the train depot back home. The fire box was round and tall, the top was about even with Willie's eyes as he stared across the stove waiting for an answer.

"Willie, I know you understand people. My problem was liquor, not how much I drank, but where I drank it."

"Preacher, I didn't mean to pry, but that day I started to tell you people was buying too much 'shine...." Willie stood up and moved over to warm by the stove, opening the door and putting in some more cobs. "You got nervous and didn't want to talk about it, but you never got hard on me. You still ain't."

"Why did you say people was buying too much?"

"Ah, I don't know. It's just some folks get carried away with whatever they do."

"Why does that bother you?"

"I hate to see anybody hurt by it." Willie finished his toddy. "Liquor's probably got its place, but since Prohibition there's been a lot of bad 'shine made, and too much of it drunk."

"Willie, I don't understand you," Ed went back and sat down on the sack leaving Willie by the stove. "Do you make a living selling 'shine?"

"Preacher, it's hard to say how I make a living. I sell a little timber, I sell some hogs, I sell all of my steers, and we've always sold some 'shine."

"I still don't see why you'd care about what happens to 'shine after you sell it." Ed hoped to find out more about Willie by using this approach.

"Preach, let's put it this way: a good 'shine buyer's got to have money, he needs to be able to work." Willie came back over by the door. "If a feller buys too much and becomes a drunk, he gets to where he won't work. He starts wanting 'shine on the credit, his family starts suffering. I have to cut 'im off."

"Why don't you quit?"

"And take a chance of my good customers gettin' poisoned on some of this rot gut that's being made?"

"But, Willie, you know it's hurtin' more people than it does good...it don't do any good."

Willie opened the door and they went back through the side room to the outside.

"Ed..." They stopped in the bright sun that was now shining. "I quit four years ago for a while after Ellen found out I'd sold Jess Still a pint the night he fell off the bluff. The next week John House got poisoned on some stuff he bought from some folks up the creek. He didn't die, but he still cain't work."

They went back to the wagon. Ed climbed on the driver's seat and pulled close enough for Willie to throw the hay in the wagon for the cows down the creek. Willie didn't ask if he was going with him to finish feeding, they just loaded the hay with the preacher stacking the bales after Willie threw them onto the wagon.

"What I meant about people buying too much was this," Willie said after he climbed up beside the preacher "I sell it for two uses. One is for toddy or snake bites, and any other kind of medicine, and then if a guy should need a drink for his bad feelings, to pep him up."

Willie pointed toward the gate below the bridge and hopped off to open it for Ed to drive the wagon through. "I'll just leave it open 'til we come back." Willie swung back up on the wagon.

"Willie, how can you say that when you know not many people are doing what you just said with the whiskey you sell?"

"Are you gonna quit preaching because your Christians don't do like you want 'em to?"

Ed drove the team of mules in silence thinking, *Lord, how do I handle this?*

"Preach, I feel real bad sometimes about things. Take this farm here. Ol' man Scarbrough worked hard chopping off that hill land and pulling all the stumps, took him about four years 'fore he got it cleared." Willie pointed to the fields on top of the bluffs. "I started letting him have 'shine at two dollars a quart on the credit 'til he got to owing a hundred dollars. I didn't know he was drinking all of it 'til his wife came and jumped on Ellen. I gave 'im four hundred more dollars for this farm, and they moved back to Mississippi."

The mules stopped to drink from the creek before they crossed again.

"I'll bet that family'll hate me 'til they die."

Ed was learning things about Willie he'd never guessed as he listened to him. He was amazed he worried about his people that bought 'shine from him.

"Preacher, if you and me drunk a toddy once a day," Willie paused as he saw the expression Ed got, " not to get drunk, but for our nerves and for our colds, do you think God would still let you preach?"

Ed stared down the black leather check lines at the mules as he drove the wagon. He wondered if he'd made a friend, or was Willie possessed by some demon trying to destroy him?

"Preach, I'm sorry I asked. I's just thinking about the scripture in Proverbs that says, 'Give strong drink unto him that is ready to perish.'" Willie looked at Ed. "I believe that's in the sixth verse of the last chapter."

"Willie, I don't know about that scripture, I just know we can't drink much and expect to go to heaven." Ed was almost too shocked about Willie knowing the scripture to answer.

They finished feeding in silence and when they did begin talking again it was about cattle and farming the fields along the creek.

Willie took the preacher to his horse. He'd enjoyed having him around all morning, but he felt bad about the liquor, wished he'd never had his toddy or even talked about it. *I'll never mention it again nor will I drink in front of him,* he thought. Willie made the resolution as he watched Ed ride back toward Big Flat.

CHAPTER 17

Ed rode back from the bridge through the hills above Cedar Creek rather than following the road. He needed to be alone to think.

Was Willie his tempter, the way Christ had been tempted? Could he ever win a man who seemed to be so well in control of his life? How much could Willie really know about him?

The questions were buzzing through his mind while the horse picked its own way through the wagon trail that had grown up in bushes and briars since the road in the bottom hollow was built. Ed knew he liked Willie. He liked his apparent honesty, he liked his generosity, and he just enjoyed his company. He was so relaxed now, easy going and he wasn't nervous around the preacher anymore.

The question Willie asked about, if he thought he could still preach if he drank the liquor, seemed to be still piercing through his mind. He remembered the arguments in the churches back home. To Drink Or Not To Drink had been the title one evangelist gave his sermon the last night of a revival. He remembered how proud the people were it was the last night. It saved them the trouble of running the preacher off in the middle of the week.

Ed came back into the road. He felt better. It was like he needed the trip through the woods to clear his mind.

"I've got to put a stop to this. I can either visit Willie like he is or I can quit going to see him completely." Ed whispered under his breath. "If I keep going he's going to catch me in a weak moment and I'll drink with him."

The thought caused Ed to sit up straight in the saddle. He began visualizing what it would do to Willie if he did drink a toddy with him. *I wouldn't have to worry about him telling anybody.*

He stopped his horse to let him drink from the pond beside the road. He'd been riding the horse harder than he realized. There was lather oozing from the hair next to the girth and around the saddle blanket.

His mind went back to Willie telling him how he acted each time he got the whiskey. *He was offering me a drink each time because he thought I was acting like I wanted one. Was I?* Ed pulled the horse's head up with the reins and started on toward Big Flat. He was still trying to decipher his own feelings as he rode the last mile and half home.

He knew Willie was probably the most open person he'd ever been around. *I may never convert him, but I'm going to continue trying.* Ed resolved that in his mind as he got off his horse and began removing the saddle.

He hung the saddle on the peg in the tack room he'd built at the same time the men had helped him build Noah's room. As he began using the brush and curry comb on the sorrel horse, he felt peaceful for the first time after a visit to see Willie. Always before he'd imagined himself like Daniel going into the lion's den each time he'd gone to see Willie. He was always the knight in shining armor while

Willie was the devil himself. He'd thought the only way to win was to go over there to Willie's and have Willie declare that he was changed, a complete turnaround. Now Ed could see it was going to take time for Willie to change. He also had a problem trying to keep thinking of Willie as being all bad. The concern Willie showed for people. Although, his excuse for selling 'shine so his customers wouldn't get poisoned had to be the first time he'd ever heard of a sin being committed for a good cause. Willie Sitton was the first good sinner he'd really met; most people drew a line where preachers were concerned that they would not allow the preacher to cross. Except for that first day, Willie had allowed him to ask anything he wanted, to say whatever he wished.

Liz yelled for him to come to the house. He gave the horse a slap on the rump, and the horse went to roll in the dirt as soon as he was away from the tack room and stall. Ed watched the freshly curried and brushed coat of the gelding as he rolled in the dirt. The currying was staying clean, just like his sermon's effect seem to last, not very long.

"What do you need, Liz?"

"It's Noah, he's got such a stuffy nose."

Ed went in where the month-old baby lay laboring trying to breathe. He felt of his chest. He could feel a rattle with each little breath

"Hon, let's try some of Sister Rhodes' camphor." He stood up and listened for Liz's answer.

"Didn't you say you thought that had liquor in it?"

"Yes."

Liz didn't argue, she just brought the salve, or camphor as Mrs. Rhodes called it. Ed began rubbing it on the baby's chest. In just a minute he was breathing easier.

"Let's give him a taste of the tonic." Ed took the bottle from Liz and placed a drop on Noah's tongue. They both watched in amazement as little Noah smacked like he did when Liz let him nurse. Before the hour was over Noah was sleeping peaceful, and when he woke up, he felt good. *That's why it was so hard to stop liquor completely back home, and it's the same way here,* Ed thought as he watched Liz let Noah nurse. *If I'm going to preach here, I'll become a part of the community, I'll just preach temperance and try to slow 'em down. They'll all agree getting' drunk is wrong.*

Ed went to feed his horses. The clouds moving in were a dark blue, a blue northerner. It might be the first snow of the season.

Today had been a good day. He'd seen Willie, he felt he understood him now. He'd seen Noah helped by the remedy Mrs. Rhodes made. It changed his mind about there being no good that could come from the 'shine, and now he was asking himself if he'd just made a compromise with these people, or the devil.

The people. He now realized he'd been looking at them as being separated from him and Liz. They were not part of the perfect religion he'd received that Sunday afternoon in Batesville. The experience of his three visits with Willie made him aware there was more of himself still part of these folks than he realized.

God may have called me to preach, but He's still part of everyone's life, too. Ed's answer to his questions came slowly, but he was going to go back to see Willie and not worry about the 'shine.

CHAPTER 18

The little log schoolhouse at Hickory was crowded for church services on this snow-covered Sunday in December.

Ed started his Christmas sermon. It was just the seventeenth, but it would be his last sermon at Hickory in 1924. As he recounted the birth of Christ, he began stressing the need for love during the Christmas season. As he went over the sanctity of the family and the fact that God's son was born into a family with a real mother and an earthly father, even though that father knew the son his wife bore him was of God, he still raised him as his own.

Willie sat beside Ellen, his hands folded in his lap. Ed could not help seeing the change in his gaze or stare. Willie no longer seemed to be studying him as closely; he was listening to the sermon more.

"Preacher, come by next week," Willie said as he shook Ed's hand. "I've got two gallons of sorghum molasses for ya."

Ed smiled as he rode the mule back through the hills to

Big Flat. When Willie shook his hand after church, everyone seemed to stop and watch, and when he said "two gallons," most of the women's mouths had come open in a gasp, anticipating Willie to say "' shine."

He was going to be busy for a few days building a new crib for Noah, working at the store, and getting all the men's haircut for Christmas, but when these jobs were finished he would go see Willie.

As Ed worked on the crib for Noah, he tried to keep his mind off the visit to see Willie. He wasn't worrying anymore about Willie offering him a drink. He'd decided to cross that bridge when he got to it.

January was cold and wet the first week. There wasn't much snow, just ice and some sleet. It had been almost a month and he still hadn't got to go get the molasses. Ed put on extra clothes. He would ride to Hickory and see how the people felt about having church this next Sunday, and stop by Willie's and pick up the molasses.

The mule was going slow down the hill above the bridge. Ed would be glad when he got down to the bottom because the wind was bitter cold coming up the side of the hill. He'd been cold all day. The trip down the hollow from Big Flat and up the Bratton Hollow and across to Hickory had all been facing the wind. His nose was cold, but at least he had feeling in it. But he wasn't sure about his feet. There wouldn't be any church Sunday. He just wished he'd postponed the trip until warmer weather.

"Willie! Willie!" Ed yelled from the front gate before getting down from the mule.

"Preacher," Ellen Sitton said from the door, motioning for him to come in.

Ed went in the house. The heat from the stove felt good. He stood warming himself before saying anything. As he turned around each time he got a little warmer. He'd never been this cold before.

"Sister Ellen, where's Willie?"

Ellen handed him a cup of coffee before she answered. "He's been gone for over an hour to see about one of the sows under the bluff." Ellen Sitton went to get herself a cup of the coffee. "You know where the hog pen below the house is?" She pointed toward the north end of the house. "No." Ed felt better after drinking a couple of swallows of the hot coffee.

"'Course you know Willie, he may be at the bridge."

"If he doesn't come back in a minute, I'll go look for him."

"How's Noah?"

"Sister, I know it's probably because we wanted a baby so long before he came, but he's our whole life."

"I don't think it's just because you had to wait. Me and Willie had our kids right after we got married. We had all three of 'em before he was twenty-one." Ellen stopped. "I ain't tellin' how old I was, but we just loved 'em to death and still do."

They sat quiet for a while, waiting for Willie.

"I'll go find Willie."

"Preacher, thanks for visiting Willie." Ellen stood up and followed Ed to the door. "If he's not at the hog pen, you'll find him around the barn."

Ed rode the mule in the direction Ellen had pointed. He heard the hogs snort as they smelled the mule, but when he got closer, Willie was not at the pen. He turned and rode down the trail to the bridge. Willie was standing in the door of the side room of the barn.

"Come in, Preach." Willie turned and went back to the grain bin. Ed followed without saying hello.

"I like to froze to death helping that sow and I've been trying to warm up ever since." The little stove was roaring and Willie put in two more hands full of corn cobs. "Burns good, but don't last long," Willie said, "Just what I need for a fire here at the barn."

"I almost froze to ..." Ed sneezed hard "...death this

morning."

"Preacher, you shouldn't a come out today."

Willie sat down by the stove. Ed looked around for the pot. He figured sure Willie would be drinking toddies in this weather.

"You quit making toddies?"

"No." Willie went to the door and thought as he looked out. *I made a promise not to mention it, and now he brings it up.* When he turned back he looked at the preacher's eyes as they watered. *Maybe he wants one for his cold,* he thought.

"Preach, you want a toddy?"

Ed dropped his head. He stared at a hole in the board floor, thinking how Willie ought to patch it or plug it with something. A lot of grain could go through the hole, or a mouse could get in. *Lord, I'm sitting here worrying about a hole in the floor and he's making me a toddy.* Ed felt fear grip him. Was he about to commit an awful sin? *I should say no,* Ed thought as he heard Willie pour the water in the pan.

The whole problem at the seminary flashed before his eyes. Was he about to be ruined again by liquor?

"Preach, I'll put some mullein syrup in it, that makes the strongest cold remedy."

Ed watched as Willie added the syrup to the hot water, but he turned his head away as he poured the 'shine in.

Willie walked around to Ed where he was still staring at the hole in the floor.

"Here, Preach."

Ed took the tin cup without looking at Willie. The smell of the liquid was almost overpowering. It was the same thing as Noah's tonic. *I gave it to the baby,* Ed thought, and he took his first drink in thirteen years.

"Willie, this is good."

Willie grinned and took a drink from his own cup.

CHAPTER 19

They sat relaxing after having split the toddy left over from their first cup.

"Willie, what do you think people around here would think if they knew I just drank a toddy with you?"

"Do you mean what they'd say or what they'd think?"

"I don't know. What do you mean?"

"Well, very few people actually say what they think. People say what they think you want to hear, and then they try to find out what everybody else thinks so they can be on the side that's popular." Willie leaned back into the pile of corn. "You come after your sorghum?"

"I guess." Ed looked straight at Willie. "How do you know so much about people?"

"I don't." Willie leaned forward. "I'm still learning, but Preacher, don't worry about yourself. You're honest."

"Honest? Willie, that's a question I pray a lot about. In church it's so hard to tell who's honest."

"I know some of my 'shine buyers lie to me all the time.

Some let on they're picking it up for somebody else, some of them do pick it up for other folks. Some buy it to get drunk, while others buy it to use like we do."

We. The sound of "we" in the last sentence gave Ed a pang in his conscience. *Already he's thinking of us as drinking buddies, and I've just had one toddy, or a toddy and a half,* he thought.

"I'm sorry, Ed." Willie stood up. "I just meant I don't see anything wrong with what we did."

"Willie, I'm confused," Ed said and he took a deep breath. "Did you know a preacher don't know anybody? I mean I've got very few friends, no, I mean I don't really get to know anybody well enough to be friends."

"Preacher, explain what you're trying to say."

Ed leaned forward toward Willie. They were facing each other not more than a foot apart.

"I mean most preachers try to appear perfect. We're, well, we're God's men. Most preachers want everybody to look up to them, and people do."

Willie laid back on one elbow. He'd slid down into the pile of corn. He listened as Ed continued.

"After a while our world becomes artificial. People act a certain way around the preacher. When I walk up they quit cursing. They start trying to talk religion, and act better than they are."

"I don't cuss, never did."

"Willie, I'm not talking about you." Ed stopped and looked at Willie. "How come you don't cuss?"

Willie turned away from Ed. "Preacher, you remember me telling you Mama read the Bible through to me when I's twelve?"

"Yeah."

Willie turned back with tears in his eyes. "I promised her I wouldn't cuss."

"Well, what I meant was people don't act themselves around a preacher. They try to show me how good they are.

It gets so bad a preacher don't really know anybody. Some preachers aren't even smart enough to know they're ignorant about people."

"I don't pretend when I'm around you, Preach."

Ed looked at Willie. He was an unusual sight, just over five feet tall. The legs to his overalls were not over two feet long. His eyes were a piercing blue, almost a sky blue. He was almost as broad as he was tall. Sprawled out on the pile of corn, Willie looked everything except pretentious.

"Willie, I've visited you four times and now I wonder if I'm coming to try to convert you, or am I coming so I can talk to you?"

"Preacher, do you know me?"

"I guess." Ed was surprised by the question "Why? Do you know yourself?"

"Preacher, this talk is crazy. 'Course I know me. I love my family, I hate liars, I like you, I like to farm, but I have to make 'shine to make a living. I pay off the county sheriff to let me do it. I give money to the church, and I make sure Ellen takes the girls every week. I've been to hear you three times in the last year. I pay my bills, I collect my debts and I try to always tell the truth—if I can."

"Willie, you're the most honest person I've ever met. The problem I have in church is that I'm never sure who's being honest. Some preachers go by their feelings, and I do that, but I like to know about people, too." Ed stood up, dusting the corn husks off him. "Willie, I've got to go."

"Let me get your sorghum."

Willie came back with two jugs of the dark syrup. "Will put 'em in this tow sack and with a jug in each end of the sack, they'll ride across the mule's back behind the saddle and not break."

Willie went out and tied the sorghum molasses behind the saddle.

"People'll think you've got 'shine," Willie teased as he tied the leather strap around one of the jugs to keep it from flopping.

"Willie, I hope I didn't say too much."

"Preacher, what we do is always between us, you hear... everything... Ok?"

Ed nodded and mounted the mule. "Thanks, Willie...for the molasses."

CHAPTER 20

Ed rode slower back to Big Flat than he'd ever ridden before. Because of the cold wind, he spent most of his time trying to ride sideways to keep from facing into the wind.

"What I don't understand is how I could ride four different directions today and always be facing the wind." He made the statement as a matter of fact not as a complaint. He felt too guilty to take a chance on griping about being cold, although he would have loved to complain. Either the morals or people were less important than he thought, or he was getting use to Willie. He'd actually enjoyed this visit even though he wasn't sure he would ever go back again. He enjoyed it, but.... He was disturbed more by this trip to see Willie than he'd ever been before because of having the toddy with him. Now he could see how people felt in the church who always said they did things without meaning to do them.

The reason he felt worse now than after he'd drank it was he wondered if there would ever be a chance to convert

Willie since he'd drunk with him. Another point Ed didn't understand was the fact that Willie knew a great deal about the scriptures. He'd always thought of church people having an exclusive understanding of the Bible.

The common ground he'd found with Willie was good for their relationship but he was confused by it. How could anyone know as much as it appeared Willie did and still not be willing to come to church? Could it be they saw through the people who went to church?

What kind of preacher am I? Ed remembered his promise, years before, to never touch any form of the liquor again. The experience with Noah's cold had caused him to reconsider his position, but could he justify the drink by using Noah as an excuse? The promise to the Lord he'd made over ten years earlier, did that promise still hold true today?

The church always seemed to live a comparative religion. You could consider yourself good and righteous if you didn't do things any worse than the other members of the congregation, but was this a valid way to determine if a person was living a Christian life?

The ride was a good opportunity for him to clear his mind, but then he began to worry about Liz and how he would answer her questions. She was a good hand to see right past his thoughts and motives, and she was becoming suspicious of his visits with Willie. The first visit was accepted as part of his regular church efforts, but Ed believed she could see the battle he was having the last two trips. *Do you suppose she'll be able to tell I've drunk that toddy?*

The question sent a shudder up Ed's spine. He began having visions of everyone finding out about the toddy and his whole ministry falling apart, like his experience at Bible school.

If Liz can tell, I'm in trouble. He knew she would be hurt more than she'd show at first. *I'll just go home and tell her, there's no need frettin' about it and being afraid she'll find out from somebody else.*

With that resolution made, Ed went home a little faster, turning to face the cold wind, forgetting he might freeze because of the cold wind.

He curried the little red mule for the first time in months. After telling Liz, the mule was a good diversion away from his troubles. Although, he'd been a little bit dishonest when he told her the story. He'd exaggerated his cold and told her the remedy Willie fixed was identical to the tonic Sister Rhodes had made for Noah. Liz's answer that he should have Willie make about a quart so they would have plenty on hand for emergencies made him feel even worse. *Why did I have to get carried away with the lie?*

Ed was beginning to understand more every day how people get caught up in situations and not know how to get out.

Preaching had always seemed to be a profession where a man became a partner with God. *Why am I having these temptations?* Ed asked himself as he finished currying the mule.

He thought about going back in the house and telling Liz he'd lied, but then he realized that would only start a new problem. Had he really lied? He didn't know, but he felt he was better qualified to preach on the art of deceit than ever before. Sometimes when he would read the story of King David, he'd wonder why God would let man's life with all the problems David had be recorded as a "man after God's own heart."

I'm getting close to blasphemy, comparing my problems with King David. Ed was sure he would have to reconcile his conscience or he wouldn't be able o face his congregation.

I told her I went into the barn sneezing, and Willie made the toddy for me with the same stuff sister Rhodes put in the tonic for Noah. Where I lied was I didn't tell her I was going to drink it before I found out Willie was making the same stuff we gave Noah. He stopped trying to decide if he could solve the problem by telling her about his intent to drink the toddy before he knew Willie was putting the mullein syrup in to make it a cold remedy.

I'll just forget it.

Ed went to the house with a better outlook on life. Criticism had always been the main theme for a lot of sermons. A preacher would find a sin that he knew a member of the church was guilty of committing and then he would use it for his text. Ed took pride in never using that approach but once when he preached against the moonshine. Now he was proud he'd only preached against it once, at least he didn't have to worry about any other sins.

He realized he might have wanted to go see Willie because of the 'shine. He knew the hardest thing in the world for a preacher to admit was that he was still human. Was the desire to drink always in the back of his mind, or did his just happen?

The questions running through Ed's mind were getting worse as he ate his supper. Since coming back in the house he had said absolutely nothing.

Does Liz think I'm worried about Willie or does she suspect something? He knew the guilt he was experiencing was the same type he'd warned his church members about so many times from the pulpit. *Where do I go for help?* It seemed hard for there to ever be an answer; not today.

Ed went to bed without reading his Bible for the first time since the Sunday afternoon in Batesville over ten years earlier when God gave him what Ed was sure amounted to a call into the ministry.

The next morning was a clear day, and the fresh air seemed to relieve part of the guilt as Ed fed the horses.

He knew telling anyone about how he felt would not

help. He could tell Liz, and hurt her even more than when he left Memphis. Or he could tell Willie. *A preacher is sure in a bind when he needs to confess.* The thought was the first time he'd been able to smile since leaving the bridge. *I could tell Willie.* Ed didn't know what good it would do to share his problem with the old bootlegger, but the thought caused a sense of relief.

I'll tell Willie and just see if he has an answer. Ed continued to plan his next talk with Willie. He knew he was not going back to the bridge for at least a month.

Thursday was reserved for cutting hair. At twenty-five cents a head he made $3.00 lots of days, plus he was able to visit with a lot of men who never came to church. As Ed cut each man's hair he sub-consciously conducted a poll. He began by mentioning his cold, then he led the questioning to kinds of remedies.

Each of the men who seldom ever came to church readily admitted to either a straight toddy or a combination of Willie's liquor with everything imaginable. The deacon of the Cozy church wouldn't admit his cold remedy had 'shine in it, but he did say his wife had Sister Rhodes bring it over when she came to visit.

Ed went home feeling better. His guilt had diminished all day after each customer. He would go back to see Willie and not worry about a confession. He did all these comparisons to his church members without ever thinking he was actually living by comparative morals, something he was sure would be the biggest reason for people going to hell. He'd forgotten the scripture in the eighth chapter of Romans, "For as many as are led by the spirit of God, they are the sons of God." Preacher Ed was consenting to follow the crowd…to Willie Sitton's again.

CHAPTER 21

In the next few weeks spring came to the hills, the worry about morals were forgotten, lost in the beauty of the dogwood blossoms. The spirits of everyone were becoming better with each day of the warmer weather.

Preaching became easier, too. Ed quit trying to control the people. He decided to preach God's love, and forget the fire and brimstone messages. All of his life preachers had tried to win people by either scaring them with the possibility of going to hell, or by emphasizing God's love for them, and they, being fair minded, ought to repay His love by working for His kingdom.

Since the toddy incident, he'd adopted a style that started each sermon on a theme of obedience to God because of His love, and closed with an exhortation for everyone in attendance to start their new life of dedication immediately.

There was other excitement in his life besides preaching. Liz had fretted for ten years because they couldn't have children until they had Noah. The excitement of having Noah didn't have a chance to soak in until Liz realized he would not be an only child on his third birthday.

Ed had teased her that if they'd worked fast enough the second baby might have been big enough to share the birthday cake, but Liz thought the comment was off color for a Christian, and especially a preacher.

The biggest problem Ed faced as a preacher was deciding what he could and couldn't say. If he joked with Liz about anything intimate, she would laugh before she realized what he'd said, then become very serious and pensive, usually ashamed she'd laughed.

When he read the Bible, Ed was always amazed how plain the verses were when dealing with sex or any other subject that he was forbidden to discuss openly, even with Liz.

Where did all this get started? The question nagged at his mind most of the time.

It seems the world wants a church above reality, while the Bible dealt with things as they were when it was written, and most people are still the same today. Ed had resolved the question to his own satisfaction with this thought.

He knew most things he really enjoyed were not sinful, but at the same time the devil usually took something sacred and used it in a way that became wrong. Maybe Liz was right, the bond between them was holy, and any joke he made regarding their relationship was wrong.

He wondered if the fear she'd experienced early in their marriage kept her from becoming pregnant. She had been afraid it was wrong for her to enjoy their relationship too much.

I should start a sex education class on Sunday nights. The thought brought a smile to Ed's face as he looked at the Bible laying open before him.

Liz finally was able to explain to him the year before

Noah was born how hard it was for her to relax and enjoy doing something she'd been taught was wrong for the first eighteen years of her life, and only bad girls ever thought of doing.

I can understand that. Ed looked at Liz sleeping peacefully with the light of the lamp casting an amber glow in the room. Noah lay sleeping next to his mother, his arms were stretched upward as if to praise her for the comfortable place she was providing for him to lay.

That's it, that's it! He repeated himself as he realized his thinking about Liz's attitude toward sex had answered a question he'd always been puzzled about.

The Christian world works hard to convince people they were wrong, then if someone becomes a convert they were given a set of rules to live by, with time to change. They received a great revelation spiritually, but then they were faced with a burden of rules of conduct, and some of them had no basis in scripture except that it was the way they were supposed to live.

The new converts were supposed to immediately change their attitude just as quickly as Liz was supposed to instantly change her attitude about sex when we got married. He saw how that was impossible.

Ed went to bed feeling better about the problems he'd been fretting about, knowing that an external conflict could never harm him, but confusion in his own mind could destroy him. He knew his convictions were basically unchanged over the last eleven years, but his perspective of those same convictions when he tried to transfer them to his congregation had become mellowed by toleration for other people's point of view. He slept.

Friday before Easter was cold in 1925. Big Flat would be the host church for the Easter services this year. Because of her pregnancy and tending to Noah, Liz didn't feel like cooking and preparing eggs for the egg hunt Sunday afternoon, but she was busy cooking fruit pies and making cookies. Noah was sleeping late this morning and she was thankful for the peace and quiet.

Ed was still trying to come up with a sermon for the morning service before the dinner. He would preach the story of the resurrection at the sun rise service, but his mind wandered....

The smell of the cookies made studying even harder. He wished it was Thursday all over again. While he cut hair most of his customers gave him ideas for a sermon, but watching the wind blow the Easter lilies, and smelling Liz's cooking didn't seem to bring a sermon to mind.

I could talk about the crucifixion again. Ed remembered the sermon from last year. *No, I'll talk....* He paused, trying to express himself, his mind still going back to the difference between reality in the Bible and the world Christians were trying to create.

Then he realized that the death of Christ was the link between man and God; it was at that point where God brought man back to Him.

I'll preach a message that God bridged the gap caused by sin and that we can pass over from where we are because of it. Ed stopped. *No, that don't sound right.*

He was having trouble, as usual, trying to understand the relationship of Christ's death, the resurrection, and the new birth. He knew that blood was the symbol of life. *But how can I explain that Christ's death by shedding his blood provides eternal life through faith?* The question could be answered by prayer.

Ed began meditating, trying to pray. He took a walk to the horse lot. Somewhere in his contemplation he knew an answer would spring forth.

As he walked he reviewed every dispensation from innocence, human government, conscience, promise, law and grace. Where did the change occur? When did God decide on his son as the perfect sacrifice?

Finally, he stopped. Ed knew that the answer was not his

to have. God is sovereign. That's what faith is: accepting God's plan without knowing all about why it works.

I'll preach knowing God. He walked back to the house feeling better, with a new slant for his Easter sermon. He would show that faith was to be placed in God's plan. He would preach that an understanding Christian didn't need to know more than the evidence of things not seen or the substance of things hoped for. Just having faith was enough.

God's creation reveals enough, just believe and you'll be saved would be his closing line. He paused. *I wonder if Willie will come?* The thought was the first time he'd wanted to see Willie since the toddy. *If he doesn't come, I'll go see him.*

The resolution was made. Ed began to plan another trip to the bridge, his first one in three months. He felt he needed to go because *a preacher could lose his sense of right and wrong without someone to....* A chill went over Ed as he finished the thought, *...tempt him?* He could taste the toddy when he thought of being tempted.

CHAPTER 22

"Preacher, I've been expectin' you." Willie was sitting in the door to the side room.

"Why?' Ed answered as he slid out of the saddle, turning the reins loose without bothering to tie up the mule.

"You better tie that thing up or he'll be half way home before you're ready to go."

"I can't stay long."

"Yeah you can. We need to talk."

Ed went to get the mule. As he tied the reins to the corral fence, he tried to understand the meaning of Willie's demanding tone today.

April 1925 had been warm and Easter was early. Sunday's egg hunt was almost like a fourth of July picnic. The weather was so nice. The mule stretched its neck trying to graze on the grass growing by the corral fence. While Ed finished tying the reins, Willie watched, waiting for him to come to the side room.

I'll find out what he wants in a minute, Ed thought as he

went to join him.

Willie turned and went through the side room with Ed following him into the grain bin. Willie began making them a toddy.

Ed stood looking at the sacks of grain. He felt of each one. There was corn in one stack, wheat in another stack, something ground really fine in another, and either salt or sugar in the last stack.

"This room is full of supplies for the still." Willie answered Ed's questioning stare at the last stack. "That's sugar, and the stack before is wheat shorts."

Willie poured them both a toddy, and they went back out through the side room. Ed followed Willie around the barn to where the bright April sun shone on an old wagon. They sat down on the back of the wagon.

For five minutes they enjoyed their toddies and watched a squirrel trying to frighten a blue jay away from its young. The squirrel's nest was occupied by at least four young squirrels, born late, not quite ready to leave. The blue jay and its mate needed the nest, but they were going to have to wait, judging from the hissing and barking of the gray squirrel.

"Preach, it sure is peaceful."

"Yeah," Ed answered, thinking how the peace he was sharing with Willie was in the middle of the turmoil between the bird and squirrel.

"Church was good Sunday," Willie commented.

"Everybody was happy."

"Preach, you've changed." Willie turned to look at Ed.

"What do you mean?"

"I don't really know, you've just changed."

"How?"

"Well, you're more tolerable toward people."

"You mean I don't seem so religious."

"No, not that. You're more willing to let people be themselves."

"How can you tell that?"

"I watched you all morning. You were happy, first time I've seen that."

Ed studied the empty tin cup. He'd drank the toddy without even thinking about it, and now he was listening to Willie tell him he was different. Was he?

"Willie, you're right." Ed didn't elaborate.

"I just noticed you're not pushing as hard as you did."

"Willie you know something," Ed turned to face him, "I just realized last year that church is voluntary. A lot of preachers treat their congregation like they were in the army or something. I used to try that, too."

"Is that the difference?" Willie's eyes were more questioning than his voice.

"Part of it." Ed paused. "Why were you expecting me today?"

"I knew you wuz coming from watching you while you preached Sunday."

Ed stood up, stretching as he listened.

"Besides, I need to know something."

"What?" Ed sat back down on the side of the wagon and leaned back against the barn.

"When are you religious?"

"All the time." Ed smiled as he answered.

"That ain't what I meant." Willie slid off the wagon leaving Ed leaning against the barn. As he started around the corner of the barn he stopped, turning back to face Ed. "Throw me ya cup."

Ed threw the cup to Willie. The first toddy had left him feeling warm and relaxed. *Willie might be bringing another,* Ed thought as he watched the sun begin to sink toward the top of the hill above the creek. *I've got to go,* he thought, but remained seated on the side of the wagon, comfortably listening to the sounds of spring and waiting for Willie.

"What I meant to ask..." Willie handed Ed's cup to him.

Ed sipped his second toddy as Willie tried to climb up in the wagon beside him. "…was how do you tell who's got religion and who don't?"

"Willie, everybody around here is religious in their own way. Aren't you religious?"

"Sort of." Willie looked serious as he stared toward the setting sun.

"Willie, you know it's impossible for me to know who's a Christian and who's got religion."

"What's the difference?"

"A lot of Christians don't act very religious because they're ashamed of church people, and a lot of church people are religious, but they're not Christians." Ed took a drink and watched Willie's face become an expression of puzzlement. "That make sense?"

"No."

"Well, Willie, you see my biggest problem is knowing the church people. A member can fool me. I may think they're real good people when really they're not. Or I may think somebody's sorry and no good when they're really OK in God's eyes!"

"Now Preacher, are you tellin' me you don't know who's what or who in the church?" Willie sounded insistent as he continued, "If you don't, then who does?"

"The Lord."

"I see."

Willie and Ed sat quiet finishing their drinks. The sun was now casting a shadow toward the barn and wagon. As the shadow got closer the woods below the barn got quieter. The birds were through singing for the day, the fight between the squirrel and the jay had ended sometime during their conversation.

"Willie, let me ask you this. When would you be a Christian?"

"When…I…." Willie stopped, looked at Ed, then at his cup, back at Ed, and then looked toward the creek below the barn.

"When you what?"

"I don't know, Preacher, I just know I'm not."

"How?"

"Well, I don't act like one."

"Why?"

Willie got up, kicking at the rotten straw in the bed of the wagon. He was irritated by the question. He jumped down from the wagon. Ed followed him to the front of the barn.

"Willie, I'm sorry, I didn't mean to upset you."

Willie stared at the preacher, his eyes were cold, almost full of hate. They faced each other like two fighters trying to figure out his opponent's next move.

"You didn't upset me," Willie smiled, breaking the tension. They went in the side room together.

CHAPTER 23

For over an hour they had been sitting in the grain bin. They were both on the same side of the room with Willie laying against sacks of wheat, and the preacher sitting on a sack of corn.

Willie's question had been answered. He knew now why Ed seemed so different when he preached the Easter sermon. He was seeing good in all people and trying to let God decide who was a Christian.

The time they'd spent in the side room had been spent mostly in silence. Ed wasn't sure how many toddies Willie had made during the hour. He was feeling guilty, he was feeling...warm, comfortable, at ease...could he be getting drunk?

The question shocked him, as he looked at Willie slumped across the sack of wheat. He no longer thought of Willie as a prospective church member, but as his friend, instead.

Friend? The thought sobered Ed. "Willie, you know what a friend is?"

"Sure." Willie gave Ed the same questioning stare he always gave him when he thought the preacher was asking a stupid question.

"No, really." Ed sat straight. "Do you know?"

"I've got lots of friends." Willie's voice was garbled, a thick tongued, drunken slur.

"Who are they?"

"Everybody." Willie smiled and made a sweeping gesture with his hands as if to point in all directions.

"I know everybody, too, but are they all my friends?"

"What you trying to say?" Willie looked puzzled.

"Willie, I don't know how you'd ever know who your friends are." Ed shifted his weight on the sack of corn. "I know there's three kinds of people." Ed stared intently at Willie and then they looked away from each other toward the door of the grain bin. "One kind is people I've met, I don't really know much about them besides their names."

"Yeah, that'd be most people." Willie nodded in agreement.

"Then there's people I associate with. They're my friends, sort of, most of the time." Ed laid back on the pile of corn sacks, trying to think of what he was saying. His mind seemed to be moving in two directions at once. One part of his mind, conscious of the situation, he was a preacher drinking too much. The other part of his mind was trying to express things he'd never thought of before. Friend was a word he thought he knew, but now he wanted to say more than that...just a word wasn't enough.

"But you know, Willie." Ed thought he knew how to say it.... "There's a friend, not many people like this, but someone who is close to you, not for what you do for them or what they can do for you—just your friend. You don't have to agree with them on everything, nor do you have to tell them how you feel. They understand and like you without saying it—just you. Am I making any sense?"

Willie stood up and poured the last of the toddy from the

pot into cups.

It was getting dark. The room was warm, but the cold damp air from the creek was moving up the hollow.

"Yeah," Willie finally answered.

"My Friend," Ed stammered. "Willie, I've never had a friend before."

"You ain't got a friend?"

"I've got lots of friends," Ed answered sharply.

"Now, Preacher, let's see. You've got friends, but they're like the first two kinds of people, but you ain't got a friend like the last one."

"Unless it's you?"

"I ain't got any, either." Willie stopped and looked away from Ed. "Unless it's you."

Silence once again filled the room while they finished the last toddy. Ed's mind was still trying to explain the meaning of a true friend, not realizing how much affect the liquor was having. He felt lonely, but he felt close to his friend, Willie.

"A friend sticks by you, Willie." Ed couldn't see Willie across the dark room. "It don't make no difference what I do if you know me and I'm your friend, you'll still have faith in me." Ed listened, trying to give Willie time to answer.

"When I'm wrong...like now...you'll know I don't or didn't mean nothing by it, and you'll still be my friend."

"Preacher, are you worried 'cause we've drunk a quart of 'shine?" Willie's voice sounded far away in the dark room.

"Quart?" The sound of that shocked Ed. His mind began to question what he was going to do. "I can't go home...I've got to go home...." Ed stopped thinking, staring toward Willie in the dark wondering how this would end. The preacher was definitely not sober minded.

"You ain't got to worry about me telling about this, Ed." Willie stressed the preacher's name. "Preacher, we won't do this no more, either...OK?"

"Willie, I just wanted to be your friend." Ed felt ashamed. "I wanted to tell you about my friend...the Lord." Ed felt almost blasphemous saying anything pertaining to the Bible while he was sitting in the dark in a bootlegger's storage room, and drunk...almost.

"Preacher, you're my friend."

"Willie, you don't know how hard it is being a preacher. I'm supposed to be perfect, but I get mad, I get disgusted, I want to quit sometimes, but I can't say that to anybody. Not 'til I said it to you." The sounds of the frogs signaled the coming of spring, a night's stillness broken in the barn by a preacher confessing to his bootlegger friend. "I don't have the right to feel bad, I've got to always tell the good news." Ed was feeling better. "The Lord knows I tell Him these things all the time."

"Preach...I'm your friend." Willie's voice slurred, and they stood up, leaning on each other as Willie walked Ed to where the little red mule was tied to the corral.

Willie helped Ed on the mule without either one saying a word. The mule walked slowly across the wooden planks of the swinging bridge. Ed Tice was hanging on...maybe a little drunk, but with a question answered in his mind. He had two friends: a bootlegger and the Lord.

CHAPTER 24

Lord, what have I done? Ed asked himself. He was feeling guilty before the mule reached the end of the bridge.

The little red mule wasn't sure if the rider was the preacher. The man riding in the old army saddle was definitely drunk, and the little mule was weaving as he walked, trying to keep his rider from falling on the hard, rocky road as they climbed the hill leaving Big Creek and the barn behind in the black of the night.

There was a crescent moon hiding behind the blue gray clouds, but Ed was not feeling well enough to notice or appreciate its beauty whenever the light found a spot in the clouds thin enough to shine through. The preacher was drunk and sick. Sick at his stomach and sick at himself. *Why?* The question ran through his head pounding from the 'shine. The warm, comfortable feeling he'd experienced while he sat on the grain sacks was forgotten in the blurred vision and effort he was using to stay on the mule.

"Lord...." Ed stopped. He felt blasphemous trying to

pray. "Why did I get drunk?" Ed almost slid off the mule, then he felt giddy. This was funny...almost. A drunk preacher trying to ride home on a mule too small to carry him when he was sober. Sober? Ed's mind was fuzzy, but being sober meant still of mind, serious, self control, and Ed's mind was being sobered by the gravity of what he'd done.

"Lord, what kid of preacher am I?" He lifted his head and arm in a skyward gesture. A mistake. Before he could grab hold of the saddle horn again, he'd gone too far and was starting to fall. He barely avoided a head first plunge by grabbing the mule's mane as he fell. He was proud he'd put off shearing the mane last week. The stiff hair had been a good handle to hang on to.

Now, can't get on this mule by myself? Ed tried to lift his foot into the stirrup. The little red mule circled in fear from the unfamiliar figure trying to mount from the right side.

"I wish Willie was here, "Ed spoke aloud. "No, I don't, he's what got me in this mess. That's human nature. I'm like Adam blaming Eve when I blame Willie for my being drunk...shh..." He put his hand over his mouth. "I mustn't tell anybody I'm drunk, not even this little red mule.

"This mule ain't made right. When I get on him I always...." Ed lifted his right foot and looked at the stirrup, then lowered it, raising his left foot. "But I'd be riding the wrong way."

The moon had been shining bright since he fell, but a dark cloud was beginning to cover it, leaving the preacher groping for the mule in the dark. Ed would never know how long he tried to mount the mule in the dark. He lost the reins twice, but the mule didn't run off. The drunk and the preacher was the same fellow...the booming voice meant too much to the little mule. A loud whoa in the dark froze him in his tracks each time until Ed recovered the reins.

Ed had been walking and leading the mule for almost an

hour, staggering from one side of the road to the other. He knew the road well, but tonight, well, the moon had been hidden for over an hour. He thought the road was heading down hill.... The moon came out just as he began to question himself.

Lord, you're in bad shape for a preacher. I've been wandering around drunk for over half the night and don't know.... He bent over and began to heave. Ed was sick. Drunk and sick.

Lord, I won't do this again.

Ed lay sleeping. How he got home and to bed was a mystery. The wind was cool blowing in the window. Liz was in the kitchen.

He opened his eyes slowly. "Lord?" He still felt blasphemous saying the Lord's name. "Thirsty." Ed's throat was too dry to swallow. "I've got to have a drink of water."

He raised up in bed and started to set his feet on the floor. His head felt like everything in it had banged together and changed places when he sat up. *This must be a hangover.* Ed held his head in his hands, *Lord, why would anyone drink if it makes you feel like this?*

A flood of fear hit Ed. *What does Liz know?* He began to sweat when the thought of what he'd done hit him for the first time sober.

He laid back down and began to try remembering. Trying to remember when he got home.

Did I pull my clothes off? He looked around the room and didn't see any sign of the clothes he'd worn to see Willie. *I could yell for Liz.* His mind was clear, but fear of the things he'd done or said last night and couldn't remember gripped him so tight that he wondered what he should do.

He was about to get up and look for some clothes when Liz came in and laid a clean shirt and pants on the dresser.

Her eyes were red; she'd obviously been crying. Ed felt

his heart almost stop at the sight of the red eyes and hurt look on her face. He was searching for something to say when she turned and smiled. A weak, soft, hopeless expression was part of the smile. Her cheeks were pale. And her expression was hollow with the swollen eyes telling Ed she'd cried ever since he got home.

"I'm sorry." Ed felt relieved when she smiled.

"I know." Liz's stern reply left Ed confused. She'd looked so helpless, but her answer had been so harsh, strong, resolute. Did she mean she knew what he'd done? Did she mean she knew he was sorry for what he'd done, or was she trying to be smart and tell him she thought he was worthless?

He fumbled putting his clothes on. He was a preacher, a man, confused about what to do.

How do I start to put myself back together? The question defied an answer as he went to the kitchen for a drink of water, still thirsty and hung over. Today would provide a new beginning...maybe?

CHAPTER 25

A throbbing head, a sullen wife, a sick stomach, and neighbors that all seemed to pick this morning to stop and visit made a miserable combination for a drunken preacher still wobbly and hungover.

"Yes, Preacher, my Albert had the same thing last week."

Ed flinched as his head continued to throb as he listened to Sister Harp continue to talk non-stop. He knew his head probably felt like her Albert's because Albert Harp was the town drunk, and everybody knew it except his poor, ignorant wife.

That's all I need is her running all over town telling about how I look and comparing me to Albert. The exasperating thought brought a surge of adrenaline from the fear of Sister Harp's story she seemed certain to start telling around the town.

Liz sat motionless, watching the old lady without even trying to answer her, content to let her ramble on talking about her Albert being sick.

"Just like you, Preacher." The phrase pierced Ed's head each time she said it, and big clear beads of sweat formed on his forehead as he tried to find an excuse to leave the room.

"Why, look Preacher! You're sweating just like Albert." She paused, looking back to Liz. "He comes home sick, and sweats just like this."

Ed left the room, heading for the horse lot behind the house. "Maybe I should curry my mule."

As the preacher stood looking at the mule staring at him, Ed thought, *Lord, what kind of shape are you in for a preacher, with a drunk whose only friend is a little red mule?*

Ed began to curry the little mule, wondering how they'd made it home. He'd just finished putting the comb on the nail inside the tack room when he saw the black army saddle in a tangled mess. The saddle was covered by a combination of salt and liniment, spilled during what must have been a rather rough trip into the little tack room.

Was I loud? Ed stood looking at the mess. As he began cleaning up the saddle, an urge to ride hit him. *I'd feel better.* Ed looked around for the bridle. He'd given no thought to where he'd ride, he just felt an urge to get away. *Run, coward.* A voice seemed to be taunting him while he watched the horse munching grass.

I haven't ridden him in a month. Ed rationalized, searching for an excuse to ride that wouldn't mean he was running away. *I need to go to Cozy.* Ed went to catch the horse, wondering how a warm feeling of closeness with his friend Willie could become a sick mess.

He remembered very little after leaving the side room, and would like to forget this morning completely.

CHAPTER 26

The plodding feet of the horse along the gravel road sent a shiver of sickness through Ed's stomach that ended with a throb in the top of his head. The horse was certainly a heavy walker compared to the mule whose gait was always a shuffle of the feet along this stretch of road.

Ed looked across the hollow at the trees turning greener as spring became more of a reality every day. The warm sun would make this a pleasant morning with the soft breeze blowing warm in his face from the west as Ed began to go down the first hill toward Cozy.

He wanted to see Brother Bryant, the superintendent of the Sunday school at Cozy. The old gray-haired gentleman was not only the pillar of the church, but the strongest man, spiritually, Ed had ever met. Everyone in the community respected him, including the men who never came to church.

"I know he'll understand," Ed spoke aloud as he began to plan his visit with the church brethren. "I shoulda been confidin' in him instead of all this time I've been spendin' with Willie." Ed lectured himself as he rode on down the hill, anxious to talk to the gray-haired Brother who always seemed so much in control.

Ed was not sure how old Brother Bryant was, but his hair was almost all a silver gray except for enough black to give him a touch of dignity, with eyebrows showing almost the same blend of gray. He was tall enough to tower over everyone except Ed at the church in Cozy. Ed always enjoyed watching the old gentleman as he welcomed everyone to church.

Liz didn't like the way Brother Bryant conveniently patted all the women on the shoulder as he greeted them, but everyone in the community seemed to accept it as part of his way of making sure people knew he cared about them. Besides, Willie had said, "Coy Bryant makes sure every woman had what she needed whether her old man took care of her or not."

Ed was feeling even worse as he rode down the steep little grade before the road began to wind along the rim of the bluff, before finally crossing the creek, almost a mile from where he first got to the sandy flats on top of the bluff. He stared at the sandy curve in the road, anxious to reach the softness of it, hoping the plodding horse would be easier to ride. Then he saw the buggy parked between two big cedars.

He recognized it as Sister Rhodes'. She always went to Cozy a couple of times a week. But what was her horse doing loose and grazing on the new grass along the ledge, and the new buggy being scratched by the briars and cedars?

Ed tied the horse up, and began the search through the cedar glade for a clue as to why the buggy was being pulled through the brush unattended. Where could Sister Rhodes be?

Ed tied his horse far enough away from the buggy to

keep the horses from getting tangled together. He looked for tracks in the moss covering the rocks above the road. There were sharp heel prints in the black sand between two of the rocks. The tracks of a small shoe pointed up the hill to the ledge above the road. Without even questioning why, Ed began following the tracks through the brush to the next level of the glade.

He was so intent in his tracking that he wasn't aware of the groaning until he came into the opening, a wide area completely encircled by big cedars. Moss covered the rocks, and early spring rye grass added to the covering over the rocks. Ed's eyes saw more than his mind could comprehend. There was the towering cedars, the open grass and moss covered rocks. The sky was clear blue. Birds singing filled the air, but the couple laying on a blanket in the center of glade, groaning in ecstasy, had left Ed frozen, watching. It was the deacon, Coy Bryant and Sister Rhodes entangled together.

CHAPTER 27

Ed couldn't remember how he left the glade, running, walking, or staggering through the brush. His mind was blurred by scattered visions of each scene that unfolded in the small clearing surrounded by the majestic old red cedars.

His first thought had been to speak to Sister Rhodes as her eyes became so large when he came into the clearing. She froze for a minute, unaware that she'd actually gotten caught in the nude with Deacon Bryant locked in her arms.

Then she'd began a wild scramble to get her dress on, and get away from her lover at the same time. Her only problem had been that Deacon Bryant had taken her gyrations as part of their love-making and became more intense, burying his face further into her neck until she'd yelled, "It's Preacher Ed!"

The sound of that yell still pierced Ed's ears. He didn't know whether he'd turned to go then or not, he just remembered that horrible sight.

The old deacon from Cozy had looked the exact opposite of his saintly Sunday morning self. He'd jumped to his feet with his pants falling around his ankles. He'd then tried to run, sprawling across Sister Rhodes, who was trying to figure a way to get in her dress while lying on the blanket they'd spread to commit this awful act on.

Ed slowed the horse. He was almost to the crossing on Big Creek, halfway to Cozy. *Why should I go now?* The question brought him out of his daze.

Ed stopped the horse. Sitting slumped in the saddle, he turned to look back at the bluff. His eyes followed the rim of the bluff. The dark green cedars were becoming lighter with new growth, pale green showing signs of spring. Birds were busy singing, building nests. Water ran off the bluff just below where.... Ed paused, looking away from the bluff.

I don't need to go to Cozy. The man he'd left Big Flat to seek help from was on top of that bluff.

Ed had forgotten his hangover, the pounding in his head was gone, but he was sick, sick at himself, sick at preaching, sick at people, sick, just.... He ran out of words to express his disgust and sat staring at the clear water of Big Creek. Usually the clear water gurgling over the rocks and swirling along the curves of the creek always made him feel peaceful, close to God.

But today, Ed's sin had been such a heavy burden ever since he woke up and saw Liz with her eyes red from crying. And now he'd just witnessed his most respected church member committing adultery with the "best woman I ever met," his usual description of Sister Rhodes.

"Why, Lord?"

The question seemed to echo across the hills along each side of the creek.

Lord, I know I'd done wrong, but why did I have to catch.... Ed stopped. Tears filled his eyes. He felt worse than he'd felt the night he'd left Liz's house in Memphis, after she'd told on him for having liquor.

People. Ed began recounting all the failures of people in churches.

Willie. He saw Willie as some kind of special person. *He don't pretend.* Suddenly, Ed wanted to see Willie. He turned the horse and began riding toward the bridge.

CHAPTER 28

Riding upstream along the banks of Big Creek was usually very pleasant for Ed. But today he was riding hard, not bothering to notice the beauty of the hills. Usually he wouldn't push his mount while riding along this stretch of Big Creek, he would study the outline of each layer of rock in the bluffs above the clear stream. The bluffs were layers of sand rock formations, with each layer a different color.

The green stripes always fascinated Ed the most. At the crossing where he'd turned up the creek toward the bridge, the stripe was high above the creek, over a hundred feet up the side of the bluff, but as he rode upstream the stripe would work its way down closer to the water.

Ed sometimes marveled at how the stripe seemed to come down to the bottom of the bluff when he knew it was an illusion. The layer of copperish green sand was on a level plane, but the creek had continued to rise as he traveled upstream. *Things seldom appear just as they are,* Ed had always concluded during his ride after watching the rock formations change.

Today he was lost in thought. The horse was following the trail without any directions from its rider. *What's happening to me?* Ed questioned himself, afraid his ministry was falling apart. A preacher that drank and members committing adultery. *They've been doing this for years,* he thought. As he remembered Sister Rhodes, he could see the scene back on the bluff. He would never forget the expression on Sister Rhodes' face as she stared at him walking into the clearing. Her eyes just seemed to pierce through him, almost as if he wasn't there.

How close was I to them? Ed tried to recall the size of the clearing surrounded by the big cedars. He finally decided he'd been about ten feet from the couple on the blanket. He still couldn't remember leaving the clearing.

One good thing had come out of the last hour's events. He had stopped feeling so bad about being drunk. *Noah got drunk, Lot got drunk.* Ed began trying to compare his sin of drinking with adultery. *There was a lot of good men that drank in the Bible; after all, Christ turned water to wine, and Paul told Timothy to drink for his stomach's sake.*

Adultery? Ed looked back the way he'd come. Down the creek bed, beyond the turns, out of sight now was the cedar glade where he'd witnessed adultery. A sin punishable by death under Moses' law. *Drinking never caused anyone to be put to death!*

Ed rode on toward the bridge. He couldn't wait to see Willie.

The hour at Willie's had been spent feeding the sows Willie kept in a pen under the bluff. The sows were all due to have pigs within a week. "The pigs will be meat hogs by December," Willie had said repeatedly during the brief visit.

Ed rode back towards home, across the wooden bridge, listening to the horse's shoes thudding on the oak boards of the swinging bridge. A few boards were working loose.

When the horse's feet hit these, they made a ringing sound much sharper than the flat thud on the boards still nailed tight. He watched the dark cracks in the boards in front of him. As the horse passed over the boards he could see straight through the crack. It became a small bit of light, allowing him a glimpse of the timbers supporting the bridge, and the ground below, just for a second, then they became dark spaces again.

It was almost dizzying to watch the change in perspective through the slits of light. *A dark spot could provide some light if I watch it long enough.* Ed was trying to make sense of something.

Willie had not mentioned their drinking. He'd asked where he was going, then asked why he came up the creek. Willie had guessed he'd been on his way to Cozy then changed his mind.

Ed had wondered for years if the bootlegger was psychic. Now he knew he was for sure. *How else can I explain his remark "You look like you just caught Coy Bryant with one of his women."*

Ed rode the horse harder, anxious to get home. *Liz has no idea what a mess I've got on my hands.*

First, he had to solve his problems. *How do I keep a good moral position without being self righteous?* Ed's questioning of himself had been intense all day.

He couldn't understand Willie's perceptive ways. Willie was able to see through everyone. But Ed would always remember Willie leaning over the rails of the hog pen handing the ears of corn to each of the sows, and telling him how hard it was to be fair.

"Everybody's got a weakness. Mine is letting people that lie bother me." Willie had looked straight at Ed. "Yours is thinking everybody's got to have the same morals." When he'd looked back at the pen, Willie'd said, "People don't mean to lie if they're protectin' themselves, and ain't no two of us can agree what's right or wrong."

Willie's tolerance for everybody helped Ed's feelings. A preacher was always expected to deny there was ever any temptations, but Willie knew better—lots better.

"Women has never bothered me," Ed said aloud. Then he remembered a few years earlier when Liz was expecting Noah, he'd gone to a church on White River to preach a three-day revival. A girl that reminded him of Liz when they first met in Memphis was sitting on the back seat. The girl had watched his every move, and seemed to hang onto his every word as she listened to the sermon.

Ed remembered asking everyone to bow their heads while he asked for sinners to come forward and repent. He was praying when he heard someone tip-toe toward him, and bow at the altar.

When he looked up after the prayer, the girl that looked so much like Liz was kneeling at the altar, her head laying on her arms folded across the top of the old oak bench. Ed remembered walking past her, admonishing someone else from the crowd to join her and repent. He remembered turning back toward her as he talked. He blushed when he remembered his next thoughts. She had on a thin cotton dress, her slip, if she had one on, had done little to conceal the well-rounded figure. He forgot his altar call while he was walking past her, and to this day he could still see every feature of that beautiful girl as she knelt, praying.

Ed remembered praying for days after he got home from the meeting, trying to decide if he lusted, or was he just tempted? Was the look he gave this girl a sin? Did anyone in the congregation suspect he'd lost his train of thought? Ed had gone back to the pulpit and bowed his head after asking some of the ladies to come and pray with the girl.

He still didn't know her name, but he knew for a split second in that church he'd been aroused by her. Why?

A preacher shouldn't notice a woman under any circumstances, especially not in the middle of an altar call. He'd tried to make excuses for himself. Liz's condition.

Total abstinence was hard, even for a preacher. He had never answered his question of when a man looking at another woman was a sin. Today as he rode back home from an adulterous scene, hungover and tired, he didn't have the answer to anything...at all.

CHAPTER 29

Ed had read his Bible for hours before he finally went to bed. He prayed...or something close to it while he read. Mostly he was trying to find meaning again to his ministry, and trying to decide what to do next.

Liz turned toward him as he lay down. He could go to sleep he decided. The squeeze on his shoulder meant more than ever before, and added to his contentment with his decision. However, neither Ed nor Liz knew the damage that had been done by Sister Rhodes.

Gossip can be spread for a number of reasons. Liz certainly didn't mean to start any gossip about her own husband. She'd gone to Sister Rhodes in desperation.

A nightmare would have been easier than worrying half the night why Ed didn't come home, and then seeing the sight of him trying to sneak in the horse lot. She'd heard him come into the yard, and was startled when she heard him tell the horse, "I'm proud you promised me...." Then he'd stopped in mid-sentence and suddenly began vomiting. Her first thought was to grab her coat and rush out to him, but then he's started laughing almost as quickly, and then finished the sentence, "...not to tell anyone I'm drunk."

"Sh, sh" would always stick in her mind as she watched the wildest scramble she'd ever seen, Ed trying to put the mule in the lot. He finally came to the house.

Almost as fast as he'd changed from sick to happy to loud and then trying to be quiet by reminding himself with a constant buzz of "sh, sh," he'd decided to become her lover.

A girl raised in the home of a prohibitionist minister, and married to a minister all of her life, was not to be blamed for going to see a neighbor she trusted after she finally got a raving, loving, drunken husband to sleep.

She'd come back the next morning only after Sister Rhodes urged her to forgive Ed.

Sister Rhodes didn't intend to ever repeat what Liz had told her about Ed, but she hadn't planned on him seeing her naked with Coy Bryant in a cedar glade, either. She'd spread the gossip as a defense "in case the preacher talks," as Coy instructed her.

Ed was sleeping soundly after he'd promised himself to be the kind of pastor to the couple of adulterers he thought was scriptural.

I'll never tell anyone about it, I'll not act embarrassed around them, I'll just preach like nothing ever happened. He'd stopped in mid-thought, thinking over his resolution, *and if they ever want to confess, I'll tell 'em to just pray for forgiveness and don't confess it to me, just to the Lord.*

Ed had resolved long ago most public confessions did nothing more than add to the sinner's embarrassment. Usually if someone came into the church and confessed publicly, they were always too embarrassed to ever come back to church.

I'll tell 'em that, if it ever comes up, Ed had resolved

before he drifted off to sleep with most of the last twenty-four hours already seeming like a nightmare that hadn't really happened.

Ed and Liz slept sounder than anyone in town, they got up later than usual, and were enjoying a good breakfast when Sister Harp knocked on the door. Liz opened the door.

"Preacher, you know what they're tellin?" Sister Harp didn't even bother to say good morning as she rushed past Liz. "They're tellin'…" She stopped top catch her breath, then looked back at Liz. "Not them, just old Sister Rhodes, she's tellin' everybody…," as she turned back to Ed, "… you got drunk."

Liz's face became still and pale. She asked in a humbling voice, "Who told you?"

"They didn't tell me." Sister Harp stood straight, proud of what she was about to say. "They tried to tell me Brother Ed came home drunk Monday night, but I told 'em I knew better 'cause I wuz over here Tuesday morning and you wuz sick, just like my Albert gets."

"Who told you?" Liz repeated.

"My Albert's brother's wife."

Ed was usually amazed by Sister Harp's round about way of telling who she heard something from, but the question in his mind this morning was how Sister Rhodes knew about his being drunk, not how Ned Harp's wife, Wanda, found out.

"Why, Wanda even tried to tell me she knew you'd been drinkin' with Willie for a long time." Sister Harp sat down at the table and continued her story. "I told her you might buy whiskey to make medicine with just like my Albert." Her eyes narrowed. "Did you know if it wasn't for the tonic I make for my Albert from Willie's 'shine that I believe he would die when he starts sweatin' and shiverin' cold at the same time." Sister Harp stood up to leave.

"Don't you go worrying none, Preacher." Sister Harp

leaned toward Liz, who was even more pale than before. "Anybody else try to tell this story to me, I'll tell 'em you just had what my Albert had."

The visitor left through the open door Liz had never closed after she'd burst into the kitchen, interrupting what had started as a quiet breakfast.

Ed stared at his plate, a half-eaten sausage patty between a biscuit, and part of two eggs, but he'd lost his appetite.

"How did Sister Rhodes...?" Ed half whispered.

Liz was crying softly.

Noah stood looking at his parents, still too young to understand, but aware something was wrong.

Ed walked past Liz and their child to the kitchen door. As he watched Sister Harp stalking back up the hill to her house he wished everyone was as innocent and gullible as she was. "She may be ignorant, but at least she's happy," he said as he came across to their cook stove.

Ed took the coffee pot and poured himself a refill. As he placed the pot back on the stove, Liz sobbed even louder.

"I told Sister Rhodes."

Ed sat down and began sipping the strong coffee. *Being sober after a drunk ain't so great,* he thought. *Maybe this is why people become alcoholics,...people are hard to cope with.*

After almost a minute, Ed asked, "When?" finally realizing what Liz had said.

He'd been so lost in his own thoughts about Sister Harp trying to help by telling everyone he just had what "my Albert" had all the time.

"The night you got home." Liz looked at him for the first time since Sister Harp's visit. "But she said she'd never say a word. Why did she?" Liz began crying again.

Ed leaned forward, taking a big swallow of the black coffee.

Liz watched him, the veins on his neck bulged as his expression changed to anger. She watched him calm down again without saying a word.

"It don't matter." Ed finished his coffee and left to go feed the mule and horse.

CHAPTER 30

Listening to the mule chewing corn usually got on Ed's nerves, but today he was enjoying listening to the rhythmic sounds. They soothed him while he thought about Sister Rhodes.

She's told it to cover up in case I start talking.

In the heat of anger, Ed had almost told Liz about the glade. He was glad that he didn't. He was feeling better standing by the fence. Feeding the mule and the horse was good therapy for a worried preacher.

Ed's thoughts changed as he looked at the lot. The fence needed repaired, the horse trying to graze through it had pulled the wire loose, briars and persimmon bushes were growing up in the fence row. Ed remembered his dad saying, "Son, you can judge a farmer by how clean he keeps his fence row." His dad would always pause and continue, "Why, son, I knew a banker once that wouldn't loan a farmer money if his fence row was growed up, or if his tack room was in a mess."

Ed stopped, startled by the memory of his dad's voice. He felt old this morning. He'd gotten up feeling good, but now.... His mind continued to wander. Ed noticed the grass in the lot was turning green. The fresh green was mostly wild rye.... *Just like in the glade,* Ed thought as he remembered the scene. Most people in Big Flat called the grass "cheat." *A good name for the grass in that glade,* Ed thought as he looked at the pale green grass trying to grow through the mat of brown Bermuda covering the lot. The Bermuda would not be harmed by the "cheat." It would remain dormant until the end of May. By that time the "cheat" would be gone to seed and dying.

A rotting piece of the feed trough lay next to a pile of horse dung. The "cheat" was even growing in a crack of the rotting wood, and the pile of manure showed tiny threads of green grass protruding from each of the oval balls.

Ed's mind was sporadic, he surveyed the lot, the grass the fence, the bare spot of ground where the horses' wallowing had worn out the grass, the loose tin on the roof of the tack room.

The tree that furnished shade for the horse and mule from the hot summer sun, stood tall and resolute in the center of the three-acre patch. Every year Ed was sure the elm was dead, as the limbs seemed to drop off almost daily in winter, until the ground was covered underneath the tree with broken pieces of the dead limbs.

"It's dead this time," Ed said aloud, looking to the far corner of the lot where the water from the town spring ran through the lot. The horse and mule had finished their grain and were heading for the water.

"A good drink after chewing all that dry grain would be what I'd want," Ed mused.

His mind drifted back to his dad. He wondered if his father had been right when he objected to him becoming a preacher.

"Son, this preacher business is gonna be hard. Not many

people like to quit doin' the things they like. To them, if it don't hurt nobody, it ain't a sin." His dad had said that the night before Ed left for Bible school. His dad had smoked four pipes full of tobacco while they sat on the porch.

Ed remembered his mother had said, "Son, visit with him. He'll miss you." After all the fighting over Ed becoming a preacher, the visit had been hard.

Why am I remembering what Dad said now? The question leaped in Ed's mind, he'd been home, visited Wayne County, only once in over ten years. Bill Tice would never cross the Mississippi River, even if it meant he never would see his son or grandson again.

Stubborn. Ed began to try to explain his dad's reason for never giving in to anybody else's ideas. *Dad's got the best kept farm over there, he makes good 'shine, he helps everybody, but actually he don't care nothing for anybody.* Ed stopped before adding, *If they try to change him.*

Realizing his mind had been rambling from the mules chewing to the condition of the horse lot, to his dad's philosophy, to the night he left home, he now saw something in memory that he'd ignored.

Willie's a lot like Dad. The comparison made, Ed began to see Willie in the same way he saw his dad. *Was that why I was drawn to him? Did I miss Dad?*

Until this morning the memory of home with his father had been blocked out because of the whipping his dad gave his mother over Ed's becoming a preacher.

Ed stared toward the house. He'd lost track of time, he didn't know how long he'd been at the lot.

The trail back to the house didn't look familiar to Ed this morning.

I came out here to feed my stock and try to plan on how to handle this mess, and I've spent most of my time daydreaming or thinking about junk I'd forgot until now. Maybe that's the problem. Ed began to review his life as he walked toward the house along the dirt path he'd always ignored. Studying the ground seemed as sensible as most of his thoughts had been.

I've lost myself. Ed reached the house. He was confused, ashamed, and at a total loss of where he stood before God or before his neighbors.

CHAPTER 31

The rest of the morning had been spent at his desk. Dark clouds were forming. It was noon, but Ed would have to light the lamp if he read any more in the house. The first sound of thunder brought back another memory, a Wednesday afternoon in Batesville.

He still couldn't resolve the unsteadiness of his emotions. He'd feel guilty, then mad, then ashamed. He'd always felt an assurance of where he stood with God regardless of his problems, but today he'd lost his peaceful spirit.

How many times have I tried to describe a clear conscience? Ed had questioned himself all morning. Emotions are impossible to explain, Ed decided. Love, hate, nor any variation could be measured or explained, but he'd always believed they existed in degrees.

Nobody loved everybody, nobody hated everybody.

Sister Rhodes would never try to hurt him, she only wanted to protect herself. She didn't mean to sin by having an affair with Coy Bryant. Coy was handsome. She was a beautiful woman. They just got together. *Wouldn't a been a thing wrong with it if they'd been married and at home.*

That dark, cloudy afternoon had been a new beginning, a trip to church with the Carrs, the decision to send the money back to the churches. A runaway preacher boy because of liquor had become a preacher man because of the depressed guilt that had mounted during a coming storm. Now the preacher was having problems with liquor again.

Would things have been different if he'd stayed out of church that night in Batesville?

I'd never have married Liz, Ed thought as he recalled the change his life took after that day. Like all memories, there were some good things along with the bad.

The few minutes Ed spent remembering Batesville helped settle his nerves, but seemed ridiculous. It was like comparing the punishment of hanging a man for murder, and the hangman. What's the difference between the hangman and the murderer? They both took another man's life.

Ed smiled as he tried to determine when sin became sin. He realized logic wasn't the answer. *If you continued the logic of hanging everybody that took a life, you'd wipe out the human race by continuous executions of executioners. But if there was no punishment for murder, that wouldn't work, either. The hangman has to be able to execute the sentence.* Ed walked across the room. The rain had started.

Judgement. Ed turned back to the desk, picked up the Bible, wishing it was light enough for him to read some more.

Judgement is not just punishment, it's got to be correction of a wrong. Ed thought he knew now why his mind had run so wild all morning. Good judgement is love, sometimes it's not punishing the person that did wrong.

King David's punishment was his own conscience. No

one smeared his name, ever. The Bathsheba first child, died as part of God's punishment, but never was anyone blessed as much as their son, Solomon.

Ed sat down. He'd been pacing the floor, but now he'd regained his peace of mind. He remembered the woman caught in adultery and brought to Christ. Christ hadn't approved of her sin, he just asked if the accusers were worthy of punishing her.

"Neither do I condemn thee. Go and sin no more." The quote from the scripture seemed to jump out of the Bible laying on the desk. Ed stood up, the feeling inside him was just like the afternoon at the Carrs years earlier.

His first thought was to run into the street, telling everybody he was forgiven, then the second part of the verse hit him, "and sin no more."

That's going to be hard. Ed went to look for Liz. *When did she leave? Where could she have gone?*

Staring into the storm that was sending sheets of water across the rocky street in front of the house, Ed felt at ease. His reputation might be ruined, his church members might be adulterous, and Liz and Noah were somewhere out in the storm, but he felt better.

The storm was over, the sun was about to come out from behind the clouds. A cool wind was blowing, water rushed down every ditch, and huge pools were slowly draining down to become puddles in the front yard.

Ed watched the sun work its way to the edge of the cloud, a deep gray cloud stretching from horizon to horizon. A straight line of brightness divided the dark cloud from the clear blue sky.

Liz was almost in front of him before he saw her, he'd been so intent as he studied the clouds. Her face was a picture of sadness almost as drab as the lawn left strewn full of debris washed in by the rain.

When Liz looked at Ed smiling and staring at the clouds, she thought he knew something she didn't, but then she stopped and watched with him.

The sun came out. They went inside. The house seemed lighter than it'd ever been.

"Sometimes, Liz, we need a storm to help see better when it's over."

Liz didn't answer. She just wished she knew what this storm was about.

CHAPTER 32

Two people had never eaten a meal together in any more contrasting moods. Liz was close to despair, Ed was bordering on ecstasy.

He's gone crazy, Liz had thought as she washed the dishes, anxious to finish so she could join Ed in the porch swing, hoping to find out why he suddenly felt so good.

She knew Sister Rhodes better than any woman around. When they moved here, it was Sister Rhodes who helped her unpack. She remembered the way Sister Rhodes had helped her learn to cook, helped do her first laundry, helped her make Ed's shirts, sat with her on nights Ed was gone to visit sick people, made clothes for Noah. Liz continued to remember all the nice things Sister Rhodes had done over the years.

Why did she break her promise? Liz couldn't answer the question. In ten years the only fault she'd ever found in her friend was she sometimes wanted to tease about men.

Liz went to join Ed on the porch. It was too cool for her,

but she sat down next to him in the swing.

"You tired?" Ed asked.

"Not much."

"Where were you during the storm?"

"At Sister Rhodes'."

"Why?"

"I tried to find out why she told what I'd said."

"Did you?"

"Sorta." Liz stared away from Ed.

"What you mean, sorta?"

"Well, she was nervous like she was afraid I knew something when I first got there, or she was afraid I was mad." Liz paused. "Anyway, she got to acting better."

"Did she ever tell you why she told about me being drunk?" Ed wanted to hear the excuse Sister Rhodes had made.

"Yes, she did," Liz answered.

Ed knew that Sister Rhodes' story had been a good one, even if Liz was still not convinced.

"She said everybody in the church needed to know what you'd done so they'd know why to pray for you." Liz turned to face Ed. "That make any sense to you?"

"Sorta." Ed used Liz' favorite answer.

After the sun went down, it got dark real fast. The cool air was way too cold for Noah, but he stayed warm by snuggling closer to his mother. He didn't understand all that had gone on the last two days, but he knew his mother was upset but today was getting better.

The child could sense his parents' moods, but not nearly as quickly as Ed was afraid he did, nor in any great detail.

Ed wanted to go inside but he was enjoying the peace and quiet. There was just enough noise on this cool night to keep his mind from wandering back to his problems. The chain supporting the swing made a rubbing sound in the hook fastened to the rafter of the porch, a soft drone, not a squeak that bothered him. Liz' feet were sliding on the boards of the porch. They made a rasping sound, because her legs were too short for them to swing without her feet scooting back and forth.

The wind flopped the loose piece of tin on the tack room, not very loud, just an occasional sound. A dog barked in the distance, slow, almost as if it didn't have the effort to do it, but keeping at it. None of the dogs in town answered back. Town dogs that barked didn't last long in Big Flat.

A still night, too cold for the frogs to sing their spring songs like they had on Monday.

Ed's thoughts had been on the peace he'd felt, but he started remembering his problems and began to wish he was somewhere else. He dreaded tomorrow. Thursday was his day to cut hair.

Can I face the people? A question he knew would be answered by Sunday night, after spending Thursday at the store cutting hair, Friday posting the store's books, and preaching a sermon at Cozy Sunday.

Looks like this could have happened when I was going to Hickory.

He'd been so caught up in his problems, it was the first time Ed had thoughts of trying to carry on as usual. He wished he had his family in a place miles away and where they didn't know a soul. *I wish I'd never preached a word,* Ed thought almost aloud.

"Ed, you ever wish we were doing something else?" Liz' question gave Ed a start.

Did I say that, or did I think it? He questioned himself before he answered.

"Yeah." Ed tried to answer casually. "I's just thinking that."

"Me, too."

The lamp burned lower in the living room. What light there'd been from it was dimmer. The window on the porch was the smallest in the house; it didn't let in much light in the day, and the light from the lamp didn't have much effect on the porch when the lamp was at its highest.

The dark porch, the quiet night, the pensive mood, wishing they were somewhere else seemed right to Ed as he pulled Liz toward him. Noah turned, facing his dad. He liked being squeezed between them. It was warm.

Ed wished he could stop time right that instant. Liz had forgiven him. He was at peace with himself, but he wasn't prepared to face tomorrow.

He'd often wondered why anyone chose a profession where they had to face people every day whether they felt like it or not.

He'd watched politicians speak at fourth of July picnics, teachers at graduations, lawyers in courtrooms, singers on stage in Memphis, actors in plays, and wondered how many of them dreaded facing people all the time.

He'd decided there were lots of them that wished they could just do their job on days they felt like it. At least that was the way he was by preaching. There would be Sundays when he felt hopeless, his mind seemed to refuse to accept that he was a preacher. When he tried to pray, he couldn't. When he tried to picture the crowd and pray for each member of the congregation, he'd have an image flash in his mind of something silly, like the little boy at Hickory that kept pickin' his nose during his sermons, or the old fat lady that sat next to Liz one morning and scratched her whole body, it seemed, during the sermon. He'd lost his train of thought twice when the lady had gotten loud trying to scratch a leg through the homemade dress. The sound of fingernails on a feed sack material stretched over a fat leg was not a noise to preach by.

All these irritations, plus being the one person every member brought their problems to was more than he could bear at times. Ed wondered if the crowd ever sensed he wasn't in the mood to preach on those days.

Then he'd start reading his Bible. He 'd stop to think.

He'd begin to pray. And the urge to preach would be born afresh. He'd forget his complaints.

Tonight was the first time Liz had ever mentioned anything about being disgusted. Had she known about his gripes during those years? There were not many times, maybe three weeks out of the years that never had there been a reason, just his losing patience. Now there was a reason. How many problems were there in the church that he didn't know about? Could Coy Bryant have other women?

Ed looked at Liz. He couldn't imagine how a man would feel if he found out his wife was having an affair. Jim Rhodes always treated his wife like a queen. Ed wondered how she could carry on with Coy Bryant and still act like she loved her husband so much.

Liz looked toward him, catching him staring at her.

"What are you looking at me like that for?"

"How could you tell how I was looking..." Ed's voice was sharp, "...in the dark?" he added, trying to cover the harsh sound.

"I didn't mean to upset you." Liz looked away. "You was just lookin' at me kinda funny."

My Lord, this is bad, Ed thought, realizing he'd been looking at Liz, trying to imagine her in the glade like Sister Rhodes. They sat quiet again until Ed picked up Noah, and Liz followed him inside. Their nerves were on edge, but they went inside feeling close again.

CHAPTER 33

The last customer would not get a good haircut. A barber couldn't work by a kerosene lamp; a part time preacher sure couldn't. Ed finished the haircut, proud the Baker's youngest son was a quiet lad and hadn't said a word during the haircut.

He'd answered questions all day. Most of the questions pertained to moonshine.

Ed went to the back of the store to get the broom. He passed the counter where Sister Rhodes was counting the day's receipts. He looked towards her but she never raised her head. He remembered other days when he'd finished cutting hair, she would always want him to help her count the money from the day's sales.

"After all, you need to know this so you can keep the books tomorrow," was her usual remark before she handed him the cash drawer.

Not today. She didn't come to the store until mid afternoon. She'd spent most of the time since she got there measuring cloth right next to the barber chair.

Ed remembered the day she insisted on moving the bolts of cloth to the front of the store. There were two stores in the store. One in the back where the can goods were stacked on shelves. One up front where the barber chair and the domino tables were, along with the loafers' benches.

At first Mrs. Rhodes wanted to move to get more space to work the cloth. When Jim pointed out she had more space where she was, and the ladies had their end of the store with cloth and can goods, she had insisted she needed better light "up front next to the windows."

Ed could still see the insistent look on her face as she continued the argument.

"Besides, with the preacher cutting hair, the men won't talk dirty!"

He would never know why she moved, but today he was proud she had come in late.

He began sweeping. The pile of hair was not going to go in the trash can. He looked toward the back of the store. He would have to pass Sister Rhodes twice more to take out the extra hair if she didn't finish counting the money.

Ed stopped sweeping. He would wait a minute. The tension had grown since she came to the store.

She'd missed the length on two pieces of cloth for her first customer. She'd become very irritable when the customer told her she wouldn't have made the mistake if she'd cut cloth "and quit worrying about what the men's saying."

Ed began moving the chairs so he could finish sweeping. He looked at the bolts of cloth. Some of the ends were dirty from being handled by men waiting their turn in the barber chair. Yard goods next to the barber chair, the stove, and the domino table were definitely in the wrong place, and the location would never be more awkward than today.

The first customer had started asking Ed's opinion about Albert Harp.

"Do you believe that wife of his'n don't know he's a drunk?"

Before Ed had a chance to answer, he'd continued, "Course it don't bother me none for him to drink." He'd turned away from Ed, grinning at the crowd that had gathered to watch the haircut. "Course it wouldn't bother me if you drank a little, Preacher. I take a drink myself now and then."

The man had burst into nervous laughter at his joke, and stopped abruptly when no one joined him.

The rest of the morning had been a mixture of curious questions, sly comments, and a few words of encouragement.

Noon came with four men waiting for haircuts. Two of them were men whose hair Ed had cut the week before; they usually got their haircut every other month. They waited while Ed went home to get "a bite to eat," his usual way of making an excuse to rest and eat.

Ed sat the chairs back in their circle around the stove. He swept. He'd forgotten Sister Rhodes, and was unaware she'd finished counting the money and placed it in the safe. She was watching him. He was lost in thought, remembering two men more than any of the others.

Fred Hudson's hair didn't grow fast. In one week it still looked fresh cut, but he took his turn in the chair.

"Just cut what needs it," he had said as he sat down.

Ed's hand shook. Brother Hudson was the kind that didn't say much. Ed knew he'd come all the way from Cozy for more than a haircut.

"Preacher, you been alright?"

For some reason the question didn't sound curious, it didn't seem to be prying; it was concern.

"Yeah," Ed answered, adding rather weak, "I guess."

"You men don't need a haircut any more than I do." Ed had stepped back when Fred Hudson made the statement to the crowd. It seemed like forever before the old hill farmer spoke again.

The pause gave Ed time to observe him. He was a muscular man, broad shoulders, heavy arms that matched the thick muscled legs, a little thick set in the middle, but not near large enough to be pot bellied. He'd looked short to Ed the first time he went to Cozy, but when he got close to him, he knew the man was close to six foot tall.

The sandy hair had a touch of red. His face was smooth with no wrinkles, he always went close shaved, had sharp blue eyes that seemed to stare at times. He was staring now at the store and the crowd.

"Our preacher deserves better'n this." He looked at Ed. "I hope you come Sunday to hear him preach.

"Son, that's the best haircut you ever gave me," Fred Hudson said as he removed the smock and handed Ed five dollars. "I'm payin' what it's worth."

Ed had not cut a hair on his head.

Ed carried the first part of the hair to the trash barrel behind the store. He wondered if there'd be any hair to cut next week.

I could take off, he thought.

One other customer had impressed him as much as Fred Hudson. Fred came to church, he expected him to have strong feelings. The other one didn't. He was a young fellow who lived across the river from Cozy. Ed Avey was slim, the exact opposite of Fred Hudson. While Fred was neat, Ed was sloppy. Not dirty, just slouchy. He never came to Big Flat over twice a year. He didn't get haircuts then.

Ed had looked at the gaps in the haircut when the Avey boy sat down in the chair. He was sure it had been cut for at least a month, but still showed huge gaps of haircut by someone interested in getting it short regardless of looks.

"Preacher, you git drunk?"

The question came just after Sister Rhodes got to the store. Ed was nervous from her coming in and was not prepared for the question.

"I guess I did."

The store was still. Ed's voice seemed to be echoing his answer to everyone in the store.

"You think you did wrong?" The question came smooth, not harsh, just plain and to the point.

"Yes," Ed answered, dropping his head, ashamed but honest.

"I don't." The Avey boy's answer was sharp. "You've been too good to folks over the years for this to bother me. I'm startin' to church Sunday."

Ed finished the haircut without his customer saying any more. He'd finished cleaning while he remembered the Avey boy's promise to come to church.

I better start figurin' out a sermon. Ed locked the store and began the walk home, tired from more than a long day of cutting hair.

CHAPTER 34

Supper was on the table getting cold. Liz was nervous. She didn't know why, but she'd been upset ever since Ed came home for lunch. He'd sat quiet while he ate, but his face showed lines of worry, something she'd seldom seen in the twelve years they'd been married.

Watching him slowly eat the bowl of stew, Liz remembered the smile that always seemed to stay on Ed's face. He could be serious, but usually there were traces of the smile at the corner of his mouth. Today he looked stern, no sign of happiness.

The afternoon had been long after seeing the serious, worried looks. Now, the wait for him to get home was worse.

Ed walked slower than usual. He could see Liz through the curtain. She seemed to be pacing around the table. He knew dinner had been on the table at least a half hour. Liz usually read until he got home, but today had been different. Her pacing was not a surprise.

Ed looked back the way he'd come. The town looked

smaller than usual. The store building seemed to lurch over the street. The stone walls towered high above the low roof of the porch.

Ed had two reasons for walking slow. The street was muddy. He could step on the rocks, staying out of the mud left from the rain yesterday, and, he needed to think.

The store building seemed to guard one end of the street, the school stood at the other end. Half way between was the church with the parsonage across the street.

Ed liked the little house. It needed repairs, but it was home. The three churches took turns painting the parsonage. There was some confusion this year about whose turn it was to paint. Hickory painted it last, but Cozy insisted they'd painted it twice in a row before. However, Sister Rhodes said she furnished the paint, therefore Cozy still owed the store for it, or they could paint it this year and the debt would be paid, and Big Flat would not have to paint, and next year would be Hickory's turn again.

Ed stopped. *The paint doesn't look bad in the dark,* he thought as he recalled the argument at the Easter picnic. The problems in the church seemed worse tonight. The paint job was just an example of how confusing three churches trying to work together could become. Ed had lost track of who was supposed to do what. He'd planned to suggest everybody paint it together this year. This next Sunday was not going to be a time for solving the paint problem.

Ed opened the door. Liz came to meet him, something she'd quit doing after Noah was born. They sat down to eat, in silence.

The meal was delicious. Noah had eaten in silence just like his dad. Ed sometimes wondered how much a child was influenced by its parents. Tonight Noah had picked up the mood of his parents.

Ed began to clean up the dishes while Liz gave Noah his bath. They both finished at the same time. Liz joined him at the clean table.

"You cut a lot of hair?" Liz asked.

"I made twenty dollars."

"At twenty-five cents a head?"

"No. I got five dollars for one haircut."

"Five dollars?" Liz thought she'd heard wrong.

"Yeah." Ed let out a deep breath. Five dollars for a man to say what he wanted to."

"Who?"

"Fred Hudson."

"What on earth did he say?" Liz's curiosity was almost more than she could stand.

"Not much." Ed leaned back in his chair. "Just that he liked us."

"Was there much said about it?" Liz asked, referring to the drunk.

"No, just questions." Ed placed his elbows on the table and leaned toward Liz, placing his chin in the palm of his hands. "Questions all day long about moonshine."

They sat silent again, facing each other. Liz almost forgot to mention her visitor.

"Ellen came to town." Liz always enjoyed Ellen Sitton's visits. Ed waited for her to tell him about the visit.

"She's afraid you'll stop visitin' with Willie." Liz watched the curious look that came on Ed's face. She added, "You won't...will you?"

"I don't know." Ed was not prepared to answer the question. "I've not thought about it. What do you think?"

"Oh, yes, she kept asking why Ruth was so worried about you." Liz ignored the question and began talking about Ruth, or Sister Rhodes. "Ellen couldn't believe she'd told it, but she said Sister Rhodes spent an hour questioning her about things you said to Willie day before yesterday."

Liz watched the expression on Ed's face become more serious, and the veins in his neck bulge.

"What do you know?" she asked.

Ed stood up and went to the kitchen stove. He poured a cup of coffee from the pot. It was just hot enough to drink. He sipped the coffee, turning to face Liz.

"A preacher can't tell anything he knows about people in his church." Ed watched Liz's face flash red, a blush of anger that he would remind her of the importance of pastoral confidence. "I can't even tell you if I know something." Ed's answer told Liz he did, but she stopped the conversation.

Ellen brought Noah some overalls she'd made for him." Liz went to get the little pair of pants and held them up for Ed to see.

"They're just like the ones she makes for Willie." Liz sat back down. "Did you know she makes all their clothes, they just buy shoes. She even knits socks."

Liz had forgot the ministry and its problems as she talked of Ellen's visit. Ed thought she had, until she asked, "Are you gonna preach at Cozy Sunday?"

"Why?" Ed was amazed by the question. He'd never missed a sermon except for bad weather.

"Ellen just asked. She said they's going and everybody else around Hickory. Some people are tellin' you'll quit and not try to preach. You won't, will you?" Liz's question sounded hollow, like she was coming from somewhere else.

"I'll preach," Ed answered. He sounded sure, but he was afraid. Actually, he'd been so busy thinking about his getting drunk and the mess in the glade, he'd not given a thought to preaching until the Avey boy said he was coming to hear him Sunday.

"I wonder how many'll be there?" Ed asked as Liz went to fix their bed.

"Too many," she answered from the bedroom.

Ed didn't hear her. He felt his palms. They were sticky. The thought of preaching Sunday had soaked in. He began to think of preparing a sermon.

CHAPTER 35

Liz lay sleeping. Ed sat still trying to work on the sermon. The oil in the lamp was getting low. Ed had read almost half of the New Testament.

How am I going to do it? Ed asked himself. He had no idea how many times he'd stopped reading to question how he was going to be able to preach after all the gossip.

Ever since he'd been a preacher, he'd marveled at other preachers who always seemed so confident they were right no matter what they did.

There was a preacher over at Marshall, the county seat of Searcy County twenty miles west of Big Flat, who never paid his bills, chased the women, and did Lord knows what else, but he would come to church at Hickory and preach anytime the church even hinted for a few words of testimony. That type of preacher always seemed like they thought they were divine partners with God and there was no reason to feel guilty about anything they did.

Ed sometimes wished he could feel that way, but tonight

he didn't and he was proud.

"I've always told people not to worry if their conscience bothered them, just if it didn't," Ed whispered under his breath, a heavy breath that he must have been holding while he was debating his plight Sunday.

The one thing he hoped to avoid was self persecution, the second thing was to not appear self-righteous, like what he did was not important.

The balance between those two points of view was going to be hard, plus having to make sure no one suspicioned the "glade problem." Coy Bryant would be there, but would he be his calm, cool self? Would he be open and friendly or would he be cold and shun him?

Ed stood up. He would go for a walk. Sometimes he'd gotten past an impasse in a sermon by walking the length of the town late at night. Maybe tonight would be one of those nights.

The air was brisk, cool but not cold. The water in the puddles shined like dark pieces of glass under the dim moonlight. *It's not as bright as Monday night,* Ed thought as he made his second trip through town.

"Monday night?" Ed stopped. That night seemed an eternity ago, not three days.

He wondered how much his personality would be changed by this crisis. All of his life he'd watched people after something big happened to them, trying to see how much their attitude changed. He'd seen nice, quiet people become loud and boisterous after something successful happened to them. He'd also seen people become quiet and withdrawn after something embarrassing, envious after a loss, paranoid after failure, jealous after a friend's success. Ed began naming the most common changes.

How does a preacher change after the embarrassment of being drunk? Ed asked. *People survive better who go through a problem without being changed, except for growing in humility,* Ed answered this question. He smiled to himself, noting his usual diagnosis for a crazy person was someone who asked and answered their own question.

Ed stood on the steps of the school. He'd been so lost in thought that he didn't remember passing the church or walking up the path to the steps.

He knew that everyone who had a problem had to search their hearts by questioning themselves, and he was sure they eventually answered their own question. *The crazy ones never found the answer to satisfy their conscious questions.* Ed was proud of the logic. *They just kept asking and answering, never satisfied.* Ed wondered if he was going to be one of them.

Usually he would start over on a sermon by going back to the basic principle of "God is love." Tonight, he'd been so caught up in his problem he'd given no thought to God's love until he stopped to look back at the town.

Every time he looked at the town from a new angle it seemed different, but he loved it even more. Here at the school he was above all the other buildings. Some of the houses seemed smaller from this angle, while others appeared larger. The church roof seemed to smother the building.

My perception is different, Ed thought, wondering if his mood had anything to do with his view of the town.

He'd always been amazed by the things he'd notice for the first time if he looked at something from a different point of view. He was seeing part of the town for the first time.

He continued to worry about the people's opinion. Would he ever be able to preach? A nagging question.

Ed began thinking about his feelings for the town. He loved the people, and he didn't want to dictate morals to them. He'd always wanted to inspire them to look at themselves, to stimulate their will to do better and to do it without them feeling he was anything more than he was, just a man trying to be their preacher.

Ed thought of going back to the house and digging out one of the books he'd stored four or five years earlier. He'd gotten disgusted with reading nothing but the Bible. He hated most of the books, novels, history books, documentaries, or any of the other books he'd been given over the years. The author always seemed to be writing only to prove a personal point of view.

If I ever write a book, I'll just write, Ed thought. *I'll just try to let my readers see things as they are. I'll be their eyes, their ears, and all the rest of their senses.* He paused, then looked at the town, realizing how hard it was to communicate well enough to be understood. Part of the reason he'd gotten drunk was the need to be understood. Willie had been able to understand.

If I could break that barrier and just say what I mean, and quit worrying about how people hear me.

Ed started back toward the parsonage. He began planning the sermon for Sunday. He would preach about the God of the universe, a God of love, not just judgment. He'd relate to each person. *Everyone thinks of themselves as the center of the world,* Ed thought as he crossed the road to the parsonage.

He would try to show that the view people had was limited to what they could see, hear and feel. Then he stopped, looking back the way he'd come, trying to remember how long he'd been walking.

Ed realized that the problem was he was limited by being able to concentrate on only one thing at a time. If he got bogged down in a negative situation he couldn't develop the positive things. *God is able to see it all, the good, the bad, the intent, and the effort.*

Ed had reached the house, and a decision on how he'd preach at Cozy on Sunday. He would stress the good in all people, he'd point out the need to improve by eliminating their failures. He'd do it by preaching God as a basis for life through love, and the rules for good living.

I'll preach on love, and the ten commandments. Ed felt his face flush red when he thought of "Thou shall not commit adultery."

Maybe I should add an eleventh one for drinking. The humor of the thought left him in a good mood as he turned out the lamp and went to bed.

CHAPTER 36

The outline for the sermon lay finished. It was not even noon Saturday. "For a man who usually goes to church unsure of what he'll preach, I've finished early," Ed said aloud, leaning back from the desk.

The sermon outline was four pages long. The waste basket held half the pages of the notebook, parts of the outline discarded in balls of paper, usually in disgust at not being able to say something just right.

Friday had been a short day at the store. Sister Rhodes sometimes helped post the books. Friday morning Ed found she'd posted everything. All he had to do was complete the order for goods. He came home early to start preparing the sermon.

His idea for using God's love as a basis, with the ten commandments as the rules for assuring God's love, was a good one. Ed began reviewing the outline again. The sermon began on a positive note. "God Loves Man," a pause, then "Man must love God." Ed liked that. It was a good way to paraphrase the first commandment, and easy to add the need to not try to substitute anything for God. He'd found it easy to get the point of idolatry across with those two early points.

The problems with the sermon began with not swearing. He'd preached on swearing and drinking together the time he'd gotten so rough on the 'shine.

I remember saying anytime a man teaches the stuff, he becomes a stupid, swearing idiot totally unacceptable to God. Ed had stopped every time he looked at the commandment, wondering how many people would remember him saying that.

I wonder why I didn't turn mean and surly? Ed thought as he tried to figure a way to make the point against taking God's name in vain.

I didn't swear, I didn't hate anybody, I just felt like saying a lot of things to Willie I'd been afraid to say before. Ed chewed on the pencil. *It seems like I remember trying to be sweet to Liz.* He almost remembered the battle Liz'd experienced putting him to bed drunk, and trying to be her lover. (Liz's trip to Sister Rhodes was caused by this part of the drunk.)

The question of keeping Sunday holy was going to be easy; maybe it would get him by the cussin' part.

Ed could see the sermon picking up with a strong emphasis on love and respect for parents. Hill folks honored their parents. *There are grown men here in Big Flat that wouldn't do a thing unless their daddy told them it was all right.* Ed felt assured by the thought.

Murder won't be a problem. Ed had stared at Exodus 20:14. There was the problem. Adultery. The same flush of red he'd felt on Thursday night returned every time he read the verse.

If I just read it with no comment, they'll wonder why. But can I preach against it without getting' too rough and giving "us" away? Ed's questioning continued throughout preparing the sermon. He unscrewed some of the balls of paper in the waste basket. They were on adultery.

Maybe I should begin by emphasizing God's forgiveness early in the sermon. Ed got an idea for presenting adultery as just one of the common sins easily forgiven by God just for the asking.

Then he'd changed his mind, realizing how hard it would be for everyone to understand his emphasis on adultery. The community was not known for tolerating men cheating. Most murders were a result of adultery in the hills.

How does Coy stand to live in fear? Ed could not keep the problems out of his mind.

He went back over the outline, trying to find a way to move through the adultery commandment in the same way he would the others.

Most of the time Ed would begin hasseling over when the commandments were broken. "Thou shall not kill" was hard to understand. War was nothing more than organized murder. That thought usually reminded him of the argument every year in school. They started with the same question each time… 'Should a person fight for his country and kill people he doesn't know just because the leaders of the country couldn't agree?'

A lot of people had become "conscientious objectors" when the draft for the war in Europe came. Ed was proud ministers were exempt, at least he was able to delay a public decision on the question, although he never told anyone he would have gone and fought. *God killed people all through the old testament,* Ed thought as he continued to review the notes.

He was sure of one thing. Breaking the commandments depended on circumstances and intent. Ed knew there were parents not worthy of honor. He knew there were justified killings, but adultery?

Again, he was stumped. Ed skipped it and looked at his

notes on stealing. That was going to be easy, although there were two families who sat just as far away from each other as possible in the little building at Cozy, because one family accused the other of stealing pigs.

Ed smiled as he remembered his first attempt at reconciling a church fuss.

It was raining hard the morning he'd gotten to the church. It had been raining all week. The creeks were up and there had been no visitors between the communities. Ed was late because of having to ride ten miles out of his way to cross the bridge.

The crowd was large. Ed noticed the row of wagons tied to the fence below the church, and all of the buggies tied to the hitching rails. He remembered wondering if revival had broken out during the week and folks were here because of that.

He'd tied his horse at his usual spot and started the walk toward the double doors in the front of the white frame building that served as a school house, church building, and any other social function. Except those dreaded dances. Some members feared the thought of dancing would send them to hell.

The crowd was quiet. Too quiet. Ed was so late it was already time for him to preach, and with no idea why the overflow crowd was there on a day when the rain would have meant ten or twelve people at most. Ed went straight to the pulpit when Coy Bryant asked him to come forward as he entered the door.

Ed wondered if the crowd would be that big Sunday.

The church pews were a mixture of school desks and home-made benches. The building was about sixty feet long and half that wide. A fourth of the area was stage, with the small children's desks from school cluttering up all of the area to Ed's left when he stood at the moveable podium.

He was sure having the small kids up front by their teacher helped keep order during class, but Ed had felt awkward the first time he'd preached flanked by all the empty seats on one side, and "Coy Bryant's crowd" on the other.

Coy, his wife, kids, and special friends did 'most everything at Cozy, and most of the time they sat together on stage.

A frown furrowed Ed's brow as he remembered Sundays when Sister Rhodes would come to visit. The aisle was narrow, maybe four feet between the rows of desks at its narrowest point. Sister Rhodes always seemed to be most elegant, swishing her full skirt through the aisle and smiling at everyone as she went to the place Coy Bryant provided for her and John to sit with them.

The morning of the "pig sermon" had gotten more tense when Ed began preaching on covetousness and wanting what belonged to your neighbor.

It was the first time Ed had noticed the Hudsons had moved to the back, away from "Coy and his crowd," a term Ed avoided because he usually never thought of Coy Bryant in a negative sense.

The tension had increased as Ed sensed the crowd was there because of a problem. Maybe I *was in training for this Sunday?* Ed's sense of humor was alive again as he continued to recall that day.

The building's six windows down each side were serving as extra seats. There were two men sitting in each of the back windows, with women and children occupying the others. Ed remembered looking at the wires suspended from the ceiling for hanging the lanterns to light the building, and trying to find an answer to the tension. The crowd all looked at the Hudsons, who stared at the rest of the people.

Ed gave his usual close, emphasizing forgiveness and the fact that regardless of the sin, it could be forgiven. He'd stopped then. He decided to take a different approach, asking Fred Hudson to come forward.

Ed hoped this Sunday didn't turn out the same as he remembered that one. He was fumbling for words, and he thought he said...

"I don't know what's going on here," then stopped, looking at the eyes of the people trying to watch Fred Hudson work his way to the front, at the same time they were all trying to watch Ed and Coy Bryant's brother-in-law, Carl Avey.

"I was late this morning on account of high water." A long pause. Fred Hudson stood facing the podium. "Fred, could you tell me what's going on?"

Ed had started to add he knew Fred was involved, but the only thing he remembered now was the question had almost started a riot as Carl Avey jumped to his feet and began yelling at Fred.

Coy Bryant had taken charge. His son took Carl from the building with a bloody nose. After eight years, Ed still didn't know who hit him, but he would never forget the rest of that day.

The afternoon consisted of a trip through the roughest country along the Buffalo River, to a hog lot where two pigs with ears longer than their noses, and tails that drug the ground, were standing in mud to their bellies, and were too weak to get to a trough full of mash, a combination of corn and sugar used to make whiskey.

"Them hogs are mine," had been a continual stream from Carl Avey for the whole trip, and Fred Hudson's reply had been, "You cain't have 'em 'til you 'poligize for callin' me a thief."

Ed leaned forward, wishing he could keep his mind on the sermon and quit daydreaming about problems that had been settled.

At least he'd spent until dark convincing Carl to apologize for calling Fred a thief for catching two pigs. He was sure no one would ever know their real owners.

"Any court would have ruled those pigs were mavericks,

or whatever a wild pig is called," Ed said aloud. Remembering how principles had ruled the argument, obviously the pigs were going to be a liability to whoever got them.

I just hope Sunday won't turn into that kind of a mess. Ed slid out of the chair and lay down on the bed.

It was late afternoon, the breeze was swaying the curtain gently when Ed raised the window.

The room had been stuffy, but now it was cool but warm enough to be comfortable. He closed his eyes, his mind was still racing, but he was tired. He lay still as his breathing became slower and deeper. Liz came into the house carrying Noah. The baby was yelling for his daddy, but Ed didn't hear. He was asleep. He had not finished the review of the notes, and he'd gone to sleep thinking about the mess of the pigs years before.

Liz seldom looked at one of Ed's sermon outlines, but this was different. She picked it up. While Ed snored loudly, and Noah sat playing at her feet, Liz tried to read the scribbling that Ed usually referred to as "my next sermon, a dandy...I hope."

The notes seemed ordinary, a usual sermon. Liz watched Ed's chest rise with each breath. He would hold the breath for an instant sometimes, before exhaling.

He's worried, Liz thought as she admired her husband laying across the bed at an angle from one corner to the other.

He seemed so tall laying spread out on his stomach. His black hair was mussed. Ed had a habit of running his hand through his hair while he slept. The hair curled around his face. Liz looked at the lines beneath his eyes. She'd noticed them for the first time just after they found out she was pregnant.

His shirt looked too big. *I wonder if he's lost weight?* Liz questioned. The shirt was loose in the shoulders and bloused out around his waist.

Liz looked at his left hand stretched open toward her, a strong hand with callouses. Ed worked enough every week to stay in shape. *He probably chops more wood than any three men,* Liz thought proudly as she reminded herself how good Ed was to help widows, the sick, or anyone else in the community.

Liz felt a surge of pride, looking at Ed's feet hanging over the edge of the bed. His shoes were not farmer hob nails, but they were not fancy boots, either. The hair, the blue shirt, the dark dungarees, the shoes worn rough from briars and work, made Ed's tall frame seem strong enough to carry the burdens of the present.

It was Ed's strength that helped Liz to bear the uncertainty of being a preacher's wife. She remembered how disgusted her mom was at living in the country while her dad was trying to preach "a circuit" for a living. When they moved to Memphis, her mom still wasn't happy. "Just don't ever let your husband preach, Elizabeth. Preacher's wives are widows with husbands." That had been Liz's mom's constant warning behind her dad's back.

Liz thought about the times she'd remembered those words and wished she'd listened. She remembered the temper tantrums over Ed's ministry when they first got to Big Flat. She remembered the day she promised to quit being a problem.

Her eyes became misty when she thought how hard times were during the years, but then her heart burst with pride at the minister Ed had become.

He is...he's.... Liz stopped, she couldn't put into words her feelings about Ed's dedication, his devotion to the people, his continuous efforts not to become self-righteous, his belief that all people had some good in them, his conviction that he should never give up on anyone because God never gave up and quit loving them.

"Liz, we've got to do more for people to show them God loves them." Liz could hear those words as she stared at Ed sleeping, tempted to wake him and tell him how proud she was of him in spite of anything he might have done. *I'm proud he doesn't gripe about people like Daddy did.* Liz frowned as she remembered how nice her daddy would be to someone at church, and then spend hours griping behind their backs at home. *I remember all Daddy and most preachers had on their minds was the offering, or how popular they were.* Liz's face soured in disgust at the memory.

The sermon outline and the balls of paper were examples of Ed's dedication. Liz began picking through the crumpled pieces of paper from the waste basket.

"Adultery—the sins of the flesh" Liz looked at the title and the half dozen tries Ed had made at developing the thought. She picked up another wad of paper and began unfolding it. "Adultery—robbing your marriage" Liz was puzzled by the second sheet of paper being under the heading the same commandment. "Marriage the sacred ordinance" was the way his first sub-topic opened after the title, then there was a scramble of words, all of them on the danger of ruining the family by adultery.

Liz went through several more of the wads of paper, and was beginning to wonder if Ed had a fixation about cheaters in marriage. She had not suspicioned him of anything, but was still relieved to find a page entitled, "Adultery—Why I keep my vows to Liz." She felt a surge of satisfaction looking at the list of things Ed had made as reasons.

She didn't remember how disgusted she got cleaning up his messes, trying to keep all of his clothes mended, or how aggravated she got when he continually wanted to wear the same clothes to church. She had forgot the constant fear of never having any financial security.

Liz picked up Noah from the floor and sat him on the bed. Ed turned over, blinking at her as he did.

Liz grabbed the wads of paper and began stuffing them

back into the waste basket. She hoped Ed didn't notice she'd been reading them.

She grabbed the basket and left the room. She would use the paper to start a fire to cook supper. Liz wondered about the notes that had been discarded, but she was happy, not suspicious of Ed at all, and gave no thought at all to Sister Rhodes' reasons for "making sure people know why they need to pray for our pastor!"

Noah had been a good way to end the nap. Ed lay still while Noah's fingers explored his dad's face. Noah always seemed fascinated by Ed's face, but usually ended his playful petting by twisting Ed's nose until Ed squealed and made him quit.

Liz listened to the scuffle that began after the squeeze of Ed's nose, a gurgle of laughter from Noah, with threats from Ed to retaliate.

Liz, Ed, and Noah all seemed to forget their problems. She cooked supper while the playing continued.

The meal sat on the table getting cold. Liz wasn't sure she would get Ed to the table unless she could pry Noah off him. The sermon, the mess, the fuss over liquor seemed miles away, but not forgotten.

CHAPTER 37

"**I**'m goin' tomorrow," Liz said softly.

"Why?" Ed questioned Liz making a trip to Cozy when neither of them was sure how close time was for her to have their second child.

"I just want to be there." Liz sounded resolute on her intent to go with Ed for the sermon at Cozy.

"OK," Ed answered, knowing an argument would upset her.

If Liz was going, he'd have to take the car. The car. Ed always winced at the thought. In 1925 roads were almost non-existent in the hills of northern Arkansas. The gift of a car from a rich man going back to Ohio on a train had been appreciated five years ago, but unless he was going to Marshall, the car was useless.

The trip to Cozy was six miles in a buggy or four on horseback if he wanted to ride through "the gap," a hole in the bluff line that afforded a way for a trail to zig-zag down the steep hill from Big Flat to Cozy, cutting off a lot of distance between the two places. In the car it was over twenty miles. The bridge crossed at Willie's, the opposite direction from where he was going, but the car couldn't cross the creek anywhere else.

Ed finished eating and went to see if he could start the car.

He'd always started it once a week regardless of weather, except for the last two weeks. The man that give it to him made sure he understood the importance of running the motor enough to keep it working.

Wednesday night church service could have been changed to the car service. There were over twenty cars in Big Flat and except for trips to Marshall or Mountain View, they were only driven to church on Wednesday.

Few people from the surrounding farms came on that night, so there was no danger of scaring horses, and it was a good excuse to drive the cars. Ed felt silly the first night he'd driven the hundred yards across the road to church from the parsonage, but as he went to try and start the car, he wished he'd driven it somewhere during the last few days.

If I can't start it, Liz'll think I'm doing it on purpose. Ed got the crank from the rack above the cowl, the area between the steering wheel and hood.

Ed set the ignition to spark, and primed the carburetor. The hand brake was set so he moved the gear shift to neutral, and went to the front of the car and inserted the crank.

He pulled the crank back out to check the toggles for rust. The last time he tried to crank the car the toggles had stayed engaged, whirling the crank in a vicious arch over his head when the engine fired on one cylinder. Ed had been thankful the crank fell back limp to the ground and the car didn't fire but the one time.

Ed oiled the crank and inserted it into the crankshaft. He turned the crank slowly, feeling the compression build in the cylinders, a quick jerk and the crank came free and the car motor roared to life. *I just hope it'll start tomorrow.* Ed listened to the hum of the motor under the hood. He looked at the tires. The left rear seemed a little low on air. He got the air pump and began pumping air into the tire.

Ed always wished there were easier means of travel than horses, mules, or cars. A horse was undependable, sometimes hard to catch, always needing fed, sometimes sick. Ed paused in his thinking. The car was just the same; instead of hard to catch, it was hard to start. Instead of needing fed, there was always something needing fixed. The mule was the most dependable, but Ed's mind wandered. *As much trouble as it is to go places, I can see why folks just as soon stay home.*

He began cleaning the car seat, wishing he could get the back glass fixed where it would stay closed. The birds always found a way inside the car whether he tried to stop the gap with a piece of cloth, or the screen wire he'd cut to fit the hole. He suspicioned Sister Rhodes' cat tearing into the car. Of course, the cat kept the mice out of the tack room, the other half of the car shed.

While Ed was starting and cleaning the car he'd forgotten the problems and the fear of facing the crowd tomorrow. But as he walked back to the house the worry over the sermon returned. The commandment on adultery was the worst, plus the fear someone would remember his drinkin' and cussin' sermon.

He was not concerned with the commandment not to bear false witness against your neighbor. He always encouraged everyone to love their neighbor as themselves. Although Ed wanted to use the false witness for a light moment in the sermon by suggesting the commandment didn't condemn all forms of lying, just false witnessing against other folks.

I wonder if I'll feel like making a joke at all. Ed sat down on the steps of the back porch.

The night air was crisp, the town was silent, the milk cows had all settled down after bawling that usually started a half hour before milking time and ended when the calves were turned in to suck after the family needs for milk were met.

Ed remembered how loud the ruckus had seemed when they'd moved to Big Flat. On the farm in Wayne County Ed had never noticed the cows and calves making noise. In Memphis there wasn't any cows, nor in Batesville, but almost every family at Big Flat had a milch cow, and the cows seemed to enjoy making as much noise as possible twice a day.

Ed knew the sermon would be preached to a crowd that could be riled to an uproar louder than the noise of forty family cows waiting to be milked, or the crowd could be as peaceful as the dew falling on the tender grass of spring.

None of the sermon would do any harm, whether it was stealing, covetous, adultery, lying, or any other part of the ten commandments, if he could preach it with God's love as a basis for the sermon.

Love is soft like the sound of the metal roof of the house cooling since the sun had gone down, Ed thought. The roof would soon be cool enough for dew to form on it just as the grass was beginning to shine in the lamp light from the window.

If I could turn the heat of anger as quick as the roof cools, I wouldn't worry about anyone ever getting' mad, Ed mused as the tin gave a tinge of sound barely audible, caused by the shrinking as it cooled.

He got up from the steps and went inside. Liz sat rocking Noah to sleep. The baby was playing with the curls of black hair over his left ear.

"I've got to cut his hair," Ed said.

"I know," Liz answered, stroking the full head of hair. "I

just hate for you to do it."

Ed sat down in his rocker and began rocking in rhythm with Liz.

"He'd a sure been a pretty girl." Liz was still admiring the smooth black hair.

"He's looking like one."

"I don't think so." Liz tilted Noah away from her and looked at him in her arms. "His face was square jawed and looked like a little boy from the first day." Liz squeezed him back to her. "He's gonna be handsome...maybe more than his daddy."

"You'll have to get up early tomorrow." Ed wanted to change the subject.

"Around six?"

"Not that early, surely," Ed answered.

"We got to be there at ten?"

"Close to then." Ed's voice trailed off with a hint of dread sounding as he gave out a long breath.

"I might could make it if I got up at seven." Liz liked to sleep late.

"Just so we leave by 8:30." Ed hoped they could go twenty-one miles in an hour and a half.

Liz took Noah to his crib and came back and joined Ed. He felt strange sitting in the small living room on Saturday night. He was usually just beginning his sermon outline. Most sermons were prepared after supper on Saturday night from the thoughts he'd had during the week.

A lot of ideas for sermons would come from someone he visited during the week, a remark by someone in the church, or a question from someone he was trying to convince to come. Not this week. The sermon was finished, but Ed wasn't sure about the idea.

He knew it was a good one, but the question kept nagging him whether or not he was trying to justify himself by preaching the commandments.

Of course, I just stayed in the old book. Ed had always

avoided preaching Christ's expansion of commandments, and was proud he hadn't.

At least I won't have to worry about explaining how looking at another woman can be adultery, Ed thought. He'd always been curious after the girl had appealed to him during the revival, when lust actually began.

Coy Bryant has to be noticing all the women. Ed wondered if the old Deacon would be fussing over all the women as usual. *I bet Willie knows all about him.* Ed remembered Willie saying Coy took care of all the women's needs.

Liz sat watching Ed. She was always curious about his thoughts when he seemed so intense, but tonight she just sat watching the flicker of the lamp cast different shapes of shadows on the walls of the room.

"You ready to preach?" Liz broke the silence.

"I hope."

"I looked at your outline."

Ed's eyes opened wide in surprise. Liz always stayed away from his sermon materials, and usually showed very little interest in his ideas. He'd always figured she was bored with preachers after being raised by one and then marrying one. She'd heard every angle that a sermon could be preached.

"You did." He finally answered, trying to hide his surprise.

"Yes."

"What do you think?"

"I don't know." Liz had been trying to guess for the last two days what was going to happen Sunday. The worst would be for the deacons to have a meeting and fire Ed as pastor. She had wondered how they would handle that. She'd overheard one of the women saying they couldn't have a preacher that was a drunk.

Ed looked at Liz. He sat silent hoping she would continue and tell him how she felt about his sermon.

"Why'd you throw away so many notes on adultery?" Liz asked. Her voice sounded shrill and a little nervous.

Ed stared at the ceiling. His answer had to be a good one.

"You don't need to worry about it."

"I'm not," Liz paused. "I read the one on how much you love me."

Liz's smile eased Ed's mind as he studied the sparkle in her eye, wondering why it was always there when Liz tried to be sweet or was amused by something.

"Adultery is hard to deal with." Ed stood up. "The sin that's not a sin if it's done under the right circumstances.... Like murder is not murder if you got a right to kill." Ed looked at Liz, wishing he'd dropped the subject before he tried to answer. She sat watching him. Ed could sense she was hearing more than he was saying.

Ed went outside. The cool air, the bright moon, the smell of dew on the grass. Silence filled the night, but Ed's mind couldn't stop to enjoy the peaceful night. Turmoil lurked, worry for nothing he hoped, but the uncertainty of tomorrows were seldom overcome by assurances from within his own spirit, or the Bible, or from Liz.

Ed turned back inside, muttering to himself about how glad he'd be when the sermon was over.

Liz had watched the pressure build in Ed's face when he tried to answer her with the comment that she didn't need to worry about him committing adultery. She also saw the pressure become a deep concern on his face when he began philosophizing on adultery.

Over the years she'd learned Ed could cope with their problems after he'd had time to consider all the possible solutions. His philosophy of not worrying about things he couldn't change because he was powerless and worry was wasted, and not to worry about things he could change because he was in control, was supposed to mean he never worried. But Liz had always watched him try to avoid discussion of any subject that he was agonizing over. *Why was he worried about adultery? Who?* Liz stopped mid-thought. Ed had returned from the porch. She noticed the small beads of perspiration on his forehead. They made her more curious about who he was worried about, or who's he caught runnin' around?

Ed sat back down. His face was now set in a resolute expression of worry.

Not about getting' drunk, but because of adultery. Liz had never asked a direct question but one time, about someone's sin in the church, and she wasn't about to now. *I don't want a two-hour lecture on how important pastoral confidence is and how a preacher that repeats anything or even gives a hint or an opinion about someone in his church isn't fit to preach.* Liz smiled when she finished the thought, and wondered how hard it must be for Ed to keep some of the "juicy gossip" he knew to himself at times.

A contrast in their moods, Liz content with Ed, sure that he would make it past the problem stronger in spirit, "a bigger preacher now that I've grown through that experience," his usual way of reviewing a problem that had been solved; Ed, depressed, resolute, scared, feeling secure in his convictions but lost in his thoughts because of fear of problems he wasn't sure he even knew enough to worry about intelligently.

They sat silent, Liz wishing she could stroke his spirit and make Ed relax like she'd always been able to sooth his tired muscles if he chopped wood too long, or just fix him something good to eat when he was tired and worn out. None of that would help now. *Or would it?*

Liz got the preacher's hand and led him to their bedroom.

CHAPTER 38

Liz woke up first. She couldn't believe she'd slept with her head on Ed's chest. The sun was bright. Ed was still snoring.

The Sunday morning that Ed had feared with all of his might, had burst on the hills clear and crisp. The air was cool with a tinge of winter still in it, but the sun rays were beaming forth the warmth that was bringing everything to life. Spring. Ed's favorite time of year, but he lay sleeping, worn out from worry, too tired to get up on time, and too preoccupied to enjoy the world of green springing forth.

Liz nudged Ed. A gentle push on his rib cage brought him out of his slumber with a lunge as he sat up in bed. He looked confused as his eyes swept around the bedroom. Liz had never seen him so nervous. He was usually alert from the instant his eyes opened until he went to bed at night.

"You awake?" Ed questioned Liz, a sound of gruffness in his voice.

"Just now woke up," Liz answered softly, contrasting

Ed's nerves.

"I've gotta...." Ed's voice trailed off. He'd gotten up quickly, but Liz could see his mood turned from a nervous hurry to a slow dread. He'd gotten awake, today, Sunday...the day his sermon at Cozy would be so hard was back on his mind.

Ed dressed in old clothes. He would attempt to start the car before he got dressed for church.

Liz was dressing Noah. She was not giving Noah her usual attention. She picked up the wet face cloth, trying to remember if she'd washed the baby's ears. Ever since Ed had gotten up Liz had been trying to see if she could see any change in his mood. The worry was bad for her, but the pressure seemed to be killing him.

Ed paced nervously. *Why does she just piddle around?* He stared at Liz.

Being married had to be the epitome of bitter-sweet. He remembered his mom's old saying about how regardless of what you thought, "onct you get married, son...you'll take the bitter and the sweet."

A good description for this morning. Liz looked soft and pretty, dressed for Sunday. Noah in his little overalls like Willie's would definitely be described as sweet by everybody at Cozy.

Ed stopped at the thought of Willie. Then his mind raced as the events since Monday night at the bridge flashed through it. The warm feeling while he drank the toddies, the sickness after, the hangover the next morning, the embarrassment in front of Sister Harp, the guilt for the nude couple in the glade, the ride back to the bridge, the day cuttin' hair, the sermon, Liz being so forgiving, the car, the gettin' ready to go. Ed stopped. He'd come outside. This mental exercise of concentrated worry had become almost more than he could stand.

He'd made four trips to the outhouse. He'd left the car motor running so long after he got it cranked that he was worried about running out of gas before they got to Cozy. He began a silent prayer.

Liz was ready. She'd spoken to Ed twice to come and get Noah's things. He was too lost in thought to hear her.

"Ed!" Liz was almost screaming.

He turned. "What?" a sharper edge to his voice than when he first woke up.

"Let's go."

Ed took Noah from her, and Liz went back for the baby's things.

She moved slowly. The day was going to be trying for her, too. She was already tiring. This pregnancy was not like the one with Noah. The doctor told her she was in her seventh month, but she knew better. She couldn't be more than five. All the weight was not normal.

She carried the things to the car where Ed sat reviving the engine, ready to go.

I've got to go, but I hate to, Liz thought as she closed the car door, dreading the trip almost as much as Ed was dreading the sermon.

They rode in silence. The pot holes seemed almost cavernous, and Ed was busy trying to miss them by zig-zagging between the big ones. Occasionally the car would fall into one and cause Liz to lunge forward, but Noah found it amusing, laughing continually. Ed didn't notice his laugh, nor did he notice the pained look on Liz's face.

At last the church came into view. The building's foundation was too tall, and made the walls seem too high for the roof. Ed had noticed the building looked odd the first trip here, but didn't figure out what was wrong until Liz asked why the rocks were so tall under the school house the first time she saw the building.

The disproportionate design went unnoticed this morning. The road was full of people, the school yard was a cluttered mess. It was hard to park, a combination of cars, buggies and wagons.

The sight brought a smile to Ed's face for the first time all day. Every preacher's dream was to have an overflowing crowd, and his dream was coming true, even if it was part of a nightmare.

Ed drove slowly through the maze of people, horses, cars, buggies, and even some hunting dogs brought along by some first-time church goers.

The curious stares seemed to pierce through Ed as he tried to park the car. He almost hit one of the wagons. The team of mules lunged against the chain that was hooked to their bridles and fastened to the hitch ring. Their movement started a scramble of dogs barking, men running to calm their teams, kids trying to get out of the way, people screaming.

Ed stopped the car. He opened his door to get out. All the scrambling around stopped. Every eye was on Liz and Ed. He looked around the crowd. The crowd seemed to be a group of strangers, but when he looked at individuals, they were all people he knew. It was seeing them all here together at Cozy that made them seem strange.

The crowd flowed with Ed and Liz to the front of the little white building. There were more people sitting inside the building than Ed had ever preached to at Cozy before, and the crowd walking with them seemed intent on going inside, too.

Ed looked around for Coy Bryant, the deacon and superintendent of the Sunday School. Coy was sitting in his usual place. Sister Bryant was at his side smiling her usual contented smile.

"Come on forward, Preacher." Coy stood and motioned to Ed.

Liz carried Noah in front of her, hugging him with both arms as she followed Ed through the narrow aisle to the front.

"Welcome!" Coy Bryant's voice boomed, and a hush fell on the crowd.

Ed felt silly. Coy had stood and said the loud welcome just as Ed and Liz got to the front of the church. Ed looked at the small school desks on the stage to the right of the podium as he faced Coy Bryant. The desks were occupied. Kids sat at some of them, but most of them were full of women. Full was the right word. A desk designed for primary school children was not big enough for a grown person, but this was an emergency, and people were sitting wherever they could.

Ed pointed to a space at the end of one of the benches. The ladies squeezed together and made room for Liz. Liz was relieved to sit down. She didn't feel as conspicuous.

As she looked at Ed, still standing, she realized she'd began staring at her husband just like everyone else in the crowd. Her eyes surveyed the crowd. *It must a been like this the time the Hudsons fussed over the pigs.* Liz remembered Ed describing the over flow crowd. There was not even elbow room today.

Ed stood still until Liz was seated. The crowd was mesmerized with his presence in the center of the building. He looked at the altar. It seemed small. A low bench maybe ten inches high and less than ten feet long, it was the only possible place left for him to sit. Unless he sat by Sister Bryant. Ed never thought of sitting on the altar. The crude bench was still sacred, and he'd winced every time a preacher stood on it for effect during a sermon. But where was he going?

Coy Bryant's "welcome" had been the only word said. The usual songs before breaking into groups for Sunday School class should be the first thing done, but Brother Bryant seemed content to allow Ed to flounder for a way to get out of the predicament of standing up front with no place to sit.

Ed turned and faced the old deacon. The touch of gray in his temples seemed brighter, the beaming smile was like a mask over a face that was rigid and old underneath. The shoulders were square and straight, but Ed thought he could see the effort it was taking for Coy to face the crowd. There was a drooping look in his eyes.

Ed relaxed, the tension from Coy Bryant was not contagious. Ed moved toward the open space along the wall in front of where Liz had sat down. He turned with his back to the wall and faced Coy again. The deacon's eye had followed him across the room.

Ed smiled at the crowd and nodded at Coy. He crossed his arms in front of him, gripping the Bible gently with both hands. It was Coy's responsibility to conduct the service until the time for the sermon.

Coy Bryant became nervous as he looked around. Finally, he said, "Let's sing," and began fumbling through the pages of a song book.

For fifteen minutes the church was filled by sounds of singers trying to sing together for the first time. Cozy usually had the best singing of the three churches, but no one seemed sure of who was doing what today. The songs had all been off key. Coy usually left the singing to one of the Hudson men. *Why had he tried it?* Ed questioned. At least the bad effort had taken the eyes of the crowd off Ed.

Coy Bryan was wet with sweat, his eyes seemed full like he would burst into tears. He turned toward Ed and nodded, stepping away from the podium without saying a word.

Ed started onto the stage. The walk was only five or six steps, but it seemed to take forever. Coy went to "his pew." Ed watched Coy as he sat down next to Sister Bryant.

Coy Bryant's pew usually had space for Jim Rhodes and Sister Rhodes. Today was no exception. *Would they come today?* The question filled Ed's mind as he turned at the podium. Ed lay the Bible and the notes in front of him on the podium. His eyes followed the aisle to the door. A hush would not describe the expectant look on the faces in the crowd.

Most people seemed to be leaning forward. There wasn't

any of the usual whispering, even the teenagers seemed intent on hearing every word. The babies had sensed the urgent need to hear, and not a sound was coming from the crowd.

Ed's mind began to race through the sermon and the opening remarks he'd planned. The Bible suddenly looked like an awkward book, and the notes like wads of paper stuck between the pages. Ed could feel an attack of "preacher fright" worse than any ordinary stage fright coming on, the first time in years.

He bowed his head. Although his mind was blank, he felt a peace come over him. He looked up.

"Let's stand and pray." Ed's voice was steady. He waited until everyone was standing. He looked over the crowd, still quiet, waiting to hear the preacher that got drunk. Ed felt his heart fill up with emotion bursting with love for the people around him.

"Lord," Ed began his prayer with a steady voice that was quiet but still strong enough to echo throughout the building and into the church yard. "I am glad to be in Your presence this morning. I want to pray for Your guidance, especially today." Ed's voice was filled with emotion, but steady. "I have prayed for many things over the years. For mercy, asked forgiveness, for help in times of trouble, but, Lord, today is special. I need more than a prayer for me. I need to pray for a better understanding for all of us. Most of these people are here for a reason I'm ashamed of…but, Lord, I'm proud they're here. I hope You'll forgive me, but, Lord, most of all I hope You'll not let me hinder Your work, and that You'll bless these people." Ed seemed lost in his words. He was praying louder and the words were flowing.

"Lord, I'll not ask for anything but a better understanding of Your spirit," Ed stopped, raising his eyes to the ceiling, "and that these people can understand and forgive me."

There was silence. Ed didn't say his usual Amen ending his prayer. He stood still staring at the ceiling. Liz was a bundle of nerves as she watched Ed's knuckles turning white from griping the edges of the podium. *Lord, help him,* she breathed the prayer.

Ed took his hands from the podium. The tension was gone. He stepped off the stage and returned to the spot in front of the altar where he'd stood trapped by the staring crowd a few minutes earlier. He was no longer in a trap. He felt inspired to preach; he'd gained his composure.

"I don't know how to start this morning. I've got a sermon prepared." Ed turned, pointing to the Bible on the podium. "The notes are in there." He turned back to the crowd.

"There's a outline that begins with God's love. There's a sermon on each of the commandments." Ed stopped, turning once again to the podium, but staying where he was.

"I believe I'd rather talk about God's house. As I watched all of us trying to crowd in here a while ago, I thought about the strain we were putting on this old building. This is God's house. Oh, I know it's really the school house where we have church. But to me it's God's house. His school desk, the floors, the walls, the ceiling, they surround us. They let us feel we're together, they make up the limits of how many of us can get in here. This is the first time we've ever strained the limits of this house."

Ed stopped. He'd become nervous again. He'd started out knowing what he had to say, but he'd gotten lost describing the building.

"My body is in God's house." He was trying to regain the thought. "It has limits." The power to preach was returning. "My most limited part is my mind." A laugh came from someone in the back, a high pitched, shrill, nervous laugh. All eyes turned to see who it was.

"I can't always say what I mean. I say things that don't express my true feelings." Ed reached out his arms and pulled them together folding them tightly across his chest. "I can't reach out and get you and pull you toward me as a crowd, and show you how I feel. I've got to stand here and hope that I can stir up the spirit of God within your spirit, with words." Ed paused. The crowd was beginning to hear his sermon and they were forgetting the circumstance.

"My spirit is another part of my house." Ed laid his hands openly against his chest.

"Where does the spirit dwell? In the heart? In the mind? In the eyes? In the...," Ed stammered. "I don't know."

He went back to the podium, turned and changed his voice to the loud, booming voice he'd become known for as a preacher. "I do know that just as this building holds the crowd this morning, this body holds my spirit. I do know that God connected that spirit of sin, and it was from a child of God's. I do know that I have a battle every day trying to keep this body from defiling that spirit with temptations. I didn't come here today to confess my sins openly; they've been confessed to God. I didn't come here to brag about my being forgiven, thank God for that. I didn't come here to justify my wrong doing. I didn't come to tell you I am righteous. I came to preach a sermon on love and God's commandments, and how that if we loved Him, we'd keep his commandments, but...."

Ed stepped down off the stage again. He began talking in a soft tone.

"Where do we find ourselves after a failure? At a loss and unable to go on? No...if someone broke all the windows in this church or school house, would we junk it out and abandon it? No. If the wind blew the roof off, would we quit? No. I may have defiled God's house," Ed thumped his chest, "but I can't move out." A quiet hush went through the crowd; they understood what Ed was saying.

"I can't build me another...God could take my soul on...I can't hide from me. I am what I am and what I've done I've done, and my only hope is to live in hope that my spirit can be renewed in God's will and that you people can understand I'm human, a man trying to preach," pause..., "a man hoping to be a friend of all men, not just the ones that comes to church, but a man able to be trusted; reaching out a hand of love and understanding that says God loves you and you can be one of His children, and when you do something wrong, you'll realize it doesn't take any longer for God to forgive than that," Ed snapped his fingers, "and that sin is serious but not fatal, and it can be repaired just like we'd put on another roof if the wind blew this one off."

Ed stopped suddenly. Sister Rhodes was making her usual eleven o'clock entry.

He usually watched her come in with curiosity about how she managed to time her arrival just as the service changed from Sunday School to time for him to preach. The service timing was off, so was her arrival. The Rhodes' entry had everyone's attention. Jim Rhodes was gawking at the crowd as he followed his wife. Ruth Rhodes was enjoying the attention. She seemed to glide slowly down the aisle.

Ed watched. The sermon could wait. Sister Rhodes stared straight at him, her eyes wide, almost like they were when he caught her in the glade with Coy Bryant.

The thought brought the scene back to Ed's mind for a second. The nude woman in the glade and this sophisticated Christian lady were totally different. *She's a beautiful woman,* Ed thought as he looked at Sister Rhodes, remembering how pretty she'd been when they moved to Big Flat. He winced at a thought he'd had that her legs were as pretty as Liz's when he saw her in the glade. The thought came back and he visualized her body under the light blue spring dress with a hat to match.

Lord. Ed felt his face flush. He wasn't sure if he'd said

the word or just thought it. His mind scrambled as he tried to regain his composure. He had the wild thoughts during Sister Rhodes' parade down the aisle. He hoped no one detected she caused a stir in his mind.

Ed motioned for her to come on by, and shook hands with Jim Rhodes before turning back to the podium. The pause had left him totally blank about his sermon. *Where was I?* Ed thought of asking someone, but when he glanced at Liz, she mouthed, "Roof," and he read her lips. He relaxed, came off the stage and picked up the thought.

"We'd all come to fix the roof as soon as possible, we'd cover the desks to keep them dry,…we'd clean up the yard, we'd salvage every piece of material we could."

Ed turned to face Coy Bryant's pew. Sister Rhodes looked puzzled, she didn't have any idea what the gist of Ed's sermon was. She was leaning forward a little pale and still nervous. Fear was a better word to describe her than any other.

Ed felt real amusement for the first time. *She doesn't know why we're rebuilding.* The room was getting stuffy, but the crowd was not becoming restless.

"One thing we would do for sure is try to stop any further damage." Ed turned back to the crowd. "This building doesn't have feelings as the house of God, but this house," Ed laid his palms on his chest and paused, "does hurt from within." The crowd seemed to lean forward with most faces showing signs of sympathy. There were tears in several eyes.

"That's what makes today so hard. I've hurt you. I've caused some of you to doubt more than just me…you doubt my experience with God." Ed's eyes became full of tears. "Maybe," a long pause as he fumbled with the lapel of his coat, "maybe I don't deserve to be your preacher anymore. Maybe my house should be torn down."

Ed began pacing back and forth. "No. In my heart I don't believe that at all. I believe you'll help me with the salvage. I believe you'll not allow any further harm to me or the church."

The crowd smiled as a group. "We need to realize that I'm no better than any one of you. I would never try to harm any of you by revealing anything I know about you. However, I feel you have a right to expect me to live in a way you can be proud to say I'm your preacher and not worry about what I've done. I won't promise you but one thing.

"I'll be the best person possible. I didn't promise not to fail, I will. I didn't promise to be perfect, I can't. I promise to always be a person trying to live right. I'll pray for you." Ed gestured in all directions. "I'll never talk about any of you unless it's something good. "If any of you have problems, it'll be between us and the Lord, and I hope I never stand before you feeling guilty again."

Ed went back to the podium. He bowed his head, praying softly under his breath. The crowd had bowed their heads. The quiet seemed to fill the building. Ed stopped praying.

He raised his head and looked at Liz. She sat watching him, her face held an expression of pride. Ed bowed his head again.

"Lord," Ed paused. "I've prayed many a prayer to close a service. I prayed without thinking, just a prayer to close and to get on our way home. Today I want to pray especially for guidance, I didn't plan on saying the things I've said to these people, but, Lord, I've spoken what's in my heart. Now I'm asking Your help for each of us, that we'll respect each other, and that we'll continue to help one another, that we'll accept you as our savior and we'll show a love for each other, without condemnation or suspicion, that will be so great that we'll help each other through our failures and we'll care enough to never do anything or say anything that'll damage Your cause." Ed stopped. He looked at Coy Bryant and then turned to the crowd. He didn't realize he'd prayed twice in one day without his customary Amen.

Ed left the podium and Liz joined him as he stepped from the stage. He took Noah from her and they began their way through the aisle they'd come down less than an hour before. It had seemed like an eternity.

Liz watched the faces, some were blank, no expression at all, some were smiling a soft expression of understanding, a few were cold with no sign of compassion. The crowd's quietness was the strangest part of all. The people standing outside were just as mesmerized as those in the building. No one said a word as they stepped aside for Ed to pass, but they turned and watched as Ed started the car and left the church.

It was a quieter ride home than it was going to Cozy. Ed spent most of the time trying to remember what he'd said and who was there. He couldn't actually recall many individuals except Coy Bryant, Sister Rhodes, the Avey boy, a couple of the Hudson men, Jim Rhodes, of course, Ellen Sitton and Willie.

Ed stopped thinking as he felt his face flush at the thought of Willie. He'd come to rely on Willie as a friend, but he knew they had a problem. He remembered Willie's expression as they were clearing the church. Willie had stopped in the front of his wagon, alone, facing the church, and then he'd turned to watch Ed crank the car. He looked like he wanted to say something to the crowd, but all he did was sit down and look away as Ed got in the car to leave.

I wonder if there's a way I can be his friend and a preacher? Ed couldn't answer the question. The car rumbled along the rocky road back to Big Flat.

CHAPTER 39

Liz watched Noah ride the stick horse around the yard, the new puppy running in stride. The black puppy tried to cross in front of him. They became tangled and fell to the ground. The puppy's yelp of pain was short as it began licking Noah's face with Noah laughing and trying to roll away from him.

Liz's face broke into a smile, a reserved expression of satisfaction because her five-year old son was having a good time playing with his puppy.

She sat still again, the smile was gone as she let her mind drift back in memory. She always remembered Sara....

The time after "the sermon," waiting for the baby to be born, the summer of 1925 was Liz's strongest memory. The baby had been born in August, two months after the doctor said it was due.

Liz could still see Ed's face as he held her hand during delivery. She could see it as his expression of encouragement changed to agony and then to disgust.

"What's wrong with it, Doctor?" Ed's question would always ring in her ears. Through all the pain she was still able to feel the despair in the question.

What had been wrong? Liz's mind continually asked the question.

Sara was pretty, her black hair shined just like Noah's, her skin was soft and pretty. Why was her head twice the size it should have been? Liz would never know the answer to the question.

Sara had lived two months. Her skin had become blotched by red spots that became sores. Her head became soft and ugly with her tiny eyes bulging. Her death had been a relief after watching her suffering.

Sara's memory was now a nightmare. Liz stood up and walked the length of the porch.

October 1929 was warm and damp. The church building looked old and forlorn. The sun had come out warm and bright, its rays warming the damp, cold sod of the yard. Liz watched Noah; he'd grown so fast during the last year. She worried, afraid she had neglected him while she mourned for Sara.

Had she really mourned Sara or for the life she and Ed seemed to have lost in 1925?

She saw Ed on Main Street, starting his walk home. Thursday, October 29, 1929, seemed like any other day. Ed was walking back home from a day of cutting hair at the store.

Wall Street's crash could not be heard in Big Flat. It would be a day or two before any worrying began about money. Liz's worry had been almost constant since the drunk.

Liz thought how she named events in time. "The drunk,"

"The sermon," "The funeral," and all of the other bad things popped into mind under their own titles. *I wonder if other people do that?* Liz watched Ed. She knew he referred to the trip to Cozy as "the sermon," but she never mentioned any of the others.

The sermon had been the last thing they could point back to with pride. *People had forgiven Ed until....* Liz stopped in thought.

Ed was climbing the hill to the house. He still carried his head high, but at thirty-two he was losing the boyish look. Liz saw the change after Sara's funeral.

Some people had been blunt enough to tell her she didn't need to feel guilty about the baby, "It was just God punishing the preacher." Liz couldn't explain the changes the four years had made in Ed.

Maybe he's just tired. Liz questioned herself because she knew he worked harder than ever. It was his enthusiasm that seemed to fade. He would start something with a lot of zeal to get it done, and before it got started he'd lose interest. He'd talk for months about moving to some far-off place to preach, and then never mention it again. He still studied his Bible, but he no longer came up with such fresh ideas. Liz's thoughts seemed to freeze them in place with Ed plodding along the path across the yard, with Noah continuing to play, ignoring his parents.

Noah was Liz's biggest worry. She knew she and Ed had become so preoccupied that Noah had started ignoring them, finding his own world less confusing than trying to get their attention.

Liz usually got irritated at Ed for not hearing Noah, but then she'd found herself so lost in thought that Noah had grabbed her hand to get her attention.

"Liz! Mama can't you hear?" Noah had screamed her name for the first time one afternoon in 1926. Liz had burst into tears and hugged him, wishing, *Lord, let me forget our problems and love this child.*

Ed came on the porch and went past Liz without saying a word. She wondered what today's crisis was.

She followed him inside. Noah came in muddy and dirty. Their moods didn't change once they were inside. Liz glanced at the table and wondered if feeding her family the leftovers from lunch was another sign of enthusiasm lost during the last four years.

Ed went to wash up. Liz lit the lamp. Noah followed his dad to the wash room. Liz listened as Noah began his usual chatter, a mixture of questions and stories about what he'd done with his new puppy. The two weeks since the puppy came had helped Noah. Liz was thankful Ed had agreed to let him keep the stray.

"Preachers and dogs don't mix," had been Ed's answer each time Noah had asked for a puppy before, but he hadn't put up the usual argument that "a preacher couldn't keep a dog because folks wouldn't want to give an offering to help feed a dog" when Noah came in carrying the puppy.

Liz had wondered if Ellen had said something to Willie, because the puppy had been well kept, like one of Willie's, and it showed signs of being part collie like Willie's stock dogs.

Liz continued setting the table. For two years she missed the times she'd always spent with Ellen. After "the sermon" Ellen had stopped coming completely. Then one day she'd shown up with two shirts for Ed and a pair of overalls for Noah.

Ellen had visited for several times without mentioning Ed, the baby, or Noah. They'd just talked about clothes, canning, and things around the house, then while she was helping Liz shell some peas, she'd stopped and asked, "Is Ed happy?" Ellen had looked away as Liz tried to think of the right answer, but before she had a chance, Ellen continued with an answer for her. "Willie's not, either."

It had taken three month's time and a half dozen visits before Ellen and Liz had discussed Willie and Ed completely.

Liz understood when Ellen told her how Willie had changed after "the drunk." She'd watched Ed's aloof attitude at times over the years, but after the problems he'd gotten worse, withdrawn, until he got around the church crowd, and then humbling with charisma. But absent was the old fire of enthusiasm. It made her almost wish he would start going to the bridge to see Willie again.

But he couldn't do it, Liz thought as Ed and Noah got to the dinner table.

"Mama, Daddy thinks Blackie's going to be a good dog." Noah's eyes showed his happiness with his puppy.

"Yep," Ed said as Noah sat down at the table. "He's gonna be a good 'un." Ed's voice trailed off, not showing the same thrill as Noah.

"Ed, what should I be feeding him?"

"Just scraps."

"Not just bread?"

"No. Make sure he gets some meat."

Noah's eyes had followed each parent as they spoke.

"I'll feed him what I don't eat!" Noah said, with his face showing a sign of relief at the idea.

"No." Liz cut her eyes at Noah. "You'll still have to clean your plate!"

A look of disgust came over Noah. The battle over him eating enough would continue.

They finished eating in silence, and Liz prepared a tin plate from the leftovers for the pup.

Ed left the table for his nightly walk up the road from the church while Liz did the dishes. The road was in better shape than in years. The new mayor had worked with the county road commissioner, and the "gravel for everybody" slogan from the campaign was becoming a reality.

Ed's mind left the road. He thought of Noah. The child's excitement since the puppy came had helped break the drab mood around the parsonage. They needed something more still.

We've been here almost fifteen years. Ed had walked to the school house. The steps had been the point he stopped for his usual rest. He called the steps his "point of reflection."

The town never looks the same, Ed thought as he looked at the church and parsonage. He remembered other times when the town looked cold and distant, almost like he was an uninvited stranger. At times it had looked warm and inviting, almost like the place he'd dreamed of during the early days of his ministry.

Everybody's dreams for life have to be adjusted to fit reality. Ed's philosophy was threefold; the real world first, and then a world as people see it with each person's view prejudiced by their experiences, and last, the dream world with each person's dreams for the "someday" that never seemed to come.

"Our dreams were for perfection," Ed said softly. He'd realized after "the drunk" that perfection was a matter of opinion. A perfect world would not necessarily be an absence of problems. For four years now, his life had been almost sterile, total abstinence from even discussing liquor, not visiting with Willie, not even defending himself from any of the gossip. The four years had seen Liz become cold, almost frigid, like she was before Noah was born.

Life was closer to perfect before, Ed thought. He continued to think of Liz.

She's not sure why Sara died. Ed had never answered the question himself, and finally decided the answer was not theirs to have. "How can you ever say why something happens?" Ed's answer to her questioning had found solace when he decided things couldn't always be blamed on God's love or wrath without ignoring there was an evil force, too. *If you blame everything on the devil, then God becomes a weakling.* Ed's mind always added to the rationale, *I think a lot of things just happen because of nature, just like a tree always falls to the ground when it's cut. It's just the way things are.*

Ed had wished he could quit worrying about things. He'd missed Willie. He could still see Ruth Rhodes' nude body when he met her, regardless of how she was dressed. The day in the glade just seemed to stay fresh in his mind, like Willie watching from his wagon as he left Cozy, like seeing the filth of the slave quarters at Newport, like seeing Liz throw her temper tantrums, and when he was in a good mood, remembering things like Liz in her sweetest moods, or things like Noah doing things, and some of the times with Willie. Ed could never figure his memory, with large spaces of time seeming to be almost blank, while some silly things stood out as clear as yesterday.

Our lives are in a mess. Ed wasn't sure there could ever be any direction to his life again. For four years he'd wallowed in misery, watching as Liz became sullen except for Ellen's visits, as Noah grew nervous and impatient, even if he was just five years old.

The best times he'd had during the four years were while he was cutting hair. It was the only time people seemed to forget he was a preacher. Men would tell stories they normally wouldn't think of telling in front of him, but he'd enjoyed those, too, even if he'd gotten embarrassed a couple of times because he'd laughed at something not very appropriate for a preacher to hear.

Ruth Rhodes was the thing that bothered him the worst. When she'd gotten over the fear he would tell about her and Coy in the glade, she'd become really friendly at the store. She would bump into Ed at any opportunity. If she was helping post the books and a question came up, she would place the ledger in front of Ed and drape herself over his shoulder.

When she turned away she would roll herself against Ed flagrantly, using him as a cushion for making her turn. Ed had been upset at her for the first couple of years, but then he'd accepted it because Ruth was discreet keeping her distance if there were people around. And the last couple of years she'd realized Ed wasn't objecting as strongly, and she enjoyed seeing him smile at some of her suggestive language and things she'd done with her body.

This bothered Ed's conscience even more. He'd come to realize she had a problem with men, but most of all he worried because he didn't know how to handle it. It was almost like Ruth thought she had God's approval to be a harlot and Ed had become her friend again.

Then Ed began thinking of earlier in the day when Fred Hudson came for his haircut. Fred had sat down, quiet as usual. After a minute he'd said, "You been OK, Preacher?"

"Yah," Ed answered slowly, trying to answer in a mood to match Fred's.

"I've been needin' to talk to you and didn't know how to start." Fred was talking fast for him.

"Well, just say what's on your mind." Ed's curiosity was growing.

"I don't know if I should." Fred's face showed deep concern.

Ed felt his heart race. "Try me."

"Where's Jim?" Fred turned his head searching for Jim Rhodes.

"He's gone to Sylamore after a load of stuff that come in on the train."

"OK, I'll tell you." Fred breathed a deep breath. Ed had stopped cutting his hair.

"You know the big barn below the mill pond."

Ed nodded, knowing Fred was referring to Coy Bryant's barn at the mouth of Big Creek.

"I's squirrel huntin' a week ago today, you know, the rainy, cold day." Fred frowned. "That was last Thursday? Anyway, it had been drizzling and looked like it was gonna rain hard."

Ed was getting impatient as he listened to Fred tell a

bunch of details with no idea where the story was going.

"I went in the big barn to get in the dry. I got to looking at all of Coy's stuff and kinda lost track of time. I even shelled a few ears a corn, just trying out his new sheller. He'll get that thing stole. Anyway, I didn't hear the buggy, I guess on account of the noise from the sheller, until Ruth was getting' out and coming toward the barn. She'd parked in the little ole shed across from the barn. I saw her coming and started to speak, but then I thought, "What's she coming to the barn for?" Fred stopped, catching his breath.

Ed cut a few hairs above his ears, realizing the story was going to be a long one.

"My first thought was she was coming into the barn to answer a call from nature." Ed smiled at Fred's description of using the toilet.

"Before I could decide to speak, she started climbing into the loft. I was in plain sight and she climbed the ladder on the wall without even looking my way. She sat down in the hay loft in plain view of the big door by the time it'd started raining."

Fred stopped. "Preacher, I didn't know what to do. I's standing there in the hallway watching her through the cracks in the floor, and I realized she was waiting for somebody."

Ed was still cutting hair, but the story was unfolding fast enough that the glade scene came back fresh. He was sure Coy Bryant was the somebody.

"Preacher, you know it was Coy Bryant." Fred stared straight at Ed.

Ed didn't answer for a full minute.

"How would I know?"

Fred ignored the question. "Well, Coy rode up on that gray of his, jumped off, and climbed the ladder in four steps." Fred's eyes showed the excitement of the story. "I hid in a stall when I saw him coming. I can't tell all that went on in that loft 'cause I didn't see nothing. I heard a lot. They had the same blanket you caught 'em on. Ruth laughed about how wild you looked, and teased Coy about getting' tangled up in his britches." Fred Hudson's voice was stern, not a hint of humor, Ed's face was ashen as he listened intently.

"I spent over two hours hiding in that stall while they cavorted around in the loft." Fred got up. Somehow Ed had finished the haircut. "I couldn't leave. I didn't say anything. I ain't told a soul. When did you catch 'em?"

"Over four years ago," Ed answered.

"What are we gonna do? Fred emphasized *we*."

"I don't know." Ed studied Fred waiting for his answer. "What can we do? I've asked that question a lot in the last four years. Now you see the problem."

"What if Jim catches them?" Fred asked. "He will if it keeps on."

Ed took Fred's money for the haircut, and he left the store. Ed was proud no one had come in. And as he sat on the school steps remembering the conversation, he knew Coy Bryant was safe as long as no one knew besides him and Fred Hudson.

He got up and started back down the hill, still thinking about the conversation as he was walking toward the parsonage. The lamp's amber glow looked peaceful through the window, but the flicker of the flame was unsteady, kinda like Ed's emotions. For four years he'd tried to recover from the embarrassment of getting drunk, from losing a friend, and from losing a child.

He couldn't say how much damage had been done to him or Liz from any of those things, nor could he say how long it would be until he recovered, but the one thing he didn't need was for the glade problem to resurface.

Liz sat quiet, watching Ed make his way back from the school. It was warm for October, almost a summer night.

"A penny for your thoughts?" Liz asked as Ed got to the porch. He jumped, startled by her voice.

"I didn't see you settin' there." Ed joined Liz in the swing.

"Ain't it warm?" Liz answered.

"May come a storm," Ed said, "it's too warm."

"I hope not."

"I do, too."

They sat quiet for a long time. The swing was still. Ed thought about how much time they used to spend out here at night. He couldn't remember the last time they'd sat out together.

"Liz," Ed started to speak just as Liz was about to get up.

"What/" Liz's voice had a sharp edge.

"You..." Ed stopped. "I forgot what I's gonna say."

"That's not unusual. You start to say a lot of things anymore, and don't finish them."

"Like what? Ed was showing signs of irritation.

"Oh, I don't know, it's just every time we're talking you act like you don't trust me enough to tell me anything." Liz's voice was high pitched, almost to the point of being harsh.

Ed didn't really answer, just more or less grunted.

"Just like now. You're worried, mad, or something, but if I try to help, you'll lecture me about how you can't talk about it, 'pastoral confidence.' I'm sick of it." Liz leaned back to catch her breath. Ed was shocked by her outrage.

"What if I told you one thing?" Ed stopped. "We'd just both be worried then."

"At least we'd both feel the same," Liz answered. "For fifteen years we've been married. We've never had our own lives together. You've always got some big secret you're worrying about one of 'your members.' I'm just tired of it." Liz was feeling better; she was saying things she'd wanted to say a long time. "Like right now. Suppose I asked, would you tell me?" Liz turned to face Ed.

"Ycah," Ed said, astonished at his own answer.

"OK," Liz was more shocked. "what is it?"

"Something Fred told me."

"OK, what did he tell you?"

"Liz, I shouldn't tell you." Ed's voice was pleading.

"How hard is it?"

"OK." Ed thought for a minute. "Let's play a game. You tell me all the women and men that you wouldn't believe would ever run around on their husbands or wives. If you don't name the two people, I'll tell you the whole story."

Liz's mouth dropped open. "Do what?"

"You heard me. You wanted to start sharing my problems. I'm tellin' you it's two people having an affair, but I won't tell you who it is if it's someone you wouldn't believe me anyway. You tell me who you know for sure wouldn't do it." Ed was enjoying Liz's expression of shock. "You understand what I'm saying?"

"You're not serious? An affair!" Liz stopped. "People in the church?"

"Yes."

"Oh, Ed...I can't think of a soul." Liz's eyes showed her disbelief. "You're just being funny."

"OK, see, you didn't really want to know the problem, did you?" Ed was glad Liz thought he was kidding.

"Not if it's junk like that. Why, that would worry me to death if it was one of my good friends." Liz was laughing at Ed's joke. "You've proved your point; I guess I don't need to know everything. I'm just glad you were teasing about someone having an affair."

Liz scooted over close to Ed. She'd decided years ago Ed's problem about preaching on adultery was just unthinkable at Big Flat. People just didn't run around here, the place was too small. She relaxed. Ed put his arm around her."

"I'm proud you didn't get mad."

Liz was being sweeter than she had in months. Ed was too shocked to answer. He'd been prepared to tell her the whole story, but the way he wanted to do it was to relieve his conscious of just blurting out the names. Liz's assumption that he was teasing had kept the secret between him and Fred Hudson. Ed squeezed Liz, knowing life had to be crazy or he couldn't stay sane any longer.

The night had been special. Ed felt better in spite of the problems.

CHAPTER 40

Willie Sitton sat still as he watched darkness creep up from the creek. He liked the fall. The trees were in full color with the bright red of the gum and the yellow of the maple accenting all the other colors. The deep shadow of the hill made the deep hollow that held Big Creek slip into dusk while the hills above and to the east of the creek basked in bright evening sun.

Willie always wondered why the darkness seemed to creep up the hill until a moment he'd always waited for, and then almost instantly the whole valley seemed to slip into dusk at once.

Willie's thoughts were usually on his moonshine, or his cows, the sows he'd bought, or Ellen and her moods.

Religion. Willie spat in disgust as he thought of Ellen's biggest gripe. She was treating him almost like somebody until Preacher got drunk. Now things were back to normal. Life for Willie before his friendship with Ed began had been a compromise with Ellen. He paid the preacher. He kept the 'shine at the barn away from the house, and his decency was overlooked, lost somewhere among the sin of him being a moonshiner.

Their sex life was the place where sin met Christianity. No humor. Willie had to be stoic, almost like a priest giving a sacrifice, only the sacrifice was Ellen. She tried hard not to enjoy her sex relations, afraid that any strong reaction on her part might give Willie the idea she was not as pious as she wanted him to believe. Willie's favorite times were when Ellen lost control and became a writhing female enjoying her bed mate and husband as much as any woman could.

Sex and liquor. Willie smiled a wry smile, not contrite like when he spat after his first thought on religion, but more amusement at the many things that could gain control of a man. Coy Bryant and his eternal sex drive. Ed Tice, a preacher who didn't trust his own instinct around liquor. The two men occupied more of Willie's thoughts than anyone. Tonight? No different. Willie began a review of why he was an outcast. The thoughts drifted usually to worrying.

Willie's face showed lines of that worry. The times had been hard for him since the preacher stopped his visits.

Friendship with Ed had meant more to Willie than he'd realized. The worry over being around a preacher had eased when he saw Ed suffered from fear, longed for companionship, was nervous if a question lingered unanswered, all fears Willie thought a preacher was immune from. A man in a pulpit could look so composed that Willie had always placed them in a category above human desires.

Willie stopped. His mind raced as he remembered Coy Bryant's holier than anyone attitude in public. He knew Coy could bed more women in a week than most men could in a life time, but his church manner was almost like a preacher. The power to display a perfect manner, Coy

Bryant had that, too. Willie's thoughts stayed on Coy Bryant. He remembered getting' sweet on the Avey girl a year before he started seein' Ellen. He remembered the Sunday he'd gone home with her from church at Cozy. The Sittons and Aveys had been friends for years. No one noticed when he took her up the path above the barn.

Willie realized a few years later she'd seduced him rather than him seducing her. The roll on the soft ground was an awkward beginning for Willie's sex life, but the thing he remembered the clearest was the gleam in the girl's eyes as she told him, "That's almost like Brother Bryant does Mama." She'd stopped and giggled. "He's been layin' me for most of a year, now." She stopped, probably noticing Willie's shocked stare. "He lasted longer than you."

Willie had stood up and walked away, ashamed of what he'd done. He'd thought he was in love. A sour taste came in his mouth. His girl was carryin' on with a man twice her age, a man that was carryin' on with her mother, a man of wealth, the deacon as he was called. A man Willie's hate had seethed for, but a man Willie avoided.

The dark shadows of the mountain were gone from the creek, lost in darkness of the black night. Willie gazed at the night, seeing nothing, wondering how long he'd been lost in his thoughts of Coy Bryant.

Some people have a way of just always ruining other folk's lives. Coy Bryant was a person that left a trail of hurt behind, but did it under a guise of good, giving food to the needy, taking a mortgage on a farm and foreclosing after making a "charity loan," helping the wife around the place while he cheated her husband out of his labor or livestock. Every good deed Coy ever done was always balanced against the trickery of gain, plus his continual conquest of women.

Willie couldn't believe Coy's desire for women and his ability to conquer them after all these years.

"Yep," Willie said to himself, "it wasn't the drunk that ruined Ed, it was him catchin' Coy." Over the last four years he'd tried several times to guess who the preacher had caught with Coy, but he couldn't make it fit. Ellen wouldn't ever let him accuse Jim's wife of seein' Coy, but Willie was sure she was. But then, Jim and Coy were close friends, both of them deacons in the church. Coy didn't usually mess with folks that close to him.

"This whole thing stinks." Willie'd said that under his breath hundreds of times since "the drunk." Now he was sure, the righteous pretense of religion would be more of a strain than he could ever stand.

That same night Ed sat on his porch watching the shadow of the two-story school building lengthen until it reached the gate to Mrs. Haye's yard. *Never goes beyond that.* Ed thought the shadow's limit was easy to figure, but Ed's limit had reached somewhere without him knowing it.

Maybe it was Liz's coolness after the baby died, maybe it was worry over trying to be perfect, maybe...Ed would always stop. He never wanted to admit he wanted to change. He would not let his desire to be himself surface. Ever since the time he'd run away from the seminary his life had been a living apology. He'd been saying he was sorry for so long that he didn't know if he had the guts to face the world with a real answer by telling everyone he was somebody, Ed Tice, the preacher had rights. Ed stopped. Yes, he had a right to get mad at people. Paul didn't like Alexander, the coppersmith. He could notice other women. David wasn't exactly a prude. And last but not least, Noah didn't raise a crop of English peas in his first garden after the flood.

But could he change? Could he treat Sister Rhodes like an adulteress? Could he treat Liz like a spoiled brat? It seemed his whole life had been based on his begging the world to forgive him, and treating people like he thought they were all precious saints, when he really knew.

"I'll go see Willie," Ed said aloud. He smiled, a resolution was being formed, a resolution to allow himself some freedom. Just Ed Tice, a preacher, a man who cares, but not too much, a man who is sorry for his wrongs but not ever downtrodden. Ed stood up. He felt mean. Noah was gone for the night to visit a neighbor. Liz sat knitting as usual.

Ed couldn't really explain why he'd done what he did, but he was proud. Liz was sleeping peacefully with her head laying on his bare chest.

Liz was nude, completely, the first time in the history of their marriage. She'd fought at first when he threw the thread and knitting needles in the basket. A torn-up dress, strewn undergarments, and a giggling couple had come out after their shell of pretense. Liz had showered him with kisses. She'd never known such bliss.

It's times like this we've missed, Ed thought as he went to sleep.

Morning came slowly. Liz lay sleeping with her knees curled to her bosom. Ed awoke first, he had the corners.

Breakfast tasted good. Liz liked the time with Ed this morning better than last night, and last night was great!

"I'm going to see Willie," Ed mused, wondering what Liz would say.

"Bring some sorghum." Liz didn't show any sign of surprise.

Ed walked toward the horse lot. After saddling the horse, he rode across the yard. Liz stood waving.

"I may be late." Ed spurred the horse hard. The horse seemed to sense the new freedom as it broke into a fast lope toward the bridge.

The ride from Big Flat to the bridge had been easy. The horse was getting old, but the only change noticeable with age had been a softening of his steps for an easier gait.

The search for Willie had not been as long as it seemed. The barn at the bridge was empty, the hogs had been fed early, the sows were already laying down, full and satisfied, while the pigs searched the ground for single grains of corn missed by their mothers. Ed guessed Willie had been gone for over an hour.

Ed had questioned whether he still knew Willie well enough to trace his steps. He fed cows, then hogs, checked horses, went to the barn? Ed tried to think; this time of year was sorghum time. He followed the wagon tracks up the creek to the mill. Smoke, heavy smoke, was coming from under the pan, spiraling up the chimney of rocks. Willie was busy starting the fire.

A young man Ed had never seen before was feeding the cane mill, squeezing out juice. The mill was turned by a mule plodding at an easy gait in an endless and monotonous circle at the end of a white oak pole attached to the mill shaft above the boy's head.

"Howdy, Preacher!" Willie's voice shouted enthusiasm without any sign of surprise to see Ed. "That's Carl Harris," Willie nodded toward the young lad Ed been studying.

"Where you from?" Ed asked Carl, dodging out of the mule's path and getting down from his horse. Ed tied his horse to a tree out of the way of the mill.

"Here," the boy answered almost a minute after Ed had gotten back from tying the horse.

Ed studied the young man; he might be sixteen. His hair was black, maybe blacker than Ed's, with a few curls. His skin was smooth, not dark, just olive enough to fit the color of his hair. The quick hands grasping the cane as he shoved it between the rollers, showed signs of being used to hard work. He had thick fingers, the kind usually not developed by most men until they were in their mid-twenties. Ed's hands seemed frail compared to the boy's. The forearms also showed strength. However, the rest of the boy's frame was raw boned and looked under nourished. At 5'9" he looked tall. The face was like the hands, mature past his age, square jawed, serious with green eyes, a beard, just a stubble grown in three days, but too heavy for a sixteen-year old. Ed had not realized he'd been staring at Carl Harris until Willie yelled.

"You gonna gawk at the boy all day or visit?" Willie's voice boomed above all the noise of the mill.

Ed walked over and joined Willie. He meant to ask Carl why he'd never met him if he was from "here."

Willie continued on about the boy as if he read Ed's mind. "The boy's folks lived on the ledge above the mouth." Willie referred to where Big Creek joined the Buffalo River some five miles past Cozy. "Their house burned last spring. The rest of 'em went to Oklahoma. The boy come up the creek, lookin' fer work."

"How come I ain't heard about this?"

"How should I know?" Willie's voice rasped hard. He never tried to hide being irritated by a question. "You ain't exactly been here much."

"I know." Ed stood dumbfounded. Willie's attitude seemed to have changed. He'd never noticed him being sassy before.

"What're ya doing here today?" Willie's voice still sassy.

Ed picked up a piece of wood and chucked it on the fire. He couldn't answer Willie. He didn't know.

"I just come over," Ed finally said.

"Yeah?" Willie grunted.

"Yeah." Ed mimicked Willie.

"You been all right?" Willie's tone softened.

"Sorta." Ed's answer lacked conviction. "You?" Ed's eyes asked the question more than the words.

"Tolerable." Willie moved down below the molasses pan to the pile of wood. Ed followed.

"I come to talk," Ed said, watching Willie pick up the heavy oak sticks. The fire would burn all day.

"Let's go after a load of cane." Willie started toward the wagon waiting above the mill. "Ellen's coming to wash the pan."

They rode silently, Ed not knowing how to start the conversation. He couldn't explain why he'd stayed away from his friend for almost four years. He couldn't say why he'd come to see him this morning.

"I like makin' molasses..." Willie paused. "I just hate the work."

"I know," Ed answered, "kinda like preachin'. I like doin' it, I just hate the...." Ed stopped. What did he hate? He didn't know.

"Willie, I spent the last fifteen years apologizing." Ed watched Willie's expression. "I'm quittin'."

"Preachin'?"

"No." Ed's answer was sharp. "Just quittin' pretending. I'm not sure what I meant to say, just I'm tired of people. I'm tired of pettin' people to get them to do what they ought to." Ed ignored the rough ride across the cane field.

"I'm tired of pretending everybody's good." Ed caught his breath. "Like Coy Bryant and his whore chasin'."

"Who'd you catch him with?"

"Sister Rhodes," Ed answered before he thought, not realizing he'd broken pastoral confidence the first time in his life.

"I always figured he diddled her, but then she's Ellen's favorite sister-in-law." Willie spat. "Could believe that, that bitch, all the nerve...holy...." Willie stopped.

"I caught her and Coy the morning after we drunk the quart."

"You did!"

"I's going to see Coy," Ed smiled, his mind easing, glad to finally tell someone about the glade.

Willie listened intently as Ed gave every detail he could remember from the scene in the glade, and began laughing hard when Ed described Coy trying to retrieve his pants from around his ankles. Ed laughed with him.

"You know, I never saw humor in that at the time." Ed

was serious again.

"Preacher, that's been your problem." Willie's tone was not scolding, just firm. "You take everything too serious. Crap! We're just people. The mean ones just like the good ones. The good ones get hungry, like women, go fishin', tell lies, work hard, pay their bills, get disgusted, cheat on a trade if'n they can. The bad ones drink hard liquor, tell the truth, chase women, pay their debts, whup you if you cheat 'em in a trade, and keep their promises."

Ed's mind raced as he tried to keep up with Willie's philosophy. He lost track of it.

"Preacher, they just ain't very many perfect folks, and they just ain't nobody I've ever met that was completely good." Willie stopped the wagon. "'Cept Coy Bryant gets close."

"Why do you say that?" Ed sat waiting for an answer as Willie began throwing the shocks of cane on the wagon.

"Get off and help, we can talk better." Willie turned to get another arm load of cane as Ed climbed down from the wagon.

"You know what you said, Ed, about pretendin'." Willie's use of Ed's name got the preacher's attention. "Well I knew you wuz under pressure, and that usually means you ain't comfortable, and most of the time a feller puts his own self in that kind of fix. Mostly it's just tryin' too hard, expectin' too much, thinkin' folks think more of you than they do, trying to keep up with something too big for ya. That's why Coy Bryant's sorry he spends all his time foolin' people."

"How does he live like that?" Ed was enjoying Willie's answer, and the wagon was almost loaded. Willie worked harder than he talked.

"Don't know." Willie climbed onto the wagon, leaving Ed to finish loading the last bit of cane from the pile. "Couldn't keep myself straight, I'd get carried away and just do one thing, probably just seein' the women." Willie's smile was sly, and Ed joined him on the wagon, smiling broadly. Willie's mind raced, he couldn't believe the change in the preacher's attitude.

"Me and Fred Hudson's dad tried to count how many women Coy had screwed one time, and decided he was the daddy of a kid in every third house in a ten-mile circle from Cozy," Willie continued. "If a man went to Oklahoma to work in the oil field, if a man went to Rush to work in the mines, aw, I don't know how he does it, but if I left Ellen for a week, Coy'd come by just to help. Most of his flings are just a week or two, but he's got four or five, make that five countin' Jim's wife, that's gone on for years. Must be all he thinks about. He can tell if'n a woman will, and he gives 'em all a fair chance to diddle even if he don't think they will."

"I didn't come to talk about Coy." Ed's voice cut into Willie's description of Coy.

"What ya wanna talk about?"

"Me."

"You?"

"Yeah."

"OK, what about you?" Willie's question sounded the amusement he felt.

"I'm changing my mind." Ed couldn't say what he meant. "Not really my mind, but my, well, just my.... Willie, I don't know, I just wanna be able to stop trying to put on an air of perfection." Ed eased down in the spring seat propping his feet on the head gate of the wagon.

"When I got religion, it was like I'd entered a separate world, a world of ritual where everybody made themselves better by denying they were ever bad, and part of being good was criticizing everybody if you could see something they were doing that was wrong." Willie listened, understanding the part about Christians being critical of people doing wrong. "Then I got caught with liquor at the seminary. I ran away, ashamed to go home. I'd crossed that imaginary line over to being bad. When I started again at Batesville, it was a new vow. I'd be so perfect, evil would not even touch me. I came to see you the first time to stamp out a bad thing." Ed stared at Willie almost a minute.

"Save the bootlegger, make good of evil and eliminate a sin." Ed was animated as he talked. "Then we got acquainted. Your insight saw past my image. You saw me crunching inside. I lost control, I got drunk. I reinforced my will to apologize. I didn't dare speak out on sin, just ease around, the downtrodden guilt-stricken preacher. Last night I's settin' on the school house steps, I suddenly saw myself. A spineless wimp, a man creeping around, afraid, cloaking his tongue in shrouds of righteousness. I got up. I wanted to kick my rear, Sister Rhodes, Coy Bryant, half the church at Big Flat, some at Hickory, most of the members at Cozy, and Lord knows who else. I went home feeling mean. Liz was the only one I could take my feelings out on."

Willie's eyes bugged, expecting Ed to tell him he'd whipped Liz.

"No, I didn't whip her. We ruined a dress, but I left her smiling bigger this morning than ever before, and me and that gal has seen some good times."

"Preacher, I still don't understand what you're sayin'."

"I don't know, either. It's just I come to realize a few things. David and Bathsheba wasn't playing footsies. God didn't do them like I did to Coy and Sister Rhodes. But I ain't gonna start no rumors, just ain't helping her to hide no more. Why, Willie, she even rubs her bosom against me at the store, bumps her butt against me ever chance she gets, and I just take it and treat her like a saint. Makes me mad after all the talking she did about us."

"Grab a hand full of her." Willie's eyes shined. That'll shock her. Might twist whichever part you get a hold of, just for good measure. Tell her you're gonna preach on love in the glade on a spring afternoon." Willie laughed hard enough to shake the wagon seat.

Ed's mood turned sour, not sure Willie understood what he was saying to him. They rode silent for several yards.

"What're you gonna do different?" Willie questioned blandly, no hint of suggestion to the answer he was expecting.

"Mostly I'm. going to start treating people the way I feel. You know I think you're doin' wrong, bootlegging, but then you know I think you're decent in your attitudes. I'm going to stop being afraid to do what I want to. I'm coming here when I want, I'm not going to worry about when I drank, what I drank, if I drank. I'm gonna cut loose, be Ed Tice, a man." Willie listened to the sermon.

"I'm not going to try to sterilize the world. I'm going to be willing to change, and hope and pray people change for the better. I guess I said all this to say I'm tired of pushing, and I'm going to try leading for a while." Ed leaned forward in the wagon. "I'm going to relax and say what I feel. If I don't like something, I'm gonna say it. I'm quittin' trying to be popular.

The wagon wheels crunched in the loose gravel at the edge of the clearing. The team of mules pulled hard, their bodies stretching low to the ground as they extended their legs to get leverage enough to move the load up to the clearing where the sorghum mill set. A crowd had gathered.

"Let's unload in a hurry!" Willie's eyes gleamed. He jumped down and began pulling the cane from the wagon.

CHAPTER 41

Ed sat still, ignoring Willie. As usual he studied the crowd. All of them were part of his congregation, some regular members, others just sporadic, but all were familiar. They looked strange gathered around the molasses pan and cane mill. Ellen Sitton was scrubbing the copper pan. Steam rolled as she swabbed the gunnels of fine oak. Each run of copper was gleaming, even the baffles were clean. She'd done a good job.

Ellen stopped cleaning, looked at Ed, and all eyes followed hers. Ed suddenly felt out of place. He'd been studying the people, as usual, noting how different they looked in work clothes. Ragged, some of them, neat patches on some, others in clothes just taken for every day. He recognized a Redman boy's shirt on one he'd worn not many Sundays before.

Now he was being inspected. He could almost feel the questions of what he was doing with Willie.

Ed jumped from the wagon. "Hurry, Willie, let's go get

another load." Ed felt silly for a second, assuming Willie meant to haul cane instead of cooking the juice.

"Newt." Willie looked for Newt Blair. "You cook. Me 'n Preacher is gonna haul."

Ed threw the last of the cane on the pile and jumped in the wagon as Willie pulled away from the mill.

"You know, Ed, that bunch a people up there never seem to notice things me and you do." Willie felt proud having the preacher with him. "They just know the things anybody can see. They didn't see you looking past Ellen at the shine of the copper. I saw you trace every run from spigot to spout. That shows you care about bein' clean.

"I've watched you when you preach. A kid with a nasty nose, a man with a torn shirt, a woman with a full bosom, a girl in a new pair of shoes, same things I notice, your eyes stop every time you come to something in the crowd." Willie went on, Ed wondering where this conversation was heading. "I see the same thing, a woman that perks up when she's noticed. They all do something that catches your eye just like mine."

Willie yelled at the team. He had lost track of his driving, and the mules had strayed off the trail beaten out across the cane field. The wagon was bouncing.

"It's the reason I can't change from what I am. I don't just see things, I feel people's moods like Ellen. She's sulky, I just leave her alone, never bother her when she's pouting. Never have asked her what's bothering her, never will. Got enough problems of my own." Willie's rambling was bothering Ed. "Take church. Don't know how you handle it. Everybody that goes feels like they're the only ones there, ones that's happy can't stand them that's sad. Them that's sad can't stand them that's happy. I watched Newt's wife two times that I went. She's wilder than most of my 'shine drinkers. Claims she's some kind of new Christian." Willie stopped and looked at Ed. "What is it she's supposed to be?"

"Pentecost," Ed said.

"I knew it was some name like that, reminds me of money or a price of something," Willie went on. "Anyway, then there's Ellen's ma, sets in church like she's mad at the world, gripes every Sunday after her 'n Ellen gets back. Ain't nothing goin' to suit her for years."

Ed was shocked. Ma Rhodes always held his hand sweetly every time he shook hands with her, and told him how great everything was.

"That's the reason I ain't going to church. Them folks is all just alike. No real opinion, set and talk about people like they's dogs, then smile and tell them how good they are." Willie's statement shocked Ed. He was sure he'd not said a word.

"I didn't say anything," Ed winced.

"I know. I just saw your surprise at Ma Rhodes' griping." Willie stopped the wagon below one of the cane shocks. The late fall was letting them make molasses three weeks later than usual. For November it was hot. The cane was dry, the dew had been light, and the slender cane no longer glistened with moisture. Willie began loading the cane. Ed swung his feet over the side and sat with his feet dangling.

"I'm proud you woke up. People made fun of you for apologizing. Shoulda told 'em weren't none of their business, just between you and the Lord. That's what Ma always taught me. 'Keep it straight between you and the Lord, son.' What she always said." Willie was heaving the cane on the wagon. Ed was still watching.

"Have you?" Ed asked.

"Have I what?" Willie's answer seemed to miss the point.

"Kept it straight."

"Ain' none of your business. If 'n I told ya, it wouldn't be just between me and the Lord anymore." Willie jumped on the wagon and pulled to the next shock of cane.

"You load this 'n. I got hot." Willie wiped his brow and pointed at the cane. Ed climbed down and began loading the last of the cane, musing to himself how Willie always managed to quit when loading the wagon got too high above his head. Ed was tall enough to finish the load without any strain.

"I don't know I'll do anything really different." Ed had taken over the reins and the conversation. "I just decided I was miserable worrying about impressions, guilt, sin. That's what I've quit. Just that."

"Worryin'?" Willie's voice was shrill and filled with question.

"Yeah."

"That'll be a trick," Willie continued, "Everybody worries. Ever keep track of your worrying? I did one year." Willie wasn't giving Ed a chance to continue. "It 'mazed me. I always worry, but the problem you got don't last long. Very little stuff I ever worried 'bout mounted to anything, Most of it went away or worked out. Wouldn't none of the bad things I imagined ever really happened."

Willie almost fell off the wagon. "Preacher, you don't drive worth a flip, you're going turn this thing over."

Ed slowed the mules down. He knew Willie had missed their visits as much as he had, but they were not getting much visiting done today. They were just taking turns lecturing.

"Yep, ain't no use to worry, but let me know if you quit. I'd like to." Willie braced for the crossing of the creek. "You reckon worry is how the devil steals our mind?"

Willie's question sounded to Ed like some of his own philosophy.

CHAPTER 42

The air was getting a chill to it. November was beginning to feel like it was November. The heat was over.

Big Creek bridge at Willie Sitton's was a long way from Wall street. The worrying Willie and Preacher Ed Tice talked about couldn't compare to the panic corporate heads were feeling. Although these people would soon be touched by the country's financial crises, today they went home well paid. They'd visited, they'd eaten a good lunch picnic style, cooked and brought to the mill steaming hot. They went home with their pay in jars, molasses.

Willie joked to Ed that ole man Mason ought to move his jar factory closer, with jars leaving his place faster than he could get them. It was the first time Willie had alluded to the 'shine business.

Ed left for home. Willie gathered the stock, watching Carl Harris clean up around the mill. They were finished for the year. Carl walked up the hollow above the mill to the cabin Willie had fixed for him to stay in, a shed until they enclosed the front and added a floor.

Ellen and the girls had gotten carried away at fixing it up for the boy. Pauline was fourteen. Willie had never thought about his girls getting grown, then he noticed Pauline hanging after Carl. Myrtle was fifteen, but scrawny. Pauline was a girl. Carl had noticed it, too.

Willie knew he liked the boy. Now he had plans for him.

"Carl, we're through with the cane." Willie followed him to the shed. "Why don't you go back to your place and see if you can catch one of them listed sows."

Willie had wanted some Hampshire blood to mix with his Red Duroc.

"I could see," Carl answered. "You going with me?"

"No." Willie studied Carl. "They might know you. They'd be spooked of me, for sure."

"I'll leave tomorrow." Carl agreed to go.

"If 'n you locate one and cain't catch her, come back and get me, we'll get her some way." Willie was walking back toward the team and wagon.

Carl sat watching him. He'd never understood Willie until today. He knew he'd been missing something ever since he got to the bridge. Today he saw what it was, his friendship with Preacher Ed.

Dawn came slowly, the fog was heavy, and Carl could barely see the harness hanging in the barn. He hated to harness the mules. They were frisky in summer, but the cool weather made them worse. They would kick, bite, twist, and try any way they could to avoid the harness. But once they were hooked to the wagon, they were gentle. "The best team on the creek," one of the few things Willie bragged about.

Carl checked the wheels of the wagon. They were all in good shape. He loaded three lengths of rope, a length of Willie's own measurement, about 30 feet. Enough for a good lariat or a plow line. Something else Carl had learned from Willie.

Carl started down the creek, dreading the trip. At least this time he wouldn't be wading, as he had in March when he made his way up the creek looking for work at every farm, being told each time, "Willie Sitton might hire ya." The people had all given a different opinion of Willie. Some mentioned his moonshine, some his molasses, some his bacon, "best ham on the creek." But they'd all ended by saying, "He always hires help."

Willie had not been anything like Carl expected. His reputation led Carl to expect some kind of giant. A burly, rough shod, ignorant hoodlum had been the image in Carl's mind.

Willie's short, square body, smooth temper, pleasant disposition had been the best surprise of Carl's life. They never made any promises all summer. Carl wasn't sure what his wages were supposed to be. Ellen had made so many shirts for him, Carl didn't know how many he had. Pauline always cleaned the cabin while he was working. Clean shirts were left in place of dirty ones.

The wagon was grinding along as Carl daydreamed about his new life. From poverty, burned out, his family leaving with nothing but their clothes for Oklahoma. His mom buried under the oak in front of the charred ruins of the house. She died in 1927. His dad, bitter and broke. His oldest sister married to a city dude. His younger sisters malnourished and sulky. Carl's new life of plenty. And he was glad to be working for Willie, and out on his own. Pauline was helping him get over being lonesome.

Carl's mind drifted to Preacher Ed. He'd wanted to go to Cozy to church when they first moved to the ledge. But then his mother got sick. He had to quit school. Carl didn't dare mention going anywhere after that.

The morning grew warm. Carl was glad his feet were dry, but he'd opened and closed more gates than he could remember. Every crossing of the creek meant a gate was next, and it seemed the wagon road crossed the creek every

100 yards.

Carl knew where he was, the neat fields were Coy Bryant's. Coy had stolen the four heifers they'd brought from Tennessee. They were short horns, the only ones in the country, but when Carl's dad saw them in the corral, Coy said he'd bought them. Carl remembered the trip to Marshall. His dad went to the sheriff, then to the lawyers. He'd been run out of each office. "If Coy Bryant said the cows were his, that's who they belonged to." Carl still remembered how his dad's shoulders slumped after that day. A failure in Tennessee, the black sheep from a good family, a new start in Arkansas.

Carl pushed the memory to the back of his mind as he climbed back on the wagon. Today was a new day. He was back, driving Willie Sitton's wagon, dressed neat. He sat up straight, proud, hoping to meet some of Coy's bunch. Carl drove straight toward Coy's big barn.

A gun roared. The mules lurched forward. Carl almost fell backwards off the wagon seat into the wagon bed. The wagon ran forward, pushing the mules in a delayed reaction from the first lunge.

The gun roared again. Carl couldn't control the reins. He fought with the reins, and was trying hard to stay on the wagon seat and locate the gunman at the same time. He couldn't figure where the shooting was except it seemed to be in the barn.

The mules turned to the left, away from the barn. Carl tugged hard on the reins, trying to keep the team from running away. As he slowed the mules he got a glimpse of a rider leaving the barn. The mules slowed down and Carl drove them in a circle back into the road, about to the place he'd been when the first shot was fired.

He stopped the team. The barn sat serene. A crow was raising a fuss on the ridge beyond the barn. Carl studied the barn. What had happened? He started to drive on, remembering how hurt his father had been when they had to leave their only stock of any value in the corral on the far side of the barn. He had never messed around Coy Bryant's stuff because of an urge to burn his barn or some other act of retaliation. But, the shots from the barn stirred a curiosity that would only be satisfied by an investigation inside the barn.

The hallway door was still swinging slowly when Carl stopped the mules and got off the wagon seat. The mules' ears stood up straight. They backed away sideways from the barn. Carl listened, the only sound he could hear above the ruckus of the mules was the crows. They had gotten louder than before.

He dropped the reins, forgetting to tie them to the brake pole. The mules scampered, dragging the wagon about forty yards, but they stopped when Carl yelled. He went into the hallway and stopped, waiting for his eyes to adjust to the dim light. There was a rustle and a moan from the loft. Carl's mind raced as he realized there was something very serious with the gun shots.

He listened for the sound again. His eyes followed a drop of blood from a crack in the loft until it splattered in the pool formed in the middle of the manure filled hallway. Carl stepped around the puddle of blood. He suddenly felt fear grip him as he started toward the ladder to climb into the loft.

The moaning stopped. He began to climb, looking up into the loft, trying to see without going all the way up the ladder.

The barn smelled like gun powder. The musty smell of hay gave a soft tinge to the odor that still hung in the loft. Shafts of light danced on the gun smoke drifting above Carl's head. He'd climbed the ladder and his eyes surveyed the barn with his chin level with the floor of the hay loft.

At first glance the bare bodies seemed to be part of the barn. The twisted body of a half nude man clutching straw with both hands was the last signs of life left in him. Carl stared. The hole in the man's back was a dark red, contrasting with the bright red blood still oozing on to the board of the loft. The hands relaxed. Straw fell from the fingers. The movement was slow and final.

Carl couldn't see the man's face, just the back of his head. The right side showed an ugly red glob similar to the spot on his back, a contrast to the black hair with touches of gray. Carl's eyes adjusted to the dimness. The gun smoke was also clearing.

The woman's head was against a post in the center of the loft. Her head was tilted with her chin resting on her chest. Her eyes were bugged, large, in a fixed stare. It was almost as if she was staring in amazement at the wound in her left breast. She was dead.

Carl eased down the ladder, his mind racing, trying to decide what he should do. His mouth was dry, his knees were weak. As his feet touched the soft manure filled hallway, Carl felt his body sway. His mind had been racing so fast, he was not aware of how sick the scene had made him.

Carl walked toward the wagon, listening to the sound of a lone crow. A slow caw just finishing up the ruckus from a few minutes earlier. Carl got on the wagon, still unsure where he was going for help. The barn was two miles from anybody's house except Coy Bryant. Carl was sure that had to be Coy Bryant lying dead in the barn loft.

He tried to remember where he'd passed the Hollimans fishing earlier. Carl got on the wagon seat and headed the mules up the creek the way he'd come less than an hour earlier. It seemed an eternity since the gun shots interrupted his leisurely ride into the same field.

Dusk was falling. Ed sat on the wagon seat by Willie. Carl Harris was in the back of the wagon. New arrivals at the barn were asking Carl the same questions he'd answered since noon.

"Did you see the man leaving?"

"Was it Jim Rhodes?"

"Where'd you go for help?"

Ed was enjoying listening to Carl's answers.

"I just got a glance of the man as he rode around the corner of the barn."

"I don't know Mr. Rhodes."

"I went to find the Hollimans. I'd seen them on my way down the creek."

The answers were always the same. Carl was not trying to add any details for the sake of saying something.

"Ed, this make you feel funny after what we said yesterday?" Willie spoke barely loud enough for Ed to hear.

Ed watched Carl's expression, realizing in spite of Willie's attempt at whispering, the boy had heard.

"Yeah," Ed finally answered, wishing the coroner would hurry. The sheriff had been there almost two hours, but they were waiting for the county coroner to come and hold an inquest. The coroner's jury would have an easy time saying it was homicide, but whether it was a murder would depend on another jury ruling if it was justifiable.

Jim Rhodes could legally kill Coy, but how would they rule on Sister Rhodes' death? Ed felt odd as the thought came to mind. Calling someone Sister didn't seem right for a woman dead in a barn loft, shot while in the nude with Coy Bryant.

"Willie, this is a mess," Ed said, referring to the crowd. Almost a hundred people had gathered in the field. A sheriff's deputy was standing in the hallway, guarding the barn to keep the curiosity seekers from climbing the ladder to see the bodies in the loft.

"Worst mess I ever saw." Willie stopped. "Good thing it turned cold, flies would a blowed 'em if ' it hadn't."

"No," Ed rasped, "I mean all these people nosing around."

"Got as much business here as you do."

"Well, I guess." Ed didn't like Willie's way of cutting him down. "But I needed to come, after all I'm responsible." Ed's voice trailed off.

"You're what?"

"Responsible."

"How in the...?" Willie stopped before he cursed. "I don't see no way. Why, Preacher, he's been on borrowed time for twenty years."

"No." Ed's face was still. "I should of exposed them. It might of saved their lives."

The crowd was listening. Willie and Ed both had said more than they intended. They shut up. Willie began wondering if Ed was going to start another spell of sulking, acting like he did after the drunk.

"Willie, all I's saying was it might a stopped this. I ain't done nothing I'm ashamed of." Ed stressed the "ain't" with a rasp to his voice for the rest of the sentence.

"OK. I see what you're sayin'." Willie felt relieved that Ed showed some spunk. They got down from the wagon seat. The coroner was driving his buggy through the crowd toward the barn.

CHAPTER 43

Three weeks of confusion, the funerals had been almost like circus events. The crowds were large, the gossip vicious. Details no one could ever know had been filled by some vivid imaginations. Ed Tice had conducted both funerals, and went with Jim Rhodes when the sheriff questioned him.

No arrest had been made. Jim Rhodes was able to prove he was in Sylamore less than an hour after the shooting. The best horse known in the hills couldn't cover the distance in less than three hours. Jim had been seen leaving Big Flat on his bay horse; he'd arrived in Sylamore on the same horse.

Ed mused at the proceedings. He was at home. It was cold, he wouldn't get out except for the chores. It was the first time he'd stopped since the shooting.

"Ed," Liz's voice softened curiously, "you know what I think?"

"What?"

"Somebody knew about Coy. Knew he was carryin' on with Mrs. Rhodes." Ed listened, noting Liz's change from Sister to Mrs. Rhodes. "They shot him, killin' her by accident, hoping to blame Jim. It was a grudge."

"I thought of that."

"You did?" Liz questioned.

"Yeah."

"Who was it?" Liz asked.

"No way to guess. Coy Bryant had too many enemies. To hear Willie talk, Coy either had an affair or tried to with every woman in the country." Ed paused, squinting his eyes as he talked, "a cheat, a lover, a gambler, a church goer, all of these brought together done ole Coy in. No way of telling who finally got the nerve to do it. Too many people with a motive. The sheriff will give up before he solves it."

"Carl can't remember?" Liz sounded curious.

"Not really." Ed's voice trailed off, wishing there was a way to help the boy answer the questions. "The horse ran out of the barn while he was trying to control the mules. The description he gave me was like Jim, but the horse was the wrong color, and the rider went up the mountain west, away from Sylamore. The tracks proved that."

Liz's face showed concern. Ed waited for her to say for the hundredth time how she wished they would find out. She knew that whoever did it was a friend, but she just felt funny going places knowing the person that killed two of their friends was loose in the community.

Ed always mused at how a person's character improved after death. Coy Bryant was no exception. By spring, people would forget the circumstances of his death. The curiosity over the identity of the killer had helped to take attention away from Coy's deeds.

Ed had mused to himself the memory of expressions as the people passed the coffin to view the body. Women had been careful not to show emotion. Some of the men had a sly look, even an occasional smile. Coy's wife had mourned, but not in the way Ed had seen wives rant and rave. It was almost anger mixed with relief.

Jim Rhodes' expression had been stoic, totally aloof, no tears, no expression at all at Coy's or his wife's funeral. Willie did not attend either funeral, neither had Carl. Ed had gone by to see Willie the next week. Willie had said very little about any of the events, murder investigation, or funerals.

"I'll bet Willie could come closer to guessing who it was than anybody," Liz continued, interrupting Ed's thoughts.

"Probably."

"You and him ever talk about Coy?"

"Yeah."

"Ellen told me about you catching Coy and Mrs. Rhodes in the glade when she was here yesterday."

Ed sat up, shocked that Willie had told Ellen about their conversation.

"Willie was just trying to convince her Ruth was no good and deserved getting' shot." Liz was answering Ed's question before he said anything. "That's what upset you," Liz's face filled with concern, "more 'un' what you and Willie did."

"I guess so."

"Ellen also told me Willie was worried, afraid you'd start sulking again."

Ed was amazed at hearing how much Willie had told Ellen.

"Ellen said it was the first time Willie'd ever told her anything." Ed felt relieved. "He asked her to tell me."

"Why?"

"He didn't want you worryin'." Liz got up to close the curtain.

"I'm not." Ed eased down in his chair, relaxing, feeling glad to hear there was concern for his feelings.

"I've changed." Ed stopped.

"I've noticed you're different." Liz pursed her lips in

thought. "I don't know how you've changed, but I'm proud."

"I give up." Ed grinned.

"What?" Liz asked, a little shocked at Ed's remark.

"I've relaxed. I realize my limits. My dream world was too far from reality. I wanted things too perfect. My failures were like tarnish on some precious metal; when I tried to remove it, I made the spot more shiny, never could blend in." Ed's mind wandered. "Couldn't fit anywhere. Too good for some, too sorry for others. Awkward for anybody to be around. A preacher has a problem fittin' in. I just made it worse. I've quit trying. Just gonna let 'er rip and be me. No more pretending."

Liz moved over and sat in Ed's lap, waiting for him to stop talking. He did.

Ed turned the crank; starting the car on a cold morning was tough. November 23rd was cold.

Why did he promise Liz to take her to Marshall? Ed continued cranking, knowing there were men all over the world working to fill a promise made in passion. He would start the car and go to Marshall.

The wind came through every crack in the car. Liz sat bundled up in a blanket. The lantern burned brightly, sitting in the floor board. It was the car's only heater.

Christmas might be a month away. Thanksgiving was next Thursday. Dates didn't matter. Liz wanted to go shop the stores before anyone else picked through the toys. Noah could care less. He spent most of his time with the Barnes kid who lived next to the parsonage. They had volunteered to keep Noah anytime Liz wanted to go with Ed. Ed and

Liz both were not aware how much they ignored Noah. Today was no exception.

The motor roared up the steep grade over the railroad track, always a test for a car's pulling power. Ed had been amazed by how many cars had to make a second run at the steep grade on his first time to come to Marshall. Their car made it over with power to spare.

The engine quieted down. Ed eased the car along Main Street to the court house square. Finding a parking place was easy. Very few people had braved the cold weather.

"Hey, Preacher Ed!" a voice boomed as Ed and Liz got out of the car. Ed started walking toward the courthouse. It was the sheriff. He shook Ed's hand and escorted him up the stairs to his office. Liz made her way to the row of stores that made up the north side of the town square.

"Preacher, what brings you to town?" The sheriff had not said a word until now since hollering at Ed as he parked the car.

"My wife wanted to buy some stuff."

"Things quieting down any?" The sheriff asked, anxious to question Ed. Joe Carson had been Searcy County Sheriff since 1918. He'd stayed in office by knowing what to do and when to do it. He looked the way a sheriff should. Potbellied, but not too noticeable because of a frame almost 6'4" tall. His head would be too large for most bodies, with big burly ears and a large nose. Also, more hair than any man in the county, wide shoulders broad enough to dwarf two men. Joe looked just right for a sheriff. The first time Ed saw him, he thought it would be easy to see how the sheriff could convince a prisoner to go to jail peacefully.

"Some," Ed finally answered the question after spending almost a minute studying the sheriff.

"I don't know what to do." The sound of the sheriff's voice warned Ed he was being polled for an opinion on the investigation. Ed didn't say a word, waiting for the sheriff to continue.

"Ain't much I can do," the sheriff said. "I questioned Jim, you's there. I've gone over it four times with the Harris boy. I went to Sylamore. Jim Rhodes was there like he said."

The sheriff stood up, went to the window, turning his back on Ed. Ed sat quiet. The sheriff studied the street below the courthouse.

"Preacher, wanna hear an interesting theory?" Joe Carson turned around. His eyes narrowed on Ed.

"What theory?"

"Jim Rhodes killed Coy and Ruth."

"How?"

"One of the Hollimans told me how he could a done it, but it's too fantastic, nobody'd ever convince a jury."

"How?" Ed's curiosity was growing.

"The Harris boy saw the rider. His description fit Jim, but the horse is different from Jim's bay, a little too light. But it was the bay, just the bright sun and the flash of movement made the boy see a lighter horse. Jim Rhodes knew about Coy and Ruth for over twenty years. Jim's pushin' sixty. Ruth was barely thirty-nine. They couldn't have kids. I know Jim couldn't tame her, nobody in town could. Everybody tried, me included. Jim married her six weeks after his first wife died. Come here to Marshall and met her, married before a week was out."

The sheriff sat down. He'd been leaning over the desk. Ed had sat amazed. He still had not said enough to make the conversation any more than a lecture from the sheriff.

"Jim planned the shooting for weeks. He went to the barn early, stored the horse in a stall inside with blinders on. He hid himself in the hay, setting on top of the bales Coy'd stacked so high to keep the north wind out of his barn loft." Joe Carson was enjoying the story as he told it. His voice put emphasis on the barn loft.

"He waited. Can you imagine setting there with a shotgun and watching your wife undress?" The sheriff opened the desk drawer, fingering a spent shotgun cartridge.

"Federal." Joe spun the brass for Ed to read the bottom. "Found this between the bales. Couldn't find the othern."

Ed took the shell case and studied the brass. He stocked the ammunition on days he caught up posting the books. Rhodes Store was the only store for forty miles that stocked double 00 buckshot in long brass Federal brand shells. They came from Carr's Hardware in Batesville, where he'd met Jim Rhodes over fifteen years earlier.

"Don't mean a thing," Joe interrupted Ed's thought. "I pick 'em up by the case and bring 'em to Marshall. You know that. I pay my account by check."

"What you do that for?"

"The county pays for 'em." The sheriff grinned. "I give 'em to my next opponent's biggest supporters. Changes lots of minds on election day."

Ed stood up.

"Set down." The sheriff rasped almost an order. "I mean I ain't finished. You ain't in no hurry." A smile flashed on Joe Carson's face.

Ed sat back down.

"The shot that killed Ruth was the second one. The same one that went through the back of Coy's neck. Blowed Coy's right jaw off and busted Ruth's left tit. Went right through her heart."

Ed wondered how much of this kind of talk he was going to be expected to endure.

"Anyway, we know all this, but how did Jim ride west and get to Sylamore when he did?" The sheriff stood up, motioned for Ed to follow. He pointed to a map of Searcy, Baxter, and Stone Counties.

"He rode down the ridge to here." The sheriff pointed to a place on the map that Ed knew was a high bluff over one of the biggest holes of water on Buffalo River. The only way from there was back the way he'd come if a rider left

Coy's barn.

"He jumped that horse into the river, swam out, and it's less than an hour to Sylamore over smooth sandy ground on that side of the river." The sheriff pointed to a straight line he'd drawn on the map to Sylamore.

Ed left the office not ever expressing an opinion, and shocked that a sheriff would repeat a wild story concocted by one of the Hollimans. They were known for big fish stories, hard liquor, and wild living.

The cold air was refreshing. Ed began to walk around town hoping to find a better way to kill time than listening to the sheriff.

As he walked Ed thought about the hill county's politics. The sheriff was more than just the law officer. He seldom made an arrest that ever resulted in a prison sentence. The accused was usually released after a deal for cash or influence. The stories of some deals were long and interesting, told over every year after a new arrest being made. Ed knew the stories were true.

Willie Sitton was a "legal" bootlegger. A typical trip to Big Flat by the sheriff included a stop at the bridge. Ed didn't know how the deal was made, but he would never forget coming to see Joe Carson to report Willie's bootleggin'. The sheriff had listened intently, promising to do everything possible to "shut 'er down," but a sly look gave away his amusement at the young preacher from Big Flat. Years of time had not changed anything.

The lawyer's office around the corner behind the bank was probably the real center of power, but the sheriff seemed to make his decisions without consulting anyone. Ed knew whoever killed Coy had been smart. They had planned their escape. Anyone smart enough to do that was also smart enough to be in with the county politicians. They could avoid prosecution. The investigation was over.

Liz came out of a store. Ed almost passed her, he had been so lost in thought.

Depression. A word familiar to everyone would not describe the mood of the hills. Ed's change in attitude was running counter to the social change brought about by the economic changes.

A murder, a Wall Street crash, a changed philosophy by a hill circuit preacher could not reach out to the pain of people trying to find a way to survive without starving to death in a part of the country where a living meant meager supplies bought with cash earned from timber and furs, with very little else to do.

Corn liquor, 'shine, was a staple that always sold for cash. Willie Sitton had cash stowed away in cotton tobacco sacks hid in the space between the logs behind the fruit jars in the old root cellar above the main house at the bridge.

As Ed rode along the trail toward Willie's still, he had no way of knowing how important Willie was about to become economically. He usually divided his thoughts of Willie into two eras.

The evil bootlegger era, when Willie was the center of Ed's attention, a time in Ed's ministry when he believed it was possible to have the perfect community. He dreamed of all these churches being filled with people and no worry about the evils of moonshine. Converting Willie could accomplish all of that. The dream, not reality.

Those meetings with Willie. The time of a second era beginning. Willie's mystic was not there. He was open, honest. Willie saw past all pretentions. Ed's mind had always been a battle ground, but Willie had made Ed admit the battle was not a losing one, but rather, a choice of recognizing honesty would permit failures without always assessing blame, while success didn't always come because of effort, but usually meant circumstances were right to permit it.

Ed's confusion seemed to end in his mind the day he stopped trying to find an answer behind everything that happened. It was coincidental that after four years of sulking in guilt Ed found the courage to change his attitude and within a week everyone had been shocked by the murder.

Willie had just assumed Ed was back in the old frame of mind.

Willie spent the winter months teaching Carl the 'shine business. Carl had never questioned their trips to the still with the loads of corn, sugar, and wheat shorts before daylight. Carl just worked hard at keeping the mash barrels clean. The day ended by bringing back the day's cooked mash for hog feed, with jars of clear liquor riding between the sacks.

Willie thought of Ed, but then he knew there could never be any real friendship between them on a full-time basis. A preacher had to keep an image of being above a bootlegger.

February sun is ideal for making moonshine. The barrels full of mash were painted black by Willie after he discovered how much faster the dark barrels would ferment in the bright evening sun. Warm enough to sour, but cold enough to cook the mash without the stifling heat of summer.

Ed rode leisurely, not sure why he was going to the still.

Life was going at a fast pace. He'd finally realized the freedom he felt was permanent. He was not worrying anymore about the past. He had forgotten Ruth Rhodes. He knew Jim Rhodes might be her killer, but Jim was still a friend. He didn't act any different than when Ruth was alive. The store was the center of his life then as it was now. The church was second before, and it was now.

Ed thought of that. Jim was what being stable meant. His life was orderly because he wasn't shaken by events. He stuck with his life without bothering to change with everything that happened. He never seemed to swing from one emotional point to another.

The steadiness Ed had achieved really came about by his being able to look at life from a point of view that didn't always show him taking responsibility for everything and everybody. The still was a good example. Although Ed's convictions didn't condone the 'shine business, he was convinced a person working with something could do it and be completely innocent, thus he knew that labeling everybody as bad because of something they were involved with was wrong.

Carl Harris was a good case in point. Carl was innocent. He'd come to Willie with no other choice. He was an employee, Willie's 'shine business was just a normal part of the farm. Carl couldn't be held responsible for any of it.

Ed's logic of not assigning blame except in deliberate acts had made it easier to tolerate failures. He even saw impulses as excusable. Like his past problems. No intent of wrong, just embarrassing results. The change of attitude was almost complete. Ed's conscience was not bothering him as he rode up to the still.

Willie was watching the worm, the copper tube that left the cap of the cooker and wound its way through the old wooden barrel filled with cool spring water that flowed over its top continuously. The steam in the copper tubing would condense and flow into the stone jar as 'shine. Willie was careful not to boil the mash too fast. He watched the copper tube turn pale from the hot steam, a cast of green came to the pale copper. The pipe hummed for just a second. Willie glanced at the end of the tubing. A few clear drops fell into the stone jar.

"That's good, Carl." Willie turned, seeing Ed but ignoring him. "Don't put any more wood on, just make sure we don't boil her dry."

Ed came closer. He'd known where the still was for years, but this was his first trip to the ledge above the mouth of Bratton.

"Carl, help the preacher tie up his horse." Willie seemed to be joking Ed because he was sitting frozen in the saddle, staring at every part of the still.

Ed was amazed at the size of the operation. There had to be forty barrels scattered around the hill. There was a shed full of sacks. There was two of the cookers, there were jars everywhere. Carl was filling the second cooker from a barrel.

"Preacher, come to help?" Willie was nervous.

Ed got down without answering, feeling foolish and wondering what impulse had made him decide to ride by the still.

"Carl, take his horse." Willie looked around for Carl again.

"Preacher, you gonna say anything?"

"I just...." Ed stopped. He was embarrassed, his face flushed. "I just decided to come see you...here," he finally added.

"Well...set down." Willie looked around, suddenly feeling as awkward as he had the first time Ed came to the barn.

Carl led the horse away. Ed sat on a rock close enough to the cooker to feel the heat from the fire.

"Preacher, you ever been to a still before?" Willie asked.

"Once," Ed answered.

"Let me show you how we run this one."

Willie began the tour of the hillside, showing Ed all the different barrels of mash.

Ed looked inside the barrels full of grain with a white mold covering the top. Some barrels showed a greenish tint on the mold. Willie took a cup and pushed the grain to the side, a murky liquid with a golden yellow color came bubbling to the top.

"That's good beer." Willie took a sip from the cup. "Few 'shine makers know the mash could be strained and beer bottled from it. The cooking makes the whiskey from the beer. When the mash sours enough," Willie pointed to the green mold on the side of the barrel, "we start cooking it off. I run the 'shine through twice. It makes the whiskey stand up."

Ed looked puzzled. The 'shine business never seemed this complicated before. The barrels of grain, mixed with water, the sacks of sugar setting stashed in barrels covered by sheet metal with rocks laying on top of the sheet metal to keep it from blowing off. All of the parts of the still seemed far apart from the 'shine business. The still could have been a cotton gin at Batesville. The labor was hard and tedious, and it seemed honest, Ed thought, aloof to the pain it brought to people that became alcoholics.

Willie continued to explain the way the 'shine was made. He was nervous; he stopped by the cooker. "Preacher," Ed was looking at the cooker, "the only danger is if that 'worm' stops up, the still could blow up."

"Worm?" Ed remembered a fight in Tennessee over a piece of copper tubing. His dad had said the man had stolen the worm from a still. Ed remembered trying to visualize some big worm. Now he knew what it was.

Willie went through every detail about how the worm could become clogged by a piece of mash if the fire was too big and the boiling got big enough to force the solid pieces into the copper tube.

Willie stopped, out of breath from his description, and still nervous from showing Ed his moonshine production. Willie didn't think to ask how Ed knew his way through the crack in the bluff. Sheriff Carson was being paid well, the Federal men were leaving Arkansas alone, with the problem of exposing the prohibition taking up their time. The still on a bluff above Big Creek producing a few gallons compared to some of the wildcat operations was too small for the law outside to worry about. Willie knew this, so showing Ed the still was almost like showing him something as common as a sawmill producing lumber.

"Willie." Ed stopped, trying to remember the question he'd meant to ask before Willie started talking about how the still could blow up.

"You know anything about the money problem?" Ed finally asked,

"Yeah." Willie didn't elaborate.

"How's it going to affect things here?" Ed asked.

"No much," Willie answered.

"Why?" Ed asked.

"Well, we're poor people." Willie walked around the cooker and sat down on one of the rocks. "When you're as poor as we are, it's hard to go broke."

"I can see that," Ed answered. "But Jim went to Batesville to get stuff for the store and Brother Carr said lots of stuff wouldn't be made any more on account of companies going broke."

"Well, that could be a problem." Willie's eyes showed interest. "The thing I meant was lots a folks don't buy enough stuff to miss it if they didn't have any money."

"I know." Ed thought of the people who only came to the store for salt. "Willie, you know ole man Holt that lives on Spring Creek?"

"Yeah."

"He comes twice a year and gets fifty pounds of salt and fifty pounds of coffee. Gripes every time about how much he's having to spend for store bought stuff." Ed smiled as he thought of the old man.

"Yeah, he makes his own 'shine with honey instead of sugar," Willie said.

"How does he do it?" Ed thought sugar was necessary to make the mash sour.

"I won't use a hundred pounds a month," Willie answered. "The honey just makes the mash sweet, and the whiskey kind of cloudy, or yellow instead of good 'n clear like mine."

The conversation drifted from the 'shine business to the economy, Ed feeling more at ease as Willie expressed his opinion.

"Preacher, the problem with having money is trying to

adjust to amounts as they change." Willie stood up, moving toward the mash barrels as he talked, covering them with the burlap sacks.

"Most folks always have more plans than money. Every time they get their hands on a few dollars, they grab something else they think they need. Most of the time they'd made it without it. From what I've read, this problem now wuz caused by people going wild. It's happened before. Sometimes there's been war just to straighten things out. May take years, but another war may come this time."

Ed joined Willie as he placed stave cores, small triangular pieces of wood about three feet long, across the tops of the barrels he'd just covered.

"Willie, I know what you're saying. I tell Liz the catalog's got my money before I ever get it." Ed stopped as he watched the scowl on Willie's face.

"Ed," Willed sucked a deep breath, "I know it's none of my business, but anytime you spend everything as it comes in, there'll be a day you'll go wantin'."

Ed rode away feeling despair as he thought about Willie's ideas. It would certainly be a bland world if everybody did like Willie. Nothing but overalls for men, no automobiles, no trips, spend your entire life hanging on to the traditions you were born with. Ed paused in his thoughts, feeling a little better as he rationalized the balance of conservative and liberal.

The conservatives will to preserve seem to always provide a bench mark to return to when things got out of hand. But if it wasn't for the bolder souls being around, nothing new would ever come along, and it always seemed the hard-core conservative slowly accepted the best of the new, and then fought to preserve it, just as if they'd come up with the idea in the first place. The balance worked. It would work again this time. This "depression" was a crisis that would sort out the problems all the way from New York to a whiskey still on a bluff above where Bratton Creek joined Big Creek in north Arkansas.

Ed rode slowly, watching another day come to a close. It was still, too still. The air would bring a change in the weather. He was proud of the new peace he'd found in himself. He was as calm as the air was still, and he wasn't worried about things changing.

CHAPTER 44

Time had moved slow on a day-to-day basis. The worry of the depression, the coming of the New Deal. Roosevelt's promises never got a chance at reality. World war had come before they'd matured. It was June 1943.

Ed was relaxing, remembering things, clearer than on most days. Over a week, now, since Noah joined the army.

Liz was still in shock that Noah decided to join the army. He had been eighteen for several months and had not been drafted. She'd lived in hope the war would end before Noah was drafted. Her mood would not affect Ed. He was in a world of his own and had been since the depression, and the war had not changed him at all.

Ed spent most of his time reading, not just his Bible, but every newspaper and magazine that came to Big Flat, even the romances and comic books. When he wasn't reading he was working in the tack room. Ed had quit barbering in '35 and began repairing harnesses. Better than cuttin' hair and listening to gossip.

Liz had wondered why haircutting had ceased to be an opportunity to witness, but then she knew Ed's problem with liquor had returned about the same time. His hands shook. That was the reason for not cutting hair.

The metal roof popped and crackled, heating up from the June sun. Not a leaf was moving. Ed sat motionless, a part of the hot, still morning.

His mind was without confusion, his conscience had relived him of worry over ten years ago. He couldn't put a date on the change, but it had started the night he'd gotten mad at himself.

After he'd gone back to see Willie, after Jim killed Coy for foolin' around with his wife, after he'd started to sip liquor from the jars Willie left in the old stump above the road by the Wildcat Spring, a spring named for a real wildcat that used to raise a litter of kittens in a crevice above it.

Ed thought of Willie telling him where he left a quart once a week for a mysterious customer that he was sure was Coy Bryant. The old stump. The whiskey was never picked up after Coy's death. Ed had stopped, curious the first day he'd uncovered the jar, but tempted to take a drink, he caked the leaves back over it. Curious again the second time, that's how he drank the first jar. Surprised when a full one was found in its place.

Willie had told him he knew, by accident, just a slip in conversation, about Ed not ever having to worry about paying for the 'shine or anybody knowing. After that Ed had a pint in the barn, one in the car. It seemed everywhere Ed went, he'd made sure he had sippin' whiskey, a "sippin' saint." Ed's ministry had improved during the depths of the depression. People had to come to church in search of relief, not materially, but spiritually, hoping to overcome the hard times.

Maybe it was the liquor, maybe it was relaxing, whatever the change, Ed's frustration in the pulpit was gone. He no longer worried about his sermons. Some mornings he'd just tell stories, anything he could think of to make the congregation laugh. He'd always close with a plea for converts, urging people to be saved with as much fervor as he'd ever had, but the pressure was gone.

He never explained, he never pretended. He went with Willie anywhere he wanted. Willie came to church, sometimes he even came inside, might sit on the front pew. Their friendship had finally been accepted without comment. Ed had mused how that if anything persisted long enough, people would eventually ignore it.

Part of the acceptance had been Willie's role as banker during the depression. Ed had no idea how Willie had made the loans, but he knew Willie held mortgages on almost the entire community. Ed could tell when Willie had helped a family through a crisis. The husband would come to church, the wife would stop any talk against Willie. It was like a compromise of necessity. Good could not be maintained because of lack of finance. Willie's loans had moved him into a position of favor.

Ed's own situation was not much different. He could remember the panic he'd felt when Ellen Sitton didn't make it to church with Willie's offering.

Willie's money had been accumulated from the same people he was loaning it back to, the only difference now was Willie had stepped up production at the still, and was selling liquor outside the area. People would come from as far away as Memphis for a load of Willie's 'shine. The end of prohibition had not slowed it down. Ed knew Willie had done this to bring in much needed money for the area. Ed had also wondered if the standard of living hadn't actually improved during the '30s. He knew one thing for sure, the year he'd decided converting Willie would put religion in control seemed distant, too far back for memory to reach. Willie had won. He now controlled Ed, the people, and their way of life.

Ed stood up, ready to go to the bridge. He needed to see Willie. It wasn't all that bad to be controlled by someone who showed the respect Willie did for Ed.

"Liz all right?" Willie framed the question as he took a dead minnow from his hook and replaced it with a live one. It was too hot to fish, but the spring fed into the hole of water creating a haven for the bass to feed. Willie thought they might bite; at least it gave them something to do as they talked.

"Yeah," Ed answered after what seemed a minute.

"Heard from the kid?" Willie asked.

"Yeah," Ed grunted.

"Where's he at?"

"Fort Dix," Ed answered, "it's in New Jersey."

"Headin' to Germany?" Willie continued the interview.

"Probably." Ed caught a small brown bass just as he answered. Too small to keep.

"Just like that fish." Willie's response didn't make sense to Ed as he released the fish barely larger than his finger, until he added, "They're takin' our boys too young, just for cannon fodder."

"War after the depression...don't seem fair." Ed tried to make conversation.

"Ellen's son-in-laws are in Italy, or close to there." Willie referred to his two older daughters' husbands. Carl had married Pauline, and Carl had failed his army physical. Ellen had been caught in the middle. Willie was proud Carl got to stay home, even if the two daughters had moved off the farm to get away from "Daddy and Carl." Jealousy had ruined the family, but Willie seemed unabashed by it all. "They ought to win the war by themselves if they're half as important as them other girls lets on."

"Carl bothered by the fuss?" Ed asked.

"Nah." Willie threw a rock at a ground squirrel trying to cross the creek on the rocks below the spring. "He'd a been a good soldier, can't help it his heart's bad."

"Why'd everybody get mad?" Ed was sure Willie had an opinion.

"Carl's like my boy." Willie leaned back on the gravel bar. "The girls just wanted an excuse to pick on him. I never liked Myrtle's Jim or Becky's ole boy. Carl works, don't ask for nothing. Them other two don't even like my girls, they just married 'em to get by easy during them bad years."

Ed felt uncomfortable at Willie's answer, wishing he'd never asked the question.

"Ever wonder about wars?" The question went unanswered. Ed asked it, but he pondered the answer harder than Willie. Willie was busy trying to keep a horse fly from biting him.

"If everybody refused to fight on both sides, there wouldn't be a war?" Ed hoped to draw Willie out of his thoughtful pose.

"Yeah, guess." Willie had run the horse fly away. "That's dumb, though. Every leader is a leader because people think he's a leader. A good leader has to shoot people that don't fight, just like Hitler has shot people. The one's doin' the shootin' are shootin' to keep from being shot. Ain't nobody got nerve enough to stop 'cause they're too scared. So the war just goes on. Everybody that's fightin' is scared, except for some crazy people that hate everybody and just like to shoot people just to see 'em die. And some that think they can stop by killin' some more, but it ain't gonna stop 'til it's over."

Willie finished the speech. Ed sat quiet, trying to decipher what he'd said.

Ed understood following someone without realizing how they dominated you. Like Willie, Ed had been a leader, Willie was a leader. Ed had planned to overcome Willie, but somewhere Willie had won. Now Ed did what Willie wanted. He was free to object, he was free to expose Willie, but he couldn't keep his share of leadership and fight Willie.

Most people were doing whatever they did trying to protect their part of the world, A lot had been said about patriotism, and young boys like Noah probably just joined to fight for that reason, but older men like Ed and Willie would never go except by force. Either the threat of jail, trying to avoid the draft, or joining to choose their own place. It came out the same.

"Things'll never be the same," Ed finally commented.

"They never are," Willie agreed. "Ever notice how much time you spend wishing for things to go back to like it wuz?"

"Yeah." Ed remembered the year Noah was a baby.

"Cain't ever enjoy the present that way. The present is all right, and I'll bet there'll be a day me and you both'll wish things were as good as they are now, and today we both think things are bad." Willie stopped. "Your boy's gone. My girls not speaking to each other. Carl feelin' guilty about something he cain't help. Me not feeling good toward anybody 'cept maybe you, but one memory will ease the bad and we'll look back to that nice day we spent fishin'."

The horse fly dove at Willie, buzzing by his ear. "I'll bet I forget this horsefly."

Ed reeled in his line to find his minnow gone. The hook was bare, stripped by a bass during the conversation.

"Attitude." Ed said the one word, "Just a matter of how you feel. Remember twenty years ago when I's so worried about bein' perfect?"

Willie straightened his back, nodding his head as he did. A sly grin flashed and then vanished just as quick.

"My attitude was wrong." Ed stopped, "I didn't understand half what I said, and couldn't explain what I felt. Spent most of my time confused. I never did know what was real or what was a charade."

Willie perked up, curious at the last word. He'd never heard Ed use it before.

"A charade, playing a part to make a particular impression." Ed used an educated tone, a thing he wasn't afraid to do around Willie after all the years.

"Lots a people charade," Willie said clumsily.

"Willie, I know we've talked lots of times about truth and happiness, but I think I'm beginning to learn some things. Remember how I told you one time that being honest was an attitude?"

"Yeah." Willie's tone didn't show interest in a lecture as he waited for Ed to continue. Ed just stared, waiting for a better answer.

Willie sat waiting for Ed to speak, expecting the lecture. Ed was not going to continue the conversation until Willie began to contribute.

Willie finally broke the silence. "I remember 'most everything, but I never understood that day you tried to tell me the truth was the way I felt, not what I did."

Ed quickly ran a picture from his memory through his mind. From the days that everything he did he tried to explain by using an example from the scripture. Ed's face flushed when he thought how abstract some of his thinking must have been. He'd stretched the Bible to its fullest to cover some of his ideas. Now a pang of guilt, he seldom ever used the scripture to measure his actions.

Ed started, wondering how long his private daydream had interrupted the conversation.

"Willie, I know it sounds strange, but I was dishonest by trying to be so honest, and my attitude might have been right, but I was so far from reality that I had no understanding of real people." Ed paused. Willie sat still, he was listening. They'd never talked this way on a hot afternoon while they fished, stone sober.

"Yeah." Willie's tone showed some interest. "I understood that you didn't know much about what you's saying. That's why I had so much patience."

Ed flushed with anger. He was trying to explain his new philosophy and didn't need a reminder by Willie of his past ignorance.

"I just meant I expected more than people were capable of living up to. I expected the world to change to the way I wanted it. When I came to see you I had a vision of your conversion in my mind. I was going to change you completely. No more moonshine." Ed paused.

"I thought about doin' just what you said," Willie interjected.

Ed felt a surge of excitement mixed with regret as his mind raced, trying to imagine how things would have been if Willie had been converted.

"Willie." Ed said his name without any idea what he intended to say. His voice trailed off as his mind continued to flash visions of all the confused events for the last twenty years. Tragedies, did they dominate? Was life wasted? Ed thought of his philosophy of living in the present without regret. No second guessing. Too hard to do, but a good philosophy when mixed with hope and faith in the future. Ed continued his comments.

"I don't know, we could set here forever and try to undo the things we've done, and spend the rest of our time dreaming about how great things could be if we'd done different."

"I do that," Willie said flatly. "I know ever decision ever made gives me doubts and makes me afraid to make it. I think about how a little thing changes so many big things in our lives."

The sun had moved in on them. The hole of water flickered with a mixture of sunlight and shade as it affected the shadows of the trees. The sun seemed to brighten as it hit the water, making it even warmer for Willie and Ed sitting on the gravel bar. Ed liked the heat; Willie hated it. They moved farther away from the creek to the shade of a willow bending low next to the bank. Ed leaned against the bank as he sat down. The cool dirt felt good. Maybe he didn't like the heat as much as he thought.

"Yeah." Willie had started the move away from the creek, placing their fishing rods on the forked limbs left by other fishermen. They'd not said a word during the move or while they sat down against the bank. Both their minds had been racing; Willie, trying to feel his way through to explaining to Ed that his respect for him had grown over the years, Ed, trying to express the same thing.

Silence followed Ed's answer.

Ed rode slow, the heat made it hard to move fast. Two friends had spent the afternoon attempting to explain their feelings. Ed knew that life built over the years, hope changed to resolve, dreams died becoming ghosts among reality. Inspired ideals got tempered by practical problems. Ed watched the day end, proud to be alive, but sad. Changes, life's events, some planned, but most change evolving from sources Ed could never predict. Yet he'd made it. Still a preacher, of sorts, still in love with Liz, just more reserved. Still Willie's friend, with more to tie them together. Ed turned into the lot, leaving his thoughts and the day behind.

CHAPTER 45

A churning wheel on a tug boat pushing barges into the swift current of the White River, the tinkling of the water with fog rising from Big Creek on a cool October morning, the bubbling of the juice cooking as smoke swirled quietly upward from the molasses pan, the drum beat of Ed's favorite horse's hooves along the packed clay roads around Big Flat, sounds Ed had found comforting over the years.

The first time on the river he was a young man running from a problem, drinking at the seminary. On Big Creek, he was a confused minister, a dozen other problems he'd thought through as he listened to Willie's philosophy and the sound of the forge or any other chore Willie might be doing at the time.

1945. The war was over, Noah was gone, killed in training in New Jersey, Liz buried next to Noah along with the baby. Ed stared at the house, a mess, trying to remember whose turn it was to clean. Some lady from the church would come, he was sure. A preacher in need, at fifty years old, Ed felt ancient, in the constant care of the church.

Pity. Ed had wallowed in it almost continuously since Noah's death. Liz hadn't spoken a dozen words in a tone other than remorse until the doctor told her she was dying from cancer. Then she hadn't shut up for the three months before she died. A continuous lamenting of how bad their lives had been. She was relieved to be dying.

Willie passed away about three months after Liz died.

Ed's humor had left him, no more sardonic looks at scripture. He'd lost his drive. No drinking, no trips to see Willie at the bridge. The people who meant the most to him—all gone.

His sermons were automatic, no long oration, just smooth rhetoric with little response from the crowds. Cozy was no longer part of his circuit, and he only went to Hickory one Sunday a month.

Carl finished mowing around Willie's grave. He always made sure Willie's was kept neat and tidy, not overgrown and neglected looking. Some folks didn't do so good at maintaining their family's graves, but for most it was a source of pride to keep them looking nice.

Carl sat down on Willie's tombstone, nestled in the center of Rock Creek Cemetery which was halfway between Hickory and Cozy. Pauline would gripe if she knew he was sitting on Willie's headstone, but he knew Willie wouldn't mind. Continuing on in life without Willie and his counseling was hard. He wasn't sure he didn't miss the 'shine as much as he missed Willie. *Cain't nobody make 'shine as good as Willie's,* he thought. Carl didn't even try. He left the moonshine business alone.

The war and the depression seemed like a long time ago. He stared at the hills toward Big Flat where Preacher Ed was buried.

Ed Tice died in the early 1950s. He had outlived Willie by several years. *He was as lost without Willie to talk to as I am,* thought Carl as he watched the haze rise above the oak trees from the summer heat. He knew Willie's and Ed's lives had become intertwined. A mixture of moonshine and religion.

They both were a big influence in their community. One, a preacher that seemed destined to settle in Big Flat and to provide the spiritual leadership needed in the Ozark Mountains. He had grown up among people whose values were the same as the people here. He understood their way of life. The other, a shrewd businessman, farmer, and moonshiner who noticed more than people realized, which gave him a different understanding. Ed and Willie influenced each other, somehow. Best friends.

As Carl continued thinking about the two unlikely friends, he realized it was time for him to gather his tools and start the journey back to the homestead on Bratton Creek. He felt at peace with who he was, trying to follow Preacher Ed into the ministry.

After he had loaded the tools in the old pickup truck, and had the good fortune of the truck starting without having to be pushed, he concentrated on his driving along the old dirty rock road that would take him through Cozy and then down the hill to the old farmstead he had moved to in the 1940s.

He thought again about life on Big Creek with Willie in charge, and learning about life while trying to follow Preacher Ed. Both gone. Both buried with only headstones to tell their story.

Understanding that relationship was beyond Carl. "All the words I know could never describe it. Not even if I knew everything about them," he said softly as he drove. "Only God knows the whole story about the bootlegger and the preacher. Will just have to leave it there."

ABOUT THE AUTHOR

Sam Pemberton was born on Bratton Creek, at an old homestead that hadn't changed much since the pioneer days. The year was 1944. Pemberton graduated from Big Flat high school. After their graduation in 1962, Sam married the love of his life, Patricia Treat.

He has worked construction in the drywall trade for most of his life. Sam presently lives in the beautiful Ozarks and continues in construction, as well as developing a new adventure called The Gathering Place in Big Flat, Arkansas, which is a restoration of the old building that is referred to in the novel as the store. He hopes you'll stop by sometime.